on the floor

aifric campbell

A complete catalogue record for this book can be obtained from the
British Library on request

First published in 2012 by Serpent's Tail,
an imprint of Profile Books Ltd
3A Exmouth House
Pine Street
London EC1R 0JH
website: www.serpentstail.com

ISBN 978 1 84668 808 9
eISBN 978 1 84765 801 2

Designed and typeset by sue@lambledesign.demon.co.uk

Printed by Clays, Bungay, Suffolk

10 9 8 7 6 5 4 3 2

FSC
Mixed Sources
Product group from well-managed
forests and other controlled sources

Cert no. SGS-COC-2061
www.fsc.org
© 1996 Forest Stewardship Council

Ai... spent
th... Sussex.
Sh... *ntics of
M...

Pr...

'A... ve this
b... nsight,
bu... or

'S... lent of
u...

'C... deliver
u...

'S... comes
t... e that
p... tiful to
re... ng into
t... ted in
d...

'Clear-eyed, lyrical... Campbell manages to infuse the cool, lucid
language of the narrator with some truly luminous descriptions of place
and emotion... a book that demands to be taken seriously, both because
of its ambitions and the beauty of its writing' Catherine Heaney,
Irish Times

'Aifric Campbell's absorbing second novel celebrates friendship past and present and the enduring hope of redemption' *Waterstone's Books Quarterly*

'Campbell writes with lambent precision... a mesmerising study of a woman clinging to the knotted cord of adolescence, uncertain whether to go backwards or forwards' John O'Connell, *Guardian*

'Campbell's style is lyrical, revealing sharp, important truths with mesmerising intensity as Caro begins to embrace a future that is rich with possibility, hope and reconciliation' Eithne Farry, *Daily Mail*

'The imagery is evocative, the narrative well-paced and there is a genuine sense of sympathy with the main character. Thought-provoking' *Scotsman*

'The flawless depiction of a life destroyed by the devastating loss of a loved one is testament to her skill as a writer' Jennifer Ryan, *Sunday Independent*

'Campbell's eloquent prose is both beautiful and compelling, making *The Loss Adjustor* a haunting and gripping novel' *Ulster Tatler*

'A powerful and thought-provoking book... the real beauty lies in her elegant and evocative prose' *Sunday Business Post*

'*The Loss Adjustor* is a beautifully written, lyrical exploration of loss and grief. Campbell's skill as a writer, however, ensures that although this is a sad story, the overall effect is far from depressing' *Canberra Times*

Women in the money-making world,
Climbing to the top,
Women in pin-striped suits,
Clutching briefcases, hurrying,
Going up in lifts
With set jaws and anxious faces...

Surely when they entered
This daily madness,
We might have hoped that they would somehow
Do more to transmute
Its vast encompassing sadness.

Anthony Cronin

prologue

the BFT

5 march 1986
16:21
london

HERE'S HOW IT GOES, the moment of my becoming:

The call comes in at 16:09, while we're already winding down. The London market's just closed so the trading floor is quiet and the only shouting is what's spilling out of the squawk box from New York.

First thing I notice is a flurry on the Block Desk, a change in tempo, like the rumble of approaching thunder. Then the Grope strides out of his glass tower, his jawbone set like stone, the way it always is when something big is going down. And it's like a tom-tom alert has gone out, faces are bobbing up behind the rows of monitors as a Mexican wave of heads rolls right across the floor from South East Asia to the US desk.

Rob stands up at his pitch directly opposite me, slaps the receiver in his palm like he's testing a cosh. Al rises from the chair beside me and the big fat research report on waste management that he keeps telling us is the Industry of the Future. And then I'm standing too, the skirt amongst men.

The Grope stops at the Block Desk where Skippy Dolan is on his feet with the phone clamped to his ear. His elbow sticks out at a right angle so you can see the sweat circle darken his blue armpit. And I'm thinking it looks bad, Skippy standing there leaking like that, he's the only Yank on the floor who doesn't wear a white shirt with a vest underneath to mop up the juice. The Grope leans into the Reuters screen and we're all craning our necks like prairie dogs, trying to see whose vitals he is checking.

'I'm guessing it's Fido on the line,' says Al. 'Skippy said he's getting real tight with them.'

And Skippy is ranting into the phone, nodding his strawberry meathead as if he's in spasm, as if he can't stop. His free hand chops the air space in front of him into big empty pieces and after 352 days in this job I can read all the signs: Skippy's client is a seller in size who wants out NOW. And I can tell from the way he's bent double and winding the phone cord around his neck, that if we don't pull the trigger soon, Skippy's client will trade away.

'Let me call Felix Mann.' My voice is very loud and very clear. The Grope snaps round. Heads swivel. Rob turns to face me with a flopped jaw. Al is sucking wind through his teeth.

The Grope hoovers up the space between us and leans across Rob's desk to fix me with that killer stare.

'Felix Mann is the only one who can do this,' I say, the receiver smooth and warm in my hand like a favourite toy.

You make your own luck. You pick your moments and this is mine.

'Two minutes,' Skippy squeals, air-slicing his throat. 'Or my man takes his business to Goldman's.'

'OK, Geri, let's smile and dial,' says the Grope, all soft and dangerous. And then he tells me what Skippy's got to show.

It is midnight in Hong Kong but Felix answers on the first ring.

'Cemco,' I say. 'I have a seller in size.'

I hear his fingers flutter across the keyboard. Picture his pale face spotlit in the darkened office, the harbour lights twinkling behind the black glass.

'I've got 56 million shares on offer at 224.'

Al is a still life beside me. The Grope and Rob like a tableau on the other side of the monitors. And behind them an audience is assembling to witness my circus animal performance. The truth is I have no fucking clue what Felix thinks of Cemco. Or the price. Or anything. But I know that he's the only one who can do this right here, right now.

'And I've got one minute,' I tell Felix. Skippy is in panicked silence, his fingers counting down the seconds to expiry.

There is a lurch in my chest like a part of my lung has just collapsed. The tickers whizz green across the black tape and I reach out to touch my Reuters like a sacred stone. In the corner of my eye I see Al's finger tapping his desk, he is keeping time with Skippy's countdown as I hurtle towards my own funeral.

'Geri,' the Grope's voice hits me like a blow to the temple.

'Felix,' I say. 'We're out of time.'

There's a crackling on the line and I imagine my voice sinking undersea, picture starfish gliding dumbly over the transcontinental cable, a scuttle of claws across the silent floor. Al stops tapping the desk and the faithless audience leans in to get a better view of Geri Molloy choking on the slime of reckless ambition.

Felix's voice shoots to the surface and into my ear.

'He'll pay 223 for the lot,' I look up into the Grope's blinkless stare. Skippy holds three frantic fingers in the air. The Grope nods quick and tight and I raise my trembling thumb level with his head and say loudly, so everyone can hear: 'You're done, Felix, 56 million Cemco sold to you at 223.' And Skippy is thumping into his phone now, he's spinning round and unravelling the coil, waving the blue ticket above his head. 'Thank you, Felix.' I kill the line, write out a pick ticket and slam it in the timestamp. It is 16:21 on 5 March 1986 and everyone is gawping like I just became someone else.

''Kin-ell, Geri,' roars Rob and a hoot goes up. Skippy lunges across the monitors and my palm is burning from a machine gun of high fives.

Then the Grope is beside me showing the full set of white teeth.

His hand lands hard and heavy on my shoulder like it has never done before. He lets it linger for a moment while he looks down at me, differently somehow, like I'm not the person he thought I was. For I am now reborn and in my hand is a piece of living history: the biggest ticket ever written on Steiner's trading floor.

This was how I became a legend in my own lifetime.

This was the Big Fucking Ticket that made me everything I am.

1

time delay

monday 14 january 1991
05:17
london

AND FOR A LONG, LONG TIME after the Big Fucking Ticket, things had all the appearance of being on an upward trend. I met Stephen and fell in love, the '87 Crash came and went, stock markets kept roaring ahead and I was coining it at Steiner's. So who could have guessed just how much trouble lay down the road? Who could have known that Stephen would dump me in Venice four years later, Felix Mann would be forcing my relocation to Hong Kong and I'd be lying here on the floor at 5:17 a.m. with an empty bottle of Absolut, watching a million troops line up in a desert theatre of war?

For a while I chose to believe that things just snuck up when I wasn't paying attention, but I've since figured out that this downward trend started exactly 737 days ago. It was 1988 and all through that summer I'd been dreaming about Kit Kats. The whole country was in meltdown about the nation's favourite chocolate bar being gobbled up by the Swiss and Stephen was working flat-out on the takeover bid, so I barely saw him.

'You know it's the ultimate compromise,' I told him one December morning in Kensington Gardens. 'The Kit Kat is the bar you buy when you can't decide what you really want.' Rex ducked his head encouragingly, a twist of red tinsel around his collar and a slimy tennis ball in his mouth. I slipped my arm through Stephen's. He was wearing that navy pea coat and the mohair was tipped with frost.

'STAY,' he raised a hand but Rex lolloped off towards the Round Pond. 'I don't know why you even have a dog when you can't be bothered to train him,' he muttered and crunched away across the frozen grass. And I was struck by how easily my arm had given up its position, like a leaf falling on seasonal cue, as if this surrender was preordained and nature was ushering in the future of singledom that has since come to pass.

That moment was an early warning signal, like a bell tinkling faintly in thick fog to warn of rocks ahead. So the end, when it finally came 181 days ago, was surprising not for the event, but for what Zanna still calls my disproportionate reaction. I did not struggle or cry out. I let Stephen sneak off at dawn without a word, for how can you cling on to what isn't there? I packed my bag and flew back home to crouch cross-legged and hyperventilating in my sleepless bed as if each lung was a dying animal panting in my hands.

Zanna diagnosed a 'viral grief', which she had seen before, since Manhattan is years ahead of London in matters of the heart. So she marched me over to Finsbury Circus and into the consulting rooms of her private doctor who cradled her hand in both of his as if he might kiss it. 'Geri needs to sleep and she needs to chill,' Zanna announced, while I sat mute in a creaking Chesterfield. The doctor nodded gravely behind his outsize desk and took my blood pressure and I left with scrips for Valium and Mogadon. 'Look around you,' said Zanna as we stood on the steps outside. City workers streamed past on the pavement below us, shouldering their jackets in the August heat. 'And remember who you are,' she turned to face me. 'You are Geri Molloy, the biggest producer on the trading floor. You are the girl who bagged the elephant and this is nothing more than a temporary setback.'

Zanna's prognosis was largely correct, although I seem to have discovered some kind of biochemical resistance to sleeping pills which means I still average only 3.4 hours a night. But I am holding my own in some quantifiable ways. I am still doing 25 million dollars of business a month with Felix. I am still the number one call to Steiner's biggest client. I have partially recovered my sense of humour. And my emotional lapses are mostly private although Zanna told me last night at Zafferano's that they are leaking into the public domain.

'You look—' she scanned me up and down, considering a range of possibilities, 'dismantled.'

'I only just got back from Hong Kong yesterday.'

'You don't look good at all.'

'I think I just need to eat,' I tugged at my sagging waistband.

'What you *need* is to cut down on this,' she tapped a scarlet nail on the side of my empty glass. 'A good night's sleep would help,' I rattled the ice cubes. But Zanna refuses to indulge my chronic insomnia, as if starving it of oxygen might make it cease to exist. I suspect she thinks I am either some sort of pharmaceutical mutant or guilty of gross exaggeration, so I have driven my debilitating frailty underground since I can't anyway account for my nocturnal horrors or the suspicion that some small rodent is scurrying round inside my chest, its sharp claws palpitating the raw muscle of my heart.

'You absolutely *have* to take that job in Hong Kong,' said Zanna, batting the waitress away before I had a chance to order another drink. 'Felix Mann is your meal ticket and it would be career suicide to turn it down, Geri.'

'But I don't want to go.'

'You've got the biggest hedge fund in Asia eating out of your hand and he wants you out there where he is. In Hong Kong. Every other sales person on the Street would be chewing their arm off for this opportunity.'

'I can do the job just as well from London.'

'Well, your number one client doesn't think so. And Felix calls the shots. You told me yourself that your competition is shipping out to Hong Kong – Merrill's, Morgan Stanley, Goldman's – they're all putting salespeople out there just to cover him.'

Zanna tucked a shiny blonde strand behind her ear and leant forward, elbows planted wide on the tabletop, staring straight at me across knitted fingers. I stopped prodding the polenta and lowered my fork.

'I know why you don't want to go,' she said and I recognised her look as the precursor to uncomfortable revelations about the state of a balance sheet or, in this case, the state of my heart. I have seen her assume this position in a boardroom, telling Steiner's clients that their multi-million dollar investment is a dog and they should ditch the stock fast before it blows up in their face. Unlike many other analysts, Zanna is happy to nail her true colours to the mast when necessary and she never shies away from delivering the tough sound bite that will send you reeling.

'You don't want to move to Hong Kong because of Stephen.'

'Not true,' I croaked but I couldn't offer any evidence to support this plaintive denial or any convincing reason for resisting what is clearly the logical career move.

'Oh, Geri,' she shook her head sadly, 'if you lose Felix Mann's business you're history.' And Zanna slid her hands wide on the tabletop like she was clearing space – for what? For the wreckage I am becoming?

'You don't know how weird he is.'

'What do you care how weird your client is if you're getting all his business? For Christ's sake, Geri, he's not asking you to marry him. He doesn't even expect you to sleep with him. Apparently.'

At a table across the way a woman idly skimmed her fingertip around the edge of a wine glass while the man opposite her gesticulated in full and earnest flow. Zanna sighed, loud enough to be heard above the swishing of waitresses and plate clearance and the sudden clanking in my head like an empty tin can being kicked around the walls of my skull.

'Anyway, you won't have a choice because the Grope will make you go. Do you really think your boss is going to let you put all that order flow at risk?'

'Felix did say he might call him.'

Zanna checked her watch and signalled for the bill. Her Sunday night rule is bed by ten except in exceptional circumstances, which this was clearly not.

'Now, Geri,' she leaned back in the chair, 'repeat after me.' And I had to return her smile because this is Zanna's old trick and I'm always happy to play along since I've discovered it is curiously therapeutic to be led by the nose.

'Repeat after me: I will move on.'

'I will move on.'

'I will give up on history.'

'I will give up on history.'

'I will go to Hong Kong.'

'Why does everybody think I should go?'

'Because everyone wants the best for you,' she shrugged. 'And you are letting things slip. Look, I'm just saying the hard stuff, the things that other people won't say. One day you will thank me for all my good advice.' She laid a cool hand on mine, gave it a little squeeze. 'I am your most effective friend.'

Zanna may well be right about the slippage since it's never great to wake up at 5:17 a.m. and find your torso on the floor, your legs up on the couch and the dog staring down at you with that look of creased sadness that is always so unbearable, even though I know it's not sadness at all, just a jowly looseness around his golden snout. 'Good boy.' I ruffle Rex's neck fur and he pricks up his ears as if he hears someone coming. I still catch him watching the door at night, the times that Stephen used to come by after a late meeting. Sometime Rex whimpers in his sleep, a weighted comfort on my legs. Perhaps he is in a dream remembering how Stephen used to throw the tennis ball for him with the straight-armed bowl of a cricketer and he'd scrabble on take-off like a cartoon dog, barrelling down the grassy slope, leaping awkwardly in the air on the bounce, tongue lolling, a little foam around his jaw. For it was

Stephen who first introduced Rex to the art of retrieval – a skill that should have been instinctive for his breed – though he preferred to fetch within a tantalizing five-foot radius and dance over the ball, a habit that Stephen, who is intimate with the attributes of good gun-dogs, always took to be an indicator of shoddy genetics. Lately I notice Rex has begun to drop the ball directly by my feet as if he has suddenly decided to demonstrate his compliance, in case it was his stubbornness that drove Stephen away, like the difficult child who suspects he may be the cause of parental separation. Or maybe he is urging me to tell Stephen, as if this transformation in Rex's skill might bring him back again and give us all another chance. He's even taken to keeping the ball in his bed at night, as if to be sure he is fully prepared for the return that Stephen is never going to make.

The alarm bleeps in the bedroom and Rex nudges my chin with his nose. I turn my head sideways and this sudden movement unleashes a shooting pain in my right temple which I recognise as the cumulative effects of dehydration, jet lag, insomnia, malnutrition and the contents of the empty bottle on the floor beside me. The clock on the stereo says 05:22 and I feel I could lie here forever, like a car stuck in the ditch, wheels spinning with no rescue in sight. And I think: maybe this is burnout, maybe my life story as investment banker is morphing into a shabby decline and fall, a blazing star in the moments before it crashes to earth. So I lie here for a while scratching Rex's head but in the end it's his persistent whining that makes me get up and take him around Pembroke Square even though his walker will be here in a couple of hours. I step out the front door and into a head spin, just make it across the street in time to throw up in the icy gutter. After that I feel well enough to stand shivering on the edge of the pavement under the yellow glow of the lamppost, watching a light snow dust the railings of the garden square, and it seems for a moment like I've stepped out of the wardrobe and into Narnia. I'm half-expecting Rex to turn into a faun as he trots down the hushed street when I think, you know Geri, it's time to pull yourself together, get a grip and some perspective, because it only takes one thread to start unravelling in your life and the next thing you know the whole jumper is gone. So I go back inside and take some Nurofen, some happy pills and a shower. Then I square up to the mirror, tell my pale reflection that I am in fact going to work, that I might as well just chin butt the day, get it over with and take what's coming. 'Because you are Geri Molloy and you have the City at your feet. It's time to take the wheel and put your foot back on the gas.'

06:21

AND I AM MAKING PROGRESS NOW, moving forwards, doing 70 along a dark and deserted Embankment with the window open to a sobering sleet spatter and the radio spilling its urgent war cry out across the black river. A defeated French voice breathes softly into the broadcast: The time to act has come after we did everything we could to avoid it. No sign, I tell you none, has come from Iraq. And that was the French Prime Minister describing the failure of France's last minute attempt to negotiate a peaceful solution to the crisis in the Gulf.

The lights on the corner of Queen Street are stuck on red and I inch a little over the white line. There is only one car diagonally opposite, coming north from Southwark Bridge and I want to screech madly forwards, but it would be insanity to draw attention to myself in this early morning desertion with a bucketful of vodka still pooled in my veins. Rain washes the empty streets and the radio keeps up its low volume war chatter. Answer me this? Would you pull out of your own house? Would you pull out of California? Kuwait is our territory and our province.

We are speeding toward the UN deadline expiry in three days' time and it is just possible that the diversion of war in the Gulf might buy me enough time for this whole relocation idea to blow over. Maybe all hell will break loose next week with airports shut down, oil prices going through the roof and Felix will be so busy making money out of misery that he forgets the whole thing. By the time it's over everyone could be dead, although Felix does seem unkillable, a post-apocalyptic spectre that will stalk the financial wastelands for all eternity.

Of course this entire mess is of my own making, since I am the luckiest girl in the City with the client that everyone else wants: the reclusive and unpredictable Felix Mann, the smartest guy on the planet. Poised on the peak of Hong Kong with his two billion stockpile of funds, Felix surveys the landscape of opportunity that crowds his global horizon. The rumoured rustle of his presence in the market can kick-start a lame stock and send it soaring to new heights, the whispered mention of his name can pierce the bubble of some chart topper, unleash a herd of ambulance chasers and a bloody plummet into oblivion. Felix is ready to pounce on anything that moves. His expert claws rip the meat from a whole range of financial instruments with an extraordinary ability to extract value from chaos. He stalks the battlefield carnage, picking at the bruised flesh of failed mergers and acquisitions, resuscitating dying deals. *Wealth creation and wealth destruction, Geraldine. The most primitive of pleasures.* Felix moves markets like Jesus walks on water.

'So what the hell is it with this guy?' snarled the Grope four years ago when he flew back from Hong Kong after Felix suddenly cancelled what was supposed to be their very first meeting: no reason, no excuse and no rescheduling. 'Tell me what you know.'

'Not much,' I admitted, because the truth is that even after five years of coverage I have only an outline sketch of Felix's identity: a non-specific Home Counties accent, a wardrobe that reflects an impeccably British neutrality, no affectations or preferences, no family photos, no Ferraris airlifted in to burn off steam after a long day in the office, no appetite for showcase restaurants or vintage champagne, none of the usual trappings and accessories of Eighties' Man. A telescope in his Peak-top apartment. A collection of old weapons and war photos in his office, otherwise a cold trail of personal clues.

'I'm guessing Felix is thirty-something. Jacked in a Cambridge PhD and shipped out to Hong Kong years ago. No wife, no kids. Speaks Cantonese like a native. No one knows where the money comes from but the talk is it could be the Chinese government.'

'And you're the only one who can get past the gatekeeper. So what's your secret, Geri?'

'Kant.'

The Grope's mouth flopped open.

'No, K*a*nt! As in Emmanuel. Felix has a thing for philosophy.'

'Philosophy, huh?' the Grope narrows his eyes. 'What else?'

'He likes to watch me eat weird Chinese food. Lizard skin, rabbit tendons, that sort of thing.'

Naturally the Grope suspects I am fucking Felix, or at the very least providing some sort of sordid sexual service and therefore putting Steiner's order flow in jeopardy since I could be cast aside at any moment in favour of some sexual athlete. So every once in a while he hauls me off the trading floor and into his glass office to shoot the breeze, but I know he is really covertly checking me over for signs of wear and tear. Only last Wednesday he nabbed me just as I was leaving for Heathrow to bag Felix's order for the China Fire block and he tried to act all casual by taking out his golf club. 'You never played?' he asked, positioning his Eezee Putt against the glass wall. 'I used to spend all summer down the country club when I was a kid.' But I told him that golf wasn't such a big thing for convent schoolgirls in Dublin. The Grope took his time lining up, shifting his weight from one foot to the other, wiggling his hips. When he flunked the first shot, he held the club aloft to squint down the shaft as if his error might reveal a problem in the alignment. 'PING,' he said admiringly, 'you know the story, Geri?' and I didn't bother saying I'd heard it many times before. 'Karsten Salheim,' he continued, 'a lowly mechanical engineer at General Motors designed and made the world's best putter at his home in Riverroad, California. Just like Microsoft, it all started in a garage.' He leaned dreamily on the club and stared at his glass cabinet where a Stars 'n' Stripes stands guard over the trophies and deal tombstones, lending the display a faintly funereal air and I imagined the Grope's embalmed body laid out among his spoils like a relic of the American Dream, preserved in this airless shrine to watch over the trading floor forever.

'Never too late to start,' he offered me the Ping with an encouraging grin. 'And it sure is a helluva day out with clients.'

I shook my head. 'Felix hates sport. He thinks it's the pursuit of primitives,' and this remark had the desired effect because the Grope kicked the Eezee Putt to one side, tucked the little furry glove over his club and stashed it back by the coat stand.

'I don't know what you're doing with Felix Mann, Geri,' he said, 'and I don't want to know. Just keep it up and don't fuck it up.'

It is six years and a lifetime ago since I first heard Felix Mann's name and that was the same day the Grope threatened to rip out his fucking asshole. I'd been at Steiner's for a few months and was with my old boss, Ed Karetsky, who liked to end an evening's tequila slamming by climbing up on a bar stool to deliver Ivan Boesky's famous speech to the Berkeley class of '83: *Greed is all right, by the way. I want you to know that I think greed is healthy. You can be greedy and still feel good about yourself.* Ed had let me tag along to his meeting in the observer role of deaf and dumb graduate trainee, not realizing that by the end of that year he'd be breeding pugs in Illinois and – in an entirely unrelated but coincidental event – Boesky and the other 1980s corporate raiders would be behind bars.

As soon as we walked into the Grope's office, Ed clicked his fingers to indicate the wall space where I could disappear. He slung his leg across a corner of the conference table, oblivious to the stink of trouble in the air, the white lips of the two hotshots from Capital Markets at the table, the back of the Grope's head framed in the window like a warning sign. Ed stretched the elastic of his business school smile and just kept on swimming out to sea. *Hey, guys, howya doing?* Like they really had nothing better to do in the middle of a 200 million dollar stock placing for Cargo International than sit there and shoot the breeze, when upstairs Steiner's client – the Cargo CEO – had popped in for an update on the deal only to find himself sitting in front of the screen watching his stock spiral down 15%.

All because Felix Mann had decided to sell the shit out of Cargo.

The Grope punctured the airspace in front of Ed with a sharp and steady finger. *Karetksy. What The Fuck Is Going ON?* Ed froze, forgot to paddle and his mouth filled with water, an Adam's apple swallow jerked his tie knot upwards and he said, *Word on the street says Felix is taking a run at Cargo. That he's short selling the stock all the way down. Though we can't be sure it's him.* The Grope thumped his fist into the back of the chair. *It's got Felix Mann's butt-fucking footprint all over it. So YOU need to talk to him.* Ed chewed his cheek and muttered *Thing is he...uh ... still won't take our call.* He looked down at the familiar landscape of his shoes and the Grope stared at his bowed head as if from a great height, although it was really only a couple of inches. *This Cargo deal is sinking like a stone so I don't give a shit what you do, Karetsky, you STOP this guy.* I timed Ed's silence. After seven long seconds he nodded and mumbled *Yes*, which was all you really can say in a room where the knives are out. But the truth was Felix could sell Cargo's stock right down to zero if he wanted and there was absolutely nothing Ed could do to stop him. In fact, there was nothing anyone could do to stop Felix doing anything because no one at Steiner's had a relationship with him back then. And although this was ultimately the Grope's failure since he was Head of Trading and Sales, he needed to pass that efficiently down the food chain.

A sudden sunburst blazed through the window and the Grope flexed his shoulders, his white shirt flared yellow, like the rippling hide of a slow-motion lion tearing into a felled antelope. The two guys from Capital Markets tensed like a pair of craning coyotes and the Grope said the thing about Felix's asshole and I thought: well that's fine, but how can you rip out someone's asshole if you can't even get them to return your calls?

I half-ran along the corridor to keep up with Ed, scrambling for some upbeat remarks, trying to make him forget I'd witnessed his public humiliation, but it was too late, I had lost his good will. He stopped dead in the centre of the corridor, leaned in so close I could smell his mouthwashed breath. *Go play with the traffic, Geri*, he snarled, *I've got some real work to do* and he slammed through the double doors, leaving me to reflect on an important lesson that I was lucky to learn so early on: shit travels downhill, don't you ever forget it.

Cargo's stock fell 21% that day and the company was forced to call off the deal. Two months later, irregularities were discovered in their financial accounts, the CEO resigned on the back of the announcement and the whole embarrassing mess snowballed into a very public media witch-hunt, with Steiner's name written all over it. Felix had made an estimated eight million bucks buying back his stock and emerged from the rubble making a lot of smart guys look very stupid indeed. In the dash for cover and the ensuing whitewash, there was a rash of internal changes in the chain of command at Steiner's. A handful of analysts and bankers were quietly scalped for falling asleep at the wheel. Ed was sacked for running a sales force that had failed to develop a relationship with one of the most important clients outside of the US. When they came for him he said *I guess I should take my jacket, huh*, in a final attempt at gallows humour. *Watch your back, kiddo* he said to me but I just nodded. The rest of the desk buried their heads in the phones, shrinking from the noxious odour of failure as if it might be contagious. The security guard stood waiting by the exit like the Grim Reaper and Ed slapped him on the shoulder and turned to face down the trading floor. *I love you all, you fuckers* he bellowed but no one said a word and Ed walked out the double doors and was swallowed by the great sea, as if he had never been.

There but for the grace of God, etcetera, said Al. *God's got nothing to do with it,* Rob muttered. *Karetsky was always a tosser.*

The general consensus at Steiner's is that the Cargo fall-out cost the Grope about two career years. It was his second stumble on the power trip, the first was when his classmate James 'Moose' Hanson Jr made it onto the Operating Committee in '83 and the Grope didn't. So it's no surprise that the Cargo experience has left him with an allergic reaction to Felix Mann, like he doesn't feel safe in the jungle knowing that Felix could be out there sunning himself on a rock, waiting for the Grope to come ambling across his path with a nice big juicy deal between his teeth. But I actually think that what really bugs the Grope more than anything, maybe even more than losing out to the Moose, is the fact that that the biggest swinging dick in the investor community just ignores him, just refuses to take his calls. Even though he knows that Felix does this to everyone, the Grope can't bear the snub. Because he can't be entirely sure that it's not personal, that Felix isn't still smirking up his sleeve.

Years later, when I felt we'd covered enough ground, I asked Felix how he'd known about Cargo's slimy dealings. I was sitting opposite him on a rickety chair in some hole-in-the-wall Kowloon restaurant, battling with the beginnings of a predictable nausea. Felix leaned over the mound of tepid food that crowded the table between us and said: *The purpose of being a selective listener is to hear more clearly. To listen to the right signal, to eliminate the background noise.*

The streetlights cut out and flicker as I accelerate into the dark sweep of Lower Thames Street. Past the blackened stone of St Magnus the Martyr marooned in a cluster of office blocks, Christmas lights still bobbing gently on the leafless branches of the churchyard tree and I wonder what gruesome death Magnus suffered. If it was worse than Peter's upside-down crucifixion, Catherine's wheel or Sebastian slowly bleeding to death gazing wistfully up at the heavens, the angels' chorus bellowing in his ears as he reached that zone where pain is nullified by sheer conviction, transfixed by a dazzling vision of God's open arms and the promise of luxuriant expiry in His holy embrace.

I round Tower Hill and head up Minories. Pass a lone cab and a passenger head bent over an open *FT*, weakly illuminated by the backseat bulb. It is 06:31, not yet the half-light and I am doing record time, may even be first in, apart of course from Rob, who cannot be beaten. I crawl past his 911 at the front of the underground Porsche pack, then hang a sudden wrench on the wheel just to hear the tyres squeal. Twenty-two minutes exactly to the lift, which notches down my five-week running average to 24.2. I press 15 and the talking doll voice cuts through the silence. Of course it's entirely possible that Felix has already put his demand to the Grope. Perhaps the small matter of my consent to relocation has been overruled and I'll be met by a one-way ticket to Hong Kong as soon as I hit my desk. Or maybe the Grope has been suddenly recalled to New York for an urgent strategy session on how to get Steiner's through a war and still make a profit. Maybe all those marathons have finally caught up with him and he has keeled over with a massive coronary, is at this very moment being rushed to the Chelsea and Westminster, his wife sobbing into a monogrammed handkerchief, *I told him he should take it easy but he's always been a very stubborn man.* His left hand scrabbles weakly at his face and the paramedic lifts the fogged-up oxygen mask from his mouth. His wife leans closer, straining to catch the last words of a dying man barely audible above the siren and the engine roar and the Grope jerks his head a full inch off the trolley, expiring with a blue-lipped rasp: *Send the bitch to Hong Kong!*

2

present value

monday 14 january 1991
06:38
london

THE LIFT DOORS GLIDE APART, I step out onto 15 and already I can feel the market pulse. On busy days you can hear the roar of the trading floor right here, a blurred wall of sound that hits you like a stun gun. Time decelerates to slow motion and I cover the twenty paces to the double doors like a drifting astronaut. There are guys who bless themselves on this spot each morning and once I saw Rob kneel down to kiss the carpet. For there is no place in the world quite like this and I pause for a moment at the gateway to heaven and hell, listening to the call of the wild, the stadium pre-match rumble, the sound of money being kicked around.

There are four parallel rows of screen-laden docking stations with a walkway loosely dividing Cash from Derivatives, thirty battery-hen slots in each row. A bank of wall-mounted clocks tells the time in every place that matters and right now we are between worlds: the Asian markets are closing, New York is fast asleep and Europe is waking up for business as risk is passed like a baton from one continent to the other in this twenty-four-hour relay. High up on the overhead TVs a muted Stealth bomber bisects one screen and, on another, a troupe of soldiers in berets and Ray-Bans trudge across a sandy plain. To my right the ticker tape runs last night's closing stock prices above US Equities, a graveyard this time of day. The Grope's glass office spans a half-width of the floor and, suspended from a coat hook, is the only visible sign that he is in: the green umbrella that doubles as a golf club in his rare frivolous moments.

In the dead centre of the floor Joe Palmer sits tipped back in his swivel with his feet up on the desk, studying the football pages of the *Sun*. Behind him on the Japanese warrant desk, fifteen traders maintain an uneasy silence while studying his body language for some clue to the day ahead. Twenty-eight years old and five foot six in his brogues, Joe has a tight, wiry body and the cadaverous complexion of the shift worker, his skin a dirty grey, his eyes always red-rimmed as if he is battling an allergy. He wears his trademark blue shirt and a West Ham tie in a lurid claret and blue. His nose is a little misaligned, the legacy of a punch up on the Metals Exchange when he was a new boy. This is apparently not noticeable when you look at him full face, which I have never had the opportunity to do, because Joe does not speak to anyone who is not involved in the Jap warrant business and Felix gives all his Jap orders to Nomura since they bring in all the hot new deals.

Joe and his army of traders are the most profitable on the Street and his own trading book is the most profitable on the floor by far – maybe 50 or 60 million bucks last year – and who knows how much squirrelled away in his personal trading account. The Grope treats Joe with the indulgence you would lavish on a favourite grandchild, tormented by the fear that he will be lured away by Nomura. But Joe seems to like it here, though according to Rob, all of this is second best because football is Joe's real passion. He was signed by West Ham when he was a kid but a knee injury at seventeen cost him his future. Rob says one day Joe will buy a football club, that this is his dream, now that the first and real dream is forever denied him.

As I head towards my own window row, Joe chucks the paper in the bin, and stands up to begin a series of neck rolls. He has been here since 4 a.m. and already done his pre-market thinking. He has spoken to

Tokyo and he will not speak to anyone on the floor until precisely 6:55. His traders shuffle and stretch and fidget with their keyboards, prowling back and forth to the water cooler, circling their positions like a pack of hungry hyenas. A heavy pall of smoke hangs over their Quick machines which I covet, mainly because the screens are so cute and compact and all the text, everything, is in Japanese. We are making millions out of this market without even one person on the floor being able to speak the language but, luckily for us, all the Japanese stocks have numerical codes so you know what's going on even when you haven't got a clue. The past five years has seen the Nikkei index more than triple and Joe and his team have been riding the wave of this bull market driven up by whispers of land banks, reclaimed marshlands out near Narita, minidisks, semiconductors and tiny mobile phones that the analysts predict will soon make our clunky Motorolas a thing of the past. I picture their warrants as little scraps of torch paper, magical promises that can evaporate like those fortune cookie wrappers that ignite and dissolve on the tongues of fire, the incantation of holy words like Sony and Canon and Toshiba and Kawasaki, those monoliths that emerged from the post-war carnage to raise billions of cheap dollars with low coupon debt in the financial nirvana of Japan and an expansion that seems unstoppable. Lately there is a whiff of things going bad out there with the banks teetering under their own weight, but whatever happens we still all believe that Joe will be the last one standing. He has traded the Nikkei all the way up and then last year he made a killing even as it screamed down 39%. And incredibly, despite being the biggest player in the warrant market, Joe has never set foot on Japanese soil. In fact, he's never even been on a plane due to his pathological aversion to flying. This Christmas he treated his girlfriend to a Concorde trip to New York for a week's shopping with her mum and her sister, put them all up in the Astor suite at the Plaza.

Of course it's hard to sneer at someone's phobias when they make so much money.

■ ■ ■ ■ ■

'Nice of you to pop in,' says Rob as I approach. He sits hunched over a printout of his trading positions, his foot tapping as he calculates the risk of the dawning day. He does not raise his head.

'Nice to see you too,' I park myself on the edge of his desk. Tapered strands of brown hair rest on his shirt collar in a slight kink and I lean in to check the label of his tie. Rob won last week's tie king competition when he arrived with what looked like a vertical pattern of dollar signs made out of rope but was actually a column of naked girls snaking all the way up to his half-Windsor.

'Grope's looking for you big time,' he says.

'Any idea what he wanted?'

'Not as such. Could just have been the fact that he expected you to be here already. Of course we're only on the brink of a major war here, no pressing reason to come in at all.' He lifts his head, smiles. 'So how was Honkers? Bring me back any juicy orders from the Cat?'

'Where's the Grope now?'

'Big war chat upstairs somewhere. He'll be down for the morning meeting. But I wouldn't be in a hurry to find him, he's been a fucking animal.'

'What's all this?' I point to the mini TV perched on top of the Reuters screen, wires trailing over his desk.

'Got IT to set me up with a front row seat for all the action. Just look at this shit,' he jerks a thumb at a shot of last night's candlelight vigil in Trafalgar Square and a close up of a woman wearing a placard around her neck that reads:

HOW MANY BODIES TO THE GALLON MR BUSH?

'Give peace a chance, my arse,' he grunts. The screen shifts to a still of John Major and Rob turns up the volume. Teenage boys murdered in sight of their mothers and sisters, their bodies left on the street as garbage. Those who caution delay because they hate war must ask themselves:

how much longer should the world stand by and risk these atrocities continuing?

'So what's the word from the Grope?'

'The usual: Keep your head down, no fancy stuff, but stay in the flow. T + three days and counting. Neeeeoooooommmmmpugggggghhhhhhhh,' and his right-hand span cuts a descending dash through the airspace.

'You making money?'

'Kerfuckingching.' He taps his printout, for Rob is our lucky charm, the trader whose stock only rises and all the juniors stay close as if his pixie dust could coat them. When he first arrived the Grope had figured him for the Jap Warrant desk so he shipped him out to Tokyo to take the pulse. Rob spent a night at a club in Roppongi where the girls put minicameras in their vaginas that projected up on a big screen, and which he said was about as sexy as watching open-heart surgery. But he didn't plan on playing second fiddle to Joe; he wanted to stake out his own financial territory.

Rob is crisp in a way the other English guys aren't – snappy button-down shirts, shoes gleaming, a pristine shave. And he knows all about studying form and reading cues because his dad was a bookie so Rob used to spend Saturday nights at Harlow, crouched below the dog track with a bag of crisps, fiddling with the stopwatch, listening to the hum of the hare on the vibrating rail. One of the big trainers offered to take him on at fifteen but it was back at the bookie pitch that Rob felt at home. It was the chalked numbers on the blackboards, his dad yelling the prices and the punters scanning the odds, the men who blew their social on the first race, who'd trade their daughters for a tenner to stick on the next one, the late surge as the bell rang and they scurried over waving their desperate fivers, the crowd scrambling up the steps just as the traps sprung and the winning ticket and all of it over in thirty seconds. But Rob's dad wanted something better for him and so did Rob. On his sixteenth birthday he went on a school trip to the Stock Exchange floor and he knew immediately that he was home and dry. He cut his teeth in Futures where he wore a candyfloss jacket and roared his order execution up from the pit. Rob still mourns the end of open outcry, the migration away from an exchange floor and onto the screen. And he still goes to the dogs; took a bunch of us to Walthamstow one night where men in anoraks sidled up to mutter in his ear and he moved easily amongst them, a prince amongst thieves in his sharp suit.

Rob's got feel, his ear is finely tuned to the pitch of the markets and we have been comrades in arms since the very beginning six years ago when we met on rotation through the UK desk, sitting there wedged in between him and Jim Bain's overflowing ashtray. *See that chair you are sitting on? Know how much it costs to keep your arse in that seat?* Bain showed his stained teeth. *250,000 dollars. That's right, a quarter of a million bucks of allocated costs is what each trading position on this floor costs. So you two bozos are nothing more than overhead and don't you forget it.* Bain jabbed my shoulder. *And you're a Paddy, so you've got to work twice as hard.*

He wandered off, hitching his trousers and Rob leant in close, his eyes clear blue with tiny creases in the corner of the lids. *Top of the morning*, he grinned and I felt the smile spread across my face: we were the rookies but we were also the future and already we could sense that Bain was history. *I am hot to trot, sitting here with these old fucks. I am itching to get my hands on a trading book. Just you wait, G, you and me, the dream team.*

'So how was your trip anyway?' he offers me one of my own cigarettes. 'Another dodgy dinner date with your number-one client? What did Felix make you eat this time?'

I lean into the cupped flame and am overwhelmed by a wave of nostalgia. I long to rest my head in the shell of Rob's hands, to lay my cheek against his starched shirt, inhale his moneyed cleanness and tell him that Felix is forcing me out to Hong Kong and away from all this and I don't want to go, that there will be all this distance and a parallel life that carries on without me while I am outside the walled city of my comrades in-arms. For it was Rob who held me 152 days ago when I was ambushed by someone's sudden enquiry after Stephen and fled the heaving Jam Pot, holding my breath and the tears, elbowing through the Friday night crowd, rushing down the alleyway. 'What's all this then, G,' his arms encircled me on Lombard Street and he stroked my head while I cried into his shoulder, closing my eyes on the night around us. Rob held me for a long time with a surprising gentleness. I could almost imagine that it was Stephen, my hand inside his jacket felt the warm steady beat of his heart and I might even have drifted off for a moment into the sleep that had previously deserted me, there by the steps of the Royal Exchange with the comforting rumble of cabs, the tyres squealing on the damp street, the closing-time hurry of passing heels.

'I can't have you hanging on to me all bloody night,' Rob raised my chin. 'I'm only flesh and blood after all.' He touched my cheek with his knuckles and kissed me on the forehead. 'You can do much better than him, y'know,' he whispered and waved me off in a cab.

'You all right, G?' Rob looks up at my pricking eyes. A squawk box blares unanswered over on the Jap desk where the boys are huddled round Joe now for the countdown to their OTC market open.

'The smoke,' I blink, already walking round to my window seat on the opposite side.

'Actually I was giving odds on you getting stuck in Hong Kong for the whole war,' he calls out behind me. 'What d'you say we all go and get blasted tonight. Or shag, your choice.'

'Remind me how much I didn't miss him over the holidays,' says Al as I sit down at my desk.

'We call it Christmas in this country, mate,' says Rob but Al ignores the bait and twirls a little Stars and Stripes between thumb and forefinger, the phone crooked underneath his chin.

'Nice flag, Al. Very patriotic.'

'We're going in real soon, Geri,' he clicks the mute button. 'Thursday is my guess, soon as the UN deadline expires.'

'Al's got it all figured out,' says Rob from across monitors. 'Got a hot line to the Pentagon.'

'Under cover of darkness,' Al continues. 'These Iraqis won't know what hit 'em. The TV's gonna be awesome.' He clicks his receiver to live and plants the flag in a blob of Blu-tack on top of his Reuters.

I prop my feet on the rubbish bin that sits between our desks and doubles as a footstool. Al is the perfect desk mate to have on a trading floor because he is very neat and does not mind my untidiness or object to my smoke. He always has a supply of pens and chewing gum and he does not floss his teeth in public which is a habit that seems to be gaining ground on the floor recently. And Al also keeps a huge pile of research reports by his desk, neatly filed by date order and sector, that comes in handy for the clients I have who are not Felix and are actually interested in what Steiner's strategists and analysts have to say. Before Al was dispatched to London from our mother ship in New York, I used to sit beside Matty, who was fired for lying about an army career he never had. According to our mole in Human Resources, Matty admitted in his termination interview that he had lied about pretty much everything on his CV: he was not a county tennis champion, he never climbed Kilimanjaro and he did not have a pet cobra called Hector. None of this surprised me or Rob, since Matty had lied all the time to the few clients who would take his call, but also because Rob had been round to Matty's place in Fulham after a night's drinking and, when he asked to see the cobra, Matty said Hector was probably hiding in the chimney because snakes like the dark. But he wouldn't let Rob use a torch to look and there were no signs of any reptile paraphernalia anywhere. When we asked Matty about it the following morning he just said *Oh yeah, shame, Rob, 'cos Hector came out shortly after you left.*

■ ■ ■ ■ ■

'BANDAI, YOU FUCKING MORON,' roars Joe Palmer with a phone clamped on either side of his head. He whacks one receiver on the desk and yells 'ONE TWO', then he rams it back in his ear. 'You hear that, you shithead? TWO HUNDRED at nine and a quarter. I am buying two hundred fucking warrants of Bandai from you at 29 and a quarter.

'BANDAI' he shouts to his traders, 'hit the decks, pay up to 31,' and the boys hurl themselves on the direct lines to the competition and in a 90-second run-around they take out all the available supply of Bandai from the Street. Joe's fingers fly over the Quick keys like a stenographer, then he leans back, pats the single cigarette in his shirt pocket and watches his assistant add up the blue buy tickets. Rob reverses his swivel across the walkway and gives him a high-five. No one else would dare touch Joe, not since we once saw him punch an Ops guy flat out on the floor over some trade input error. In five hours' time he will be quietly planting the victory flag on the hill and he will take out his only cigarette of the day, which he will sit and smoke in absolute silence while his assistant tallies up the numbers. At 14:25 he will take his jacket from the back of his chair and walk over to the glass office where the Grope will leap up all toothy smiles and fuss over him like a grandma. Sometimes I wonder what they talk about, what the Grope's declarations of love are. How the big Yankee Wasp does man-to-man with this Essex boy whose girlfriend fills his thermos and packs his snack box every morning. They can't shoot the breeze about skirt because Joe is known for his disapproval of indiscriminate shagging. Joe is a family values guy who still has Sunday lunch with Mum and Dad. At exactly 14:50 he will stand up and the Grope will open the glass door and walk him out to the elevator and Joe will go home for a kick-about and a sleep and return refreshed the following morning at 4 a.m. This ritual is never broken.

'Word on the street is Bandai is going to start making edible underwear,' Rob returns to tell us. 'All those sex-crazed comic readers are in for a real treat.'

'So that's the big research story,' sneers Al. His dad didn't spend

$40,000 a year on Columbia tuition just so Alexander could coattail a casino market like Japan where fundamental research counts for nothing and barrow boys buy on the rumour and sell on the news and wind up earning five times what Al does. And of course Al himself is feeling pretty smug about the downturn in the Nikkei since he's been saying for years that the bull market has sinister overtones, that it's Japan's revenge for the bombing of Hiroshima, that Asia as a whole represents a fatal threat to the US economy because all their Toyotas and Hondas will force the Cadillacs and Chevrolets off the road and into extinction, their imports will flood the American markets and a teetering trade imbalance will topple us all into the sea.

'Hey, Geri, Geri, you gotta listen to this,' Al snaps his fingers, points to the phone crooked in his shoulder. 'I have got the ultimate shithot war trade,' and he taps his pad where he has scribbled the words *VULKAN VALVE*.

'Jurgen, my man,' Al shifts the receiver close to his mouth. 'I have come to tell you how to play this war.' He kicks his chair out of the way and starts his sales march backwards and forwards between the window and the row of desks, ever since he read an article about how standing up improves blood flow to the brain, Al makes all his sales calls upright. And as he launches into full flow beside me I can tell by the smooth patter that he's been flogging this idea for a couple of days now.

'But, Jurgen, just because Switzerland is neutral doesn't mean you can't come to the party. So here's what I'm telling you. A Saudi wellhead is only 20 metres across, and that's like *way* too small for the Iraqis to take out.'

When I started pulling in big orders from Felix, I used to think it would really get under Al's skin, him sitting beside me watching me chalk up the numbers, but he seems to relish it, as if there is some reflected glory in being my desk mate. So despite the fact that his sales numbers are a fraction of mine and his dogged pursuit of clients yields limited results, he still looks after me like an older brother. In the fallout after Stephen he behaved as if my broken heart was an extra presence on the desk that needed special care. He would surprise me with coffee in the morning or the avocado and mackerel pitta from Nadia's that he knows I like. And he was scrupulous about inviting me to any social event that came up. He even suggested I try my luck with his expat friends while he tried out mine. A sort of dating club for two. *We could like, you know, hang out at the weekend.*

Thanks but no thanks, Al. I mean I just have things to do, you know, Rex and stuff.

She's walking the dog, mate, quipped Rob. *That's girl code for fuck off.*

Shut up, Rob.

Only kidding, G. But Al's right, you know, said Rob. *You need to start getting out.*

Al slaps the desk with his free hand. 'Whoa there now, Jurgen, don't forget the MiG-29 Fulcrum: Mach 2.3, 30mm gun, six air-to-air missiles. Now that baby might be Russian but it's still one of the best fighters around and I would *not* want to be the guy sitting in a British Tornado staring that in the face. Luckily, there are only forty-eight MiGs in Baghdad, *as far as we know*. Which leads me straight to the reason for my call: Vulkan Valve.' He gives the phone cord a triumphant belt. 'No, no, it's a *British* company. No, NO, Jurgen. *Not* American, British. *Footsie listed*. Vulkan Valve has been around forever. A solid electronics business with increasing involvement in defence – comms systems, that sort of thing. And you know what these geniuses at Vulkan Valve have come up with? You know what the hot new defence must-have is? MSTAR. M-S-T-A-R,' his right hand twangs the phone cord in time with each letter. 'So what's MSTAR you say, Jurgen? Well, let me tell you. MSTAR is short for Man-portable Surveillance and Target Acquisition Radar. It's a new – and this is crucial, Jurgen – portable radar system. Imagine a tiny little dish no bigger than a – than a – Frisbee.' Al pauses and draws an imaginary Frisbee circle in the air in front of him. 'A tiny little Frisbee that gives you 180-degree cover over a range of sixteen miles. And so light you can carry it around. This baby can sniff out the enemy and provide exact positions. I mean if you want to kill people, you need to know where they *are*, right, Jurgen? Now MSTAR is state-of-the-art hardware, hot off the production line at Vulkan and rushed out to Saudi as of last week. And take it from me, if this puppy does what it's supposed to do, *everyone* is going to want one. You know how many defence budgets around the globe are getting beefed up in size as we speak? This is what I'm saying, Jurgen. Let's try and be *clever* about this war. Let's try and be ahead of the pack. The Vulkan Valve chart might look like a dog to you now, but just you wait till those MSTAR orders come rolling in and that stock takes off. Forget *de-fen-sive*, Jurgen, I'm saying let's go ballistic,' and he punches the air.

Rob holds up a Post-it and gestures at Al who leans in to read OXYGEN THIEF, while Rob is eye-rolling and mock-gasping for air. And I surprise myself by giggling because every time Rob does this in response to Al's high-pressure sales pitch, it is somehow just as funny as it was last time. Al gives him the finger and retreats to his desk, thwacking his phone cord against his leg.

'Like the man said, Jurgen,' he continues, 'the meek shall inherit the earth but not its mineral rights.' I know this quip is straight from the book he keeps hidden in his drawer called *Wall Street Wit*, and I also know that Jurgen doesn't get the joke because his English is not good enough, so he is not laughing like Al, who is chuckling into the phone now as he begins winding up the call. Without an order. And this is the nub of the problem: Al is great at coming up with stories but his closing skills stink. The Germans and Swiss appreciate his diligent attention to detail but he doesn't know when to hit the pause button. He buries clients alive with his spiel, I can picture them gasping for air as another shovel of clay hits them in the face. Al just doesn't see that sales is seduction, it is dialogue, not monologue. *Just shut the fuck up and listen sometimes*, I said to him last year when he was panicking because his numbers were flat and the Grope was leaning hard. *What you hear is worth much more than what you say. You've got to put yourself in the client's shoes.* But like most guys in this business, Al thinks it's all about him and the logic of the pitch. So he'd rather showboat than pay attention to what kind of performance pressure his clients might be under in this business of ego damage and repair. He doesn't try to imagine being Jurgen, sitting there in his dingy little cubicle at SK Zurich, newly promoted and scared shitless now that he is finally behind the wheel of the European fund just at the very moment that the world is staring down the barrel of a gun. Al won't hear the whimper in Jurgen's voice as he watches the world square up for war, he won't think himself into performance pain and until you become the only warm embrace in this bleak and hostile world, you will never have the client safely in your grip. ·

'Sure, Jurgen, sure. I'm going to be watching Vulkan real close and I'll be back.' Al hangs up and stares admiringly at his latest new toy – a black mug with "Greed is Good" emblazoned in gold on the front. His desk is an installation homage to Americana, and each time he returns from a trip home, he brings back a little souvenir. There is an NRA mug with the right to bear arms on one side and the pursuit of happiness on the other; a Coke bottle opener; an IBM drinks mat; the weighty pewter Bull & Bear statuette his father gave him when he got the offer from Steiner's; a collection of pencils with Columbia logos; a selection of Ivy League mugs that I am under strict instructions never to use; a basketball hoop that hangs on the wall behind us. Al keeps his Red Sox mitt in his locked top drawer since the last one disappeared and caused a lot of bad feeling. A varsity pennant hangs from his phone hook and the back of his chair has got a Route 66 sticker on it even though it is generally considered bad form to personalise chairs on the floor. And I see Nantucket '90, a new photo of Al in cut-offs leaping for a volleyball on white sand.

'You should personalise your space, Geri.' He has seen me looking. 'With what?'

'Some stuff that means something to you.'

'A bottle of vodka,' Rob cuts in. 'And a pack of Silk Cut.'

'How about a picture of Rex?' says Al.

'That's lovely that is,' says Rob, 'a picture of her fucking dog.'

'Or on vacation,' Al nods at his photo.

'One with your kit off,' Rob snorts.

'I don't remember this being a three-way conversation,' says Al.

I offer Rob a dark frown and then, to Al, I say, 'This is not my dorm. I don't actually live here.'

'Geri,' Julie's voice leaps out of the squawk and I look up to see her standing up at her gatekeeping post right in front of the Grope's glass box, gesturing urgently. 'He wants to see you.'

'How about later, like after the morning meeting?'

'Right now,' she cuts me short and watches like a hawk as I cross the floor, as if she senses I could disappear down a rabbit hole at any moment.

'Close the door,' he says as I turn into his office and I'm remembering six years ago when I showed up here for interview and the Grope asked me what I really wanted out of life. According to him, I said *I want to get my teeth into something*, but all I can recall is that he was the first man I'd seen with manicured hands. He had this trick of seeming not to breathe, a fat-fingered corpse propped up in a grey carver, no blinking, no rising chest, no visible signs of life. But like everybody else on the trading floor, I soon learnt to see it for the play-dead tactic it was, how he could lull you into a false sense of security just before unleashing his deadly strike. *Like watching a fucking alligator*, said Rob when I shared this observation. *The whole thing about reptiles*, yawned Al, his laundered arms stretched in a hand-lock, *is they have this transparent shield that covers their eyeballs so they don't need to blink. It's not like a deliberate thing*. Rob shook his head mournfully, *Life's just too short, mate*, and walked away, hands in pockets, sleeves up. Always the sleeves up.

'Great job last week on China Fire,' the Grope rolls into position behind his desk.

The truth is my big ticket with Felix on Thursday was a breeze since he had already made up his mind about the deal before I even arrived in Hong Kong. Steiner's had a client with a block of China Fire shares and a real nervous disposition who was forecasting World War 3 and wanted to liquidate his position before the first shot was fired in Baghdad. Felix was the obvious buyer; there was nothing I could tell him about China Fire that he didn't already know. So we could have done the business on the phone, but a ten million dollar trade was a good excuse for him to make me fly out to Hong Kong so he could arm-twist me about the relocation. First he let me run through the sales patter for the benefit of the two bifocalled gophers who stood hovering on the boardroom threshold waiting for an entry permit. One of them moved to slide a business card in my direction and Felix fixed him with a stern glare. He doesn't encourage fraternisation and I have never met the same analyst in all the time I've been coming to see him. After five minutes Felix dismissed the two lackeys with a terse nod and they slunk out of the room. Felix sat facing the door as if expecting an assassin. I waited, silent. I have long since learnt that opening gambits bore him, that he prefers to take the lead.

'You know that Goldman's are putting a sales person out here in Hong Kong next month, Geraldine. One of their top producers, in fact. A major commitment to the region.' He positioned his Mont Blanc in a precise alignment with his notepad. 'Apparently they think locally-based global coverage is exactly what I need.'

'Yes. We should talk about that.'

'We *are* talking about it, Geraldine.'

Of course we both knew that he could short-circuit the whole discussion with one call to the Grope and force the issue, but Felix prefers to amuse himself by toying with my feigned insouciance in the face of his smothering possession. It is control and its boundaries that keep him interested.

'And what are Steiner's plans for their Hong Kong clients?'

'You know we are totally committed. It's a question of—'

'I must confess that I have noticed lately a certain lacklustre quality in your performance, Geraldine. Speaking frankly, I think you would find that Hong Kong is the kind of environment where you would flourish.' Felix raised a palm to silence my intervention. 'And, of course, you wouldn't want the competition to steal a march on your business.'

'Yup, another great trade with Felix Mann,' says the Grope and leans towards me. 'And now we need to have a whole other conversation about him.'

I focus on the dead space between his eyes, tell myself this pulsing heart is just the booze and the lack of sleep. The intercom beeps. 'I have Tokyo on the line,' Julie interrupts.

'I said no calls,' he snaps.

'Yamamato-san says it's urgent.'

'God*dam*it.' The Grope slaps the desk.

'And they need you upstairs before the morning meeting.'

He frowns, checks the clock and pushes back from his desk. 'There's a very big opportunity coming your way, Geri. And we need to talk about it the minute I get back.'

He strides out of the office, leaving me sitting here staring at the TV and Saddam in his open-necked fatigues.

But this is no more than a temporary reprieve; all that's happened is I've bought a little extra time before I try to explain why I don't want to shift my ass to Hong Kong, for reasons that are not entirely clear because nothing is clear anymore, though some clarity might emerge if I applied myself to proactive thought instead of guzzling vodka and popping pills. Is Zanna right, is it really the vain hope of Stephen that makes me cling on to the non-life I have here? I am struck by the crazy thought that I should just ring him now, a desperate impulse to call and beg for his advice, but even if I could scale the 161-day ice wall of our silence, what would I actually say? The fact is I wouldn't make it past Alison, she would happily call-screen me into oblivion on the private line that Stephen never answers. *Sorry, Geri, he's in a meeting*, she used say when I rang in from trips, in a way that made me certain he wasn't. If I said I'd call back, she'd say the meeting leads straight into another meeting and all the while, in my head, I'd be carefully de-beading the strand of pearls around her neck and forcing them down her throat. I'd picture her sitting there, wondering if she could get away with not telling Stephen I called and if she did, how she would barb-edit the message. The power of being on the spot when I was ten thousand miles away. Ever since that night in Grodz when she overheard me say to Stephen it would be like fucking a fish or something. But he would never sleep with Alison, even I could tell she would cling on like dog hair, it could never just be the one fuck. Otherwise they have the same genetic profile, an intimacy with horses and Klosters and top-ranked public schools.

Sell water to a duck, fuel to a fire, a cure to a dying man, Stephen used to say to wind me up. Because he operates, of course, on a higher plane. Stephen makes history, not sales. He doesn't trade tickets, he delivers vision. Stephen raises the capital that bankrolls corporate ambition. He doesn't dance to the tune of the markets, he pioneers virgin territories, each new deal another chapter in the ongoing evolution of investment banking, another leap forward in mergers and acquisitions. He creates complex financial structures like a child dresses a doll in different outfits. In order to execute this important task, he had to organise it so he was born in the right hospital, went to the right prep school, bagged his Cambridge First and took his MBA at Harvard. Stephen has a direct line to the jugular while the rest of us suck on veins.

You have to have a nice speaking voice to work in Corporate Finance. You have to be able to hold your drink to work on the trading floor.

Behind me through the open door I hear the roar of another's day's business. Right now I should be warming up for the high point of my sales day, my phone audience with Felix, but I cannot muster the enthusiasm. Kant's treatise lies unopened on my desk although Felix told me I was to apply myself as I was leaving his office on – when? Friday and a lifetime ago. But I have not applied myself one little jot and he will use this as further evidence of my accelerating decline. There is only one way down from the pinnacle of success and that is a nosedive into oblivion.

The fact is Felix could pull the plug on a whim and I have to guard against complacency. *Such an undisciplined mind*, he snapped some weeks back when I slurred through a critique of Kant's Formula of Autonomy. *Such laziness, Geraldine.* When the line went dead I could feel the cold rush of career disintegration in my ear, for this was a foretaste of what would happen if I managed to detonate our exclusive relationship. I would find his direct line on auto-divert to his secretary, the past five years would count for nothing, Anna-Li would no longer recognise my name and I would face a future cradling an empty dial tone, that sound you never want to hear: the windswept wail of a salesperson who has lost a client, like a child screaming for its mother.

Zanna is right: Felix owns me body and soul. He structures my day and my compensation curve, a steady upwards slope to last year's peak: $872,678.14 (Base compensation $150,000 + Discretionary bonus of $722,678.14, excluding unvested stock options). Felix is the reason why my numbers exist and the reason I get paid what I do. He knows I know this, but Felix handles bonus numbers with the distaste you reserve for other peoples' shit. *I trust events yesterday were to your satisfaction?* he commented on the morning after Comp Day in December. *Fine. Everything's just fine*, which is how I always respond, DESPITE the fact that I bet I still attract a chick discount, some sort of arbitrary but in-excess-of-30% female cut, based upon Steiner's assumption that my career longevity will not match the guys around me, that it will be short-circuited by the ticking of a biological clock that will one day catapult me off the trading floor and into a Bulthaup kitchen. But I let it lie, because, hey, what's fair? You're only as good as your last trade and since when was I a feminist anyway?

A shout goes up behind me, I turn my head as the Warrant desk erupts into frenzy, all the traders are on their feet and yelling down the phones. Already these glass walls, the whole floor, is bathed in soft focus, now that I may be forcibly removed from the place where life first took shape. Something in an inaccessible place that feels like my gut is telling me that I just don't want to leave. That I just don't want to take the next logical step in the career ladder that began with a chance encounter in my final year at UCD, when all I longed for was flight. But isn't this everything I came looking for and more? Isn't this the most spectacular success?

For ten years since he emerged from the mists of Cambridge, Felix Mann has carefully constructed his own legend. But I imagine a beginning, some moment where he raised a sudden head from his books and stared into a future of petty squabbling over journal articles, frantic whispering over professorships, the breathtaking irrelevance of a life's research that would only ever amount to a soundless drop in an indifferent lake. I see him standing up abruptly, the scrape of his chair reverberating down the corridors as he flings open the college doors and disappears into a bright light. Felix walked away in search of a real-world blood sport where he could beat others at their own game, the Philosophy post-grad with no formal business training who jacked in a brilliant academic career and unearthed a treasure trove of assets that would give him the opportunity to flex his outperforming muscle.

Ten years is a lifetime in this business, the stuff of folk memory.

The view from Felix's Hong Kong fortress on the 31st floor of Exchange Square Two is littered with the sprawling bodies of enthusiastic bankers who crash and burn at his door, offering third-hand information and a menu of redundant services. Felix has never needed any hand-holding or breathless sales patter, he doesn't believe that the hungry beaks can tell him anything he needs to know in order for his fund to make a rumoured and consistent in-excess-of 40% return. Before me, he never spoke to a single sales person; execution only was always his policy, a non-partisan and strict division of non-Jap orders between the golden triangle of Morgan Stanley, Goldman's and Merrill's, with the occasional crumb dropped at the feet of the squawking competition whenever some deal inadvertently fell into their incompetent laps. Felix routed his orders straight through to the head trader of the relevant desk. He positioned himself as a reliable cornerstone in new issues, ruthlessly exploiting his barometer position in the pricing. You get Felix to commit to taking down 15% of a deal and you're home and dry.

So five years ago when I first announced to the rest of the desk that I was going to cold call the largest private fund in Asia, everyone sniggered at the idea of a rookie sales person thinking she might succeed where countless legendary big-hitters had rammed their heads on an unrelenting stone.

And when it worked, when I first had incoming from Felix Mann, they stood there gobsmacked, only to dismiss it later as the natural advantage of pussy. *No offence, Geri, but a bit of skirt will get you there every time.*

But I knew it was something else that had caught his attention.

It was 22 February 1986, some months after Cargo and Ed's demise and I was sucking wind on a virtually non-existent client base, when a blow-in from the New York office who was my temporary boss threw me a phone list one morning and said, 'Go fish for clients in Asia, it's virgin territory.' So I flew out to Hong Kong to meet a bunch of small-time institutions who liked free lunches but had little business to give. But my real target was Tom Castigliano, Steiner's dealmaker who had been based in Hong Kong for a couple of years, and had just succeeded in engineering a rare audience with Felix to discuss a complex restructuring for some Australian mining company. It took twenty-four hours of persistent pleading and ego-massaging flirtation over margaritas in the Captain's Bar but Tom finally relented and agreed I could tag along to the meeting with Felix Mann – on the strict proviso that I would be a bag-carrier with no speaking role. Eleven minutes into the torturous permutations of the deal, when Felix told Tom to change a few parameters and rework the pricing, I forgot my promise and reflex second-guessed an answer before Tom had even started working it out on his bond calculator. Felix's eyes registered my presence for the first time. He leaned back in his chair, tapping his pen on a notepad and ran a few scenario analyses by me as a test, instructing Tom to check my numbers on his calculator. Then he stood up and said, 'My, my. Quite the little performer.' Showing his yellow teeth. 'Sadly, an obsolete talent these days,' he added and pointed at the HP10 before ushering us out of the room.

'So what is it, like a photographic memory thing with numbers or what?' Tom asked later in the sinking lift.

'It's just seeing connections. Order. Sequence,' I replied.

I wondered if he was pissed off that I'd stolen the show. But I have since understood that Tom is a visionary pragmatist who adapts to the prevailing landscape, knows there are always other thunders to steal and had already realised how useful I could be. So when the doors shuddered open onto the foyer, he turned the full glow of his fuck-me eyes onto my face and smiled, 'You could make a killing card-counting in Vegas with a trick like that.'

But our unarticulated plans for sex were scuppered when I arrived back at the Mandarin to a message from Felix's secretary that he was expecting me for dinner that evening. I turned back to the street for a forty-five minute Dress Emergency, whipping through boutique rails of backless-strapless nothingness until I decided on the 500-dollar ambivalence of a forest-green silk suit. The faint flame and mandarin collar would tell Felix I hadn't gotten the wrong signal, hadn't confused him with the kind of client who spends his evening in a champagne drool down the front of your dress.

Felix's uniformed driver bowed and led me from the hotel lobby at

7 p.m. 'Where are we going?' I asked the back of his shaved head but his peak cap didn't respond. I smoothed the careful folds of my skirt as the car glided away from Central, away from the elegant hotels and the clustered nightlife I knew, speeding down into the tenemented harbour hell of Wan chai. The car stopped in a side street and I looked through the darkened window down an alley where a dog nosed through a jumble of rotting garbage.

'There must be some mistake,' I said when he opened the car door, my sandals hovering delicately just above ground.

'Please, Miss Mowoy,' said the driver and pointed to an opening in the wall where shredded blue and red plastic strips dangled in the evening breeze.

Two men sat cross-legged and smoking on a low step, squinting impassively at my legs. On the opposite side of the street, a thin-limbed boy crouched on the ground, poking a gecko with his finger. A chicken came hurtling through an open door and stopped to shit by the boy. The car moved off and I pushed through the entrance, colliding with an elbow-height old woman who pinched my upper arm and pushed me towards the threshold of a room packed with smoking locals. There was a sudden lull in the chatter as they watched me make my way towards an empty table in the middle of the room and I sat down to a mutter and a sharp burst of laughter.

'Geraldine. Delighted you could make it.' Felix materialised at the table, in full evening dress, a naked bulb casting orbs of shadow below the sockets of his cold tea eyes, his thinning black hair swept smooth and sparse over a pallid skull. 'I thought you might find it interesting to see where the natives go.' He turned to the old crone and issued a rapid-fire sequence of Cantonese while she sucked loudly on her gums.

Felix sat down and took a pen from his jacket pocket, scribbled on a notepad and slid the page towards me.

$$1 + (^1/_2)^4 + (^1/_3)^4 + (^1/_4)^4 = ?$$

'1.08,' I said. 'That's if two decimal places is close enough for you.'

Felix stroked a thumb tip along the inside of his watchless wrist.

'And the sum of the series?'

I picked up his pen and wrote: $(\pi)^4/90$.

The old woman shuffled to the table and set down a chipped bowl in front of me. 'Aren't you eating?' I asked Felix, sweat seeping though the forest of silk as she returned with a platter piled high with the smell of fetid decay.

'Thank you, Geraldine, but I prefer to eat alone.' He laid one bony hand on the other and leaned forward. My trembling palms slid on the impossible chopsticks while Felix smiled and watched me eat and gag and eat and gag my way through a stinking procession of dishes, describing each arrival with painstaking detail: 'chicken hearts on sticks, a rather vulgar snack popular with cinema crowds; deer tendon, requires the precision of a scalpel to cleanly sever it from the bone. Ah yes, bear paw, a northern delicacy with a host of medicinal properties. Did you know that the Romans used to eat flamingo tongue?'

A pale lizard picked its way along the edge of the table and Felix grabbed its tail. 'Transubstantiation, Geraldine. A rather troubling concept for an Irish Catholic child I would have thought – eating the flesh and blood of the grown-up baby Jesus?' The light bulb flickered above our heads. 'I don't remember ever thinking about it,' I said, looking away from the spasming body that dangled in the eye-level space between us.

Felix clicked his fingers and the muttering crone appeared with a small stemless glass of what looked like red wine that I immediately drained, choking mid-swallow on the viscous metallic swill.

'Turtle blood,' Felix smiled. 'Strictly speaking, a Taiwanese speciality.'

I lurched away from the table in a blurred stagger, the old woman pursuing me with a stream of high-pitched squawking, the sound of laughter and clapping from the other tables. She shoved me out the back door into a shed where I bent double in the near-darkness and spattered my dinner into a black hole in the ground. She handed me a stained grey towel and I wiped the vomit off my sandals. 'Water,' I said holding up my hands, and followed her back inside to a sink full of dirty dishes. A fly buzzed just beyond my nose, the tepid tap water trickling over my hands. She handed me a plastic cup with a flood of encouraging sounds and gestures and I drank the clear liquid that smelt reassuringly of chemical oblivion, holding out the cup for a refill. When I returned to the table Felix stood up and bowed, thanked me for a delightful evening and led me out into the alley where his driver stood by the open car door. I got in and we sped off, a wordless drive back to the hotel where I stumbled out of the lift and onto my bed, to lie in the darkness under maximum air con, breathing a slow struggle against the churn in my stomach.

At 7:30 the following morning I got a discretionary order for five million bucks worth of S&P futures contracts, phoned in by Felix's assistant while I was still puking my guts out all over the hotel bathroom.

A week passed back in London and Felix didn't return my calls. And then one morning a shout came through on the squawk box that he was on the line. My hand hesitated over the receiver, Al and Rob staring at me in slack-jawed disbelief.

'Geraldine.' Felix's voice like a light wave. 'What's your bedside reading these days?' I turned to the wall and told him I was looking for recommendations.

'*Principia Mathematica*. Call me tomorrow at 8:15.'

I spent all night poring over the musty hardback that I had tracked down in the Kensington library, a 1963 second edition, last borrowed on December 1972, thinking, where shall I start, what kind of test is this, what does Felix want to hear? I flicked to the appendix: Truth Functions and Others. According to Frege, there are three elements in judgment: recognition of truth, the Gedänke, and the truth-value...

At 8:16 the following morning Felix asked my opinion of Whitehead and when I put down the phone thirteen minutes later, I knew that I had bagged the elephant. My sales numbers rocketed and within four months I was the biggest hitter on the floor, generating eighty million dollars of orders and fuck knows how much trading p&l. Every head-hunter in town was leaving cryptic messages on my answerphone, wanting to buy me a drink on behalf of Goldman's, Merrill's, whoever, but I never returned the calls. Steiner's was right up there in the bulge bracket and I'd found my place in the sun, so why would I ever want to leave?

So now I cover Felix on everything that moves – stocks, derivatives, bonds, commodities – wherever he wants to go. He told the Grope I would be the only point of contact, the only voice at Steiner's that he wanted to hear. 'One-stop-shopping', I believe you call it, Felix's faint message like an old recording on the answerphone that the Grope played back to me in his office. Every morning for the past five years, Felix has taken my daily call at precisely 8:15. He never asks what Steiner's strategists are thinking about the markets and he hasn't the slightest interest in anything our research analysts have to say. Instead he begins each call by asking me what I have read from the list of philosophical and mathematical texts he has prescribed. Sometimes he wants me to quote entire passages or formulae, more often he will ask a question only to cut me dead mid-flow. Sometimes he just listens without remark. And these are the toughest calls, hunched over my desk amid the flickering screens and the purring phones and the roar of business, holding forth to a silent long-distance audience of one. When Felix has heard enough he says, 'Thank you, Geraldine.' As a reward for this service, I receive a party bag of two or three substantial 'No Limit' orders, one of which is guaranteed to inflict some pain on the traders.

Out of all the bobbing heads in the sea of banking, all the barking seals voice-trained to perfect sales pitch, Felix has chosen me as the interesting diversion in his day, the research experiment that he might have undertaken if he hadn't found academia so lacking in thrill and excitement. I am the engaging lab rat with the curious facility with numbers, and it seems Felix finds it amusing to test my outer limits, to explore the line between what I can absorb and what I can understand. *Investment banks are usually so unimaginative in their hiring policy. How refreshing that Steiner's should have found such a gem hidden away in a third-rate university in Dublin.* I am a favourite pet, a beacon of entertainment in his outperforming day, an antidote to some bone-crushing monotony, the taste other people leave in his mouth, a dry and bitter acidity, an undisguised contempt. *There is no one who keeps me amused like you do, my dear.* I know that Felix sees my circus trick as a delightful affliction, a genetic fault, a deformity that fascinates. He is conducting pressure tests on a rare specimen to get a clearer view of what lies behind. Felix wants to know if my maths talent has real potential, if I can apply myself to original thought. *Science is what you know, my dear, philosophy is what you don't. Did you know that the great Mr Russell did most of his thinking as a teenager? In fact he'd already stumbled on Descartes' ideas long before he actually read them.* Felix has told me he is delighted that I paid so little attention during my undergraduate days in Dublin since too much study of old philosophers creates the illusion that everything has been already thought of. *The young Mr Russell spent most of his time thinking about maths and God, concealing his theological doubts in secret code lest it cause his family pain. Your intellectual laziness intrigues me, Geraldine. It is as if something has dulled your appetite for all that you could become.*

He is right, of course, although he doesn't know why. Felix is inching closer, can smell my reluctance, maybe even suspects that which only I know: how the numbers can cloud and swim in my line of vision, how they threaten to obscure everything, their horror seduction pursuing me through the night hours. The curve of a three, the suggestion of a seven, the swimming fluidity of an eight, the compulsion to connect, their screaming demands, the drain on my attention. The slow reveal of a sequence, the fear that I may somehow lose myself in the numbers, that they may one day suck me dry.

But as long as I have Felix Mann's account I am untouchable. And if the Grope could just figure out the key to Felix's twisted heart then he could sleep easy. Every night Felix is with me as my head hits the pillow, and I know without ever having to be told, that if I didn't do my reading, there would be no forgiveness, there could never be an excuse.

It feels like phone sex, I said to Stephen once. *So your client gets off on philosophy? So what?* He turned the pages of his weekend *FT. Just go with it, Geri, don't look a gift horse in the mouth.*

But every morning at 8:15 it feels like I'm sitting naked from the waist down, feet pressed up against a glass wall, my quivering thighs splayed wide so that Felix can inspect the bits he's paying for, the thing he owns.

06:58

'HE WON'T BE BACK NOW till after the morning meeting, Geri,' Julie appears in front of me. 'Are you OK?' she bends down, peering at me with a frown. 'You look—'

I lean forward but the effort of rising from the chair is beyond me, there's a rush of fluid to my head like I've driven over a bump. Julie shoots out a hand. 'Steady,' she grabs my arm. 'You look like you're going to faint. Lean over and put your head between your legs.'

'No chance.'

'Well, sit still then, don't move and I'll get a glass of water.'

I close my eyes. Breathe. Think of a number, any number, say 167. Which is how many days it's been since I last saw Stephen in the flesh. He'd left it two weeks since the Venice dumping to collect the last of his possessions from my place. There was less than might have accumulated during the four years of our coupledom – some shirts, books, a pole that had been separated from its ski. *At least you weren't living together,* said Al. As if there is an arbitrary scale of collateral damage associated with a break-up where the maintenance of separate homes is taken as an indicator of a lack of commitment, rather than the by-product of an excess of income and a shortage of time, so that when everything falls apart it is supposed to be *less* upsetting, less painful than if you had been cohabiting. As if wealth is a fire blanket that insulates you from pain.

Stephen was not red-rimmed or dark-eyed when he called round. He showed me how polite evisceration could be done with panache while I stood affecting nonchalance in my own hallway, hands wedged in the back pockets of my jeans, trying to short-circuit a trembling sensation that was creeping down into my fingers. He was sporting a pink check shirt I'd never seen and wearing deck shoes without socks, the pale instep showing as he balanced his leg on the chair to sort through some CDs. And I was staring at his instep while he chatted on in the manner of a friend who had popped round on their way elsewhere. Perhaps an impeccable prep schooling includes lessons on how to handle awkward aftermaths with aplomb. Stephen always exuded the charm and good manners of a Foreign Office diplomat. First they offer you a sherry and then they stab you through the heart. He could talk his way out of a bandit emergency on the Khyber Pass.

I felt a lurch somewhere below my ribs and a dizzying drop in temperature as if warm fluids were being drained from my body and replaced by a formaldehyde chill. Stephen would have noticed the telltale signs of personal carnage: overflowing ashtray, dirty glasses on the floor, my unmadeness like a scripted response.

When it was time for him to leave Rex tried to shove past through the open door so I had to grab his collar. Then he lunged and I banged my head on the wall, ricocheting into Stephen who dropped the shoebox of CDs and it descended into pantomime slapstick with him making solicitous enquiries about my forehead and me trying to shovel the CDs back into the box and Rex dropping his tennis ball in between us. I kept my head bowed so my hair would hide the tears that must have been unleashed by the blow to my head, because I could not believe that I had any left for us. *Ice maybe?* said Stephen. *Just leave*, I said and grabbed Rex, held his wriggling body tight while Stephen closed the door behind him and Rex sloped off to his bed in the corner, looking reproachfully at me as if to say, it's your fault, you blew it.

Oh, Geri, said Zanna when she called round that afternoon and found me with a pile of photos dumped on the floor. *You thought he was coming back, didn't you?* she said, ferreting out my misplaced hope that Stephen's return might have been a ruse to confess his loneliness and retract his terrible error with an admission of undying love and a plea for forgiveness that would end with us collapsing in each other's arms. But Stephen is, as Zanna would say, so over me. And the fact that he could be bothered to call round to collect a bunch of possessions that he could easily replace was simply further evidence of the fact that he had already left me a long time ago.

Zanna was right. Zanna is always right about the ring of steel that encircles the heart.

'Take this,' Julie holds out a plastic cup. She nods approvingly, watching while I drink. 'If you don't mind me saying, Geri, you've lost a lot of weight recently' – and I have to admit that it may be some time since I have eaten. She opens her mouth as if to say more but decides to hold her fire. Instead she waits, twisting her engagement ring, the one we all saw before Tim's Christmas proposal when Ruben showed up from Hatton Garden, his coat pockets stuffed with shedloads of gear that he carts across town. *He does quality gear, none of your rubbish*, said Rob as we crouched down by my desk. *Like you could tell diamonds from paste without looking at the price tag*, I snorted. *I'm thinking emeralds to go with her eyes*, said Tim, carefully tipping the velvet pouch on to my notebook, holding the ring up to the overhead light. *Pay attention, Geri*, said Rob, *'cos this is the closest you'll ever get to one of those unless you buy it yourself*, his face so close I could see his scrubbed pores. *I mean, you're not really the marrying kind, are you, G? You're not interested in all that?*

Am I right? and I laughed because laughter heals a sting, a sore that goes unnoticed until it's scratched.

'How do you feel now?' Julie asks, all worried frown. I stand up unaided and turn towards the floor and the open door where life is playing out before us. Over on the Jap desk Joe Palmer is yelling at Tokyo on the hoot 'n' holler. Skippy Dolan stands tall on the Block Desk with his middle finger spiked in front of him. There's lots of air punching going down in France and over by the window I can see Rob in what looks like a face-off with Al.

'Like a million dollars,' I say and spread my arms wide. Julie smiles in broad relief, for I have been returned to my familiar self and this is the Geri we all know and love.

3

on the tape

07:11

'SO HOW 'BOUT YOU GO fucking sell 'em, Al?' Rob says. Al stands frowning on the other side of the desk, the undialled phone falters in his hand.

'Fucking waste management,' Rob batters at his keyboard.

'How was I supposed to know you went and bought them for your hedge book?'

'Put your money in Claxin Falls,' Rob mimics Al's drawl. 'The industry of the future.'

'He's been saying that for months, Rob,' I tip out a cigarette. 'And anyway, aren't you supposed to be the trader who never listens to a single word spoken by a salesperson?'

'I didn't even have an order, for Chrissake,' says Al.

'Yeah, well, why don't you have that etched on your tombstone, mate? Here lies Al, a salesman without an order.'

'Fuck you,' Al slams down the receiver and walks away.

'So you've still got that Claxin?' I ask.

Rob scowls at his screen. For months now he has been making hay on his proprietary positions, ever since the Grope told him he could take a punt on whatever he fancied as well as handling client orders.

And now Rob is furious because his precious hedge book is groaning under the weight of five million Claxin Falls convertible bonds that have been treading water since he bought them.

'Still got the fuckers. Going nowhere,' which was exactly what Felix said when I showed him the bonds before Christmas but Rob made the mistake of thinking he saw value where Felix didn't and went ahead and took them on himself. For six months now Rob's been on a roll in convertibles, a lucrative exotic that very few people truly understand and a market that Felix adores since it is imperfect and therefore awash with opportunity.

An instrument of rare beauty, traded by fools who have no idea how to value. So I buy them too cheaply from Merrill's, Goldman's, Morgan Stanley. And even from Steiner's. Felix has been the convertibles king for five years, making a killing out of these quirky little creatures that can generate vast returns. *Always pay attention to the activity at the margins, Geraldine, it is the peripheral vision that reveals the real treasure. Look at the ripples, there is so much value at the fringes.* He tapped his temple. *Shall I tell you why my returns are vastly superior to those of my so-called competitors in the investment community? I've always had a soft spot for the undervalued. The misunderstood, underappreciated, unloved asset class, a rich complexity of the hybrid that can only be truly appreciated by those with a more sophisticated palate. Those with a natural curiosity for the unusual. Like fine wines from small vineyards. You can pick them up for a song. The convertible bond is a financial hermaphrodite – outcast and frequently ignored. And I am a connoisseur of the neglected. For in the backwater lies the gem. Much like yourself, my dear.*

This is the kid of creepiness that Felix likes to taunt me with, his thin grey lips screwed into what looks like a leer but is actually the closest he gets to a smile.

'So, Geri,' Rob perks up, suddenly enlivened. 'How 'bout you work some of your sales magic? How 'bout you show Bud Light a real big hitter in action?' Rob jerks his thumb at the brown-haired boy who stands beside him like a gundog in attentive observance. Bud Light is one of the interns we ship in from Columbia, Harvard, INSEAD or even down the road from the LSE, although the American grads like Bud usually wipe the floor with local talent. He is back under Rob's wing after a brief sojourn in Operations to complete his study of the life cycle of a trade. Rob is an effective teacher who does not provide false shelter from the storms they will meet. He makes the grads run tickets at full tilt to the back office because he believes an early lesson in urgency will make them appreciate the danger of getting things wrong. They listen wide-eyed to his horror stories about lost trade tickets, little slips of pink or blue paper that can mysteriously disappear in the Bermuda triangle: the fifty-foot ocean between a trading floor and the Ops is the most treacherous water where a five million dollar trade can vanish in the ether.

'Come on, G, show Bud here how it's done.' Rob rubs his palms, elbows Bud, who nods eagerly.

'What you *really* mean, Rob, is you want me to find a nice tame client and stuff him into a landfill. So you can dump your shit position in Claxin Falls and save your ass from the Grope who wants to know why you bought such a dog in the first place. Am I right?'

'She's all heart, our Geri,' Rob grins. Bud Light follows this exchange like it's a tennis match. His real name has been erased from my memory since Rob's christening after he survived the acid test of a night's drinking and resurfaced on time the following morning only to puke up in the waste bin. Trainee survival odds lengthen dramatically when you are awarded a nickname, but Bud Light does not know this yet. Still, he has stayed the course with sturdy good humour, is happy to start at the bottom of the food chain and seems to embrace the challenge of moving from overhead to asset and understand that success is entirely his responsibility, that nothing comes to those who sit and wait. You must therefore get the coffees in or make yourself useful while simultaneously remaining invisible and exhibiting a murderous keenness. This is not as difficult as it might sound, though most of the pink-lidded rookies do not make it. Once a boy cried. He'd been despatched on a simple errand, to get a fresh stack of tickets but failed to return before Rob had actually run out. He ambled back to the desk with an insouciant grin and asked Rob where he could get a sandwich. *This is not fucking Treetops where we show you the toilet and give you a packed lunch.* Last summer when an intern showed up one morning sporting braces with dollar signs Rob picked up a marker and wrote *I am a cunt* on the kid's cheek. It turned out to be indelible ink so he had to go and get some stain remover from a hair salon and he was allergic so he went around for a week with a rash.

'Now listen up, Bud,' Rob points to the screen and reads aloud: '07:13 Pentagon confirms 680,000 allied forces in Kuwaiti theatre of operations – White House. Lesson number two thousand three hundred and four: War is opportunity. And Geri is going to demonstrate exactly what that means any minute now, aren't you, G?' Bud Light looks from Rob to me, he is soaking it all up, learning the banter protocols of head trader to top producer.

'Five million lovely Claxin Falls on special offer,' Rob dangles the receiver.

I flick my speed-dial, thinking that I *could* just do what I'm paid to and work some client up to pre-war fever pitch, make him believe that the *worst* thing to do right now would be to sell and that the *best* course of action would, in fact, be to pre-empt a victory rally and buy some quality merchandise while everybody else is sucking wind. And what could be safer than rubbish? The perfect target is, of course, Arthur at Bishopsgate Asset Management whose ulcerous paranoia about the chronic underperformance of his fund is directly correlated to his inability to resist sales chat. I signal to Rob who clicks onto my line, presses the mute button and hands the receiver to Bud Light to listen in to my call.

After a little grumbling about how I haven't been around for a couple of days and my soothing apology that I was away in Hong Kong (seeing a much more important client than him), I find Arthur at exactly the right point of frantic indecision. A few days listening to the news and staring at the screen has tipped him into a pre-war tailspin and he is borderline hysterical about some analyst from Merrill's who's just come across the tape saying that oil could drop to twenty-five bucks.

'Forget oil, Arthur,' I say. 'Number one, you haven't got any in your portfolio. Number two, it's a total red herring. As we were saying last week, you're cash rich going into this war so you're way ahead of the pack. Now what you really want to be worrying about is that you might be too *light*.'

'Light? Too light?' he mutters in a subdued scream.

'That's right, Arthur. Remember our strategist who predicted the fall of the Berlin wall? Well, I've just come out of a meeting and he's saying that the war is already in the price, it's all discounted, so what you *really* should be worrying about is the risk to performance when the war is over.'

There's a moment's silence while Arthur considers this. 'I don't know, Geri.'

'That's exactly what I'm saying, Arthur. Forget all this short-termism. I mean, you're not a day trader, are you?'

'No.'

'And you *are* running an income fund right?'

'Uh huh, but—'

'Arthur, listen. What you need to be thinking about is what your boss is going to be saying about your performance at the *end* of the year, when we're all looking back at the mother of all rallies that happens *after* the war has been won. I'm talking dollar exposure, high credit ratings, big fat coupons. You know as well as I do that there's not a lot of stuff like that around. For example. I did a run-through this morning and the only thing I could find was Claxin Falls. 7.5% coupon. Single A, 35% premium with a chart that's bursting at the seams.'

I hear Arthur tapping it into his Bloomberg.

'Look at the last two years on the stock chart now and you'll see what I mean.'

I lean over and flick open the Value Line report on Al's desk, omitting to tell Arthur that Steiner's don't actually cover the stock. In a carefully-timed passing remark, I mention that I normally wouldn't get Rob to show any size on US stuff before the market opens, especially on a day like this. But I could probably twist his arm. 'Seeing as it's you.'

'Mmmm,' says Arthur and I know I'm home and dry.

'Hey, Rob,' I point to the receiver in my hand, which I do not mute, because I want Arthur to hear the exchange. I tell Rob very clearly that I know it's risky before the stock opens in New York, but Arthur's a good guy and is there any chance at all that you could show some Claxin Falls? Rob breaks into a grin, climbs up on his desk so he can lean over the two banks of screens and says, just loud enough, 'Well, I dunno, Gerl. I don't want to get fleeced on the opening.' He lets his voice trail away and I say that I understand but Arthur really needs some high-quality exposure right now. We wait. Rob watches without moving until I give the hand signal. Then he leans over the desk and says loudly, 'OK, well, seeing as it's Arthur, I'll show five bars at 92.' He lifts his chin, smiling into my eyes.

I tell Arthur that he can have five million at 92. 'Done,' he says straight away, reminding me to give a special thank you to Rob for helping him out.

I hang up. 'You're done. Five bars at 92.'

'Once a scout always a scout,' Rob blows me a kiss. 'That's fifty grand for the good guys.' He high-fives Bud Light. 'Welcome to the dream team.' Bud Light's face is aglow with the excitement of witnessing this learning milestone in sales–trader cooperation.

'SOAPY,' Rob bellows over at the Jap desk where one of the Ops girls is emptying the ticket trays, picking her way through the gauntlet of traders, on the lookout for hands that at any moment could grab her butt or plunge a receiver in between the enormous boobs that all the boys love. But the market is roaring so they are busy and oblivious so she is safe – or maybe she misses the attention, who knows?

'Got a big one for you, darlin,' he roars and nods to Bud. 'Give that to Soapy, mate.'

'New one on me.' Bud picks up the ticket.

'As in Soapy-tit-wank.'

Bud spins round, his mouth flops open and then he looks over at me just as she pulls up.

'All right, Soaps. Meet Bud here.'

She mutters a jaded hello and Bud manages a strangled Hi while studiously keeping his flushed gaze away from her chest. Soapy doesn't linger, just takes the ticket, flicks her long brown hair over her shoulder and turns away.

I stamp my own ticket, drop it in the out-tray and open the file marked *1991 trades, GM*. I look down at the last ticket in there and the post-trade fizz flattens. And I can remember that even as I was writing *that* one I was thinking exactly what I'm thinking now: so this is it and I am getting nothing out of it, not a rush, not a buzz, it's all just a big *So what*. It used to be that one trade led to another and another, and a day, a whole week would fly by in the self-generated challenge of outclassing myself and the rest of the team. I would jump, just to jump the highest. I'd spend the whole night hanging onto the same bar rail, arguing the finer points of where any stock was going, scattering the stats and forecasts in an impressive demonstration of my circus trick. Clearing the Beechers of all hurdles – the Most Difficult Sales Pitch at the Most Inopportune moment – in one sweep used to be all it took to get me into a blisszone that didn't know day from night. But somewhere, one day when I wasn't watching, the spark must have sputtered and died. This is what Felix has been hinting at and it is just a matter of time before the Grope notices that the numbers which might look like a seasonal plateau are actually accelerating into a disinterested decline. I think about time decay, that beautiful slope that charts the death throes of an option as it screams towards a certain expiry, like a meteorite on a steady course for earth and sudden obliteration.

I turn around to the window and what's outside our world: a skyline, orange cranes, yellow hardhats. Bloated worms with a murderous hunger boring into the City – glass, steel and stone sprouting everywhere in the post-Crash earth. And somewhere out there is the beginning of all this: the little old lady takes her few quid to the building society, who wires the news to the fund manager, who gives the nod to his dealer, who picks up the phone to a salesman, who shouts across to the trader who says SOLD. So pick a number, place a bet. Look at the graph: here is the high, here is the low. Is this a breakout or a dead-cat bounce? Data is information is interpretation is action. A hundred salesmen plugged into the phone lines with a kaleidoscope of truths, a thousand different ways of looking at the same picture.

I close the file, slot it back into place beside my Reuters and remind myself that it is only 07:23 and I have already managed to do what I am paid to do – feed the bottom line. I passed on Rob's dud position to Arthur who doesn't need it but isn't smart enough to know when he is being sold a pup or strong enough to say no. I have learnt to be a good liar or, at the very least, a great storyteller, though what the truth is no one has a clue, it is all informed guesswork. Market analysts, stock experts and all of us sales people gather the facts and spin a story that sounds convincing, one which will become self-fulfilling if it creates momentum among the great herd of investors. But in the end it's no different to watching a dog race, the favourite can stumble on the break or falter at the first bend and be beaten by a rank outsider who crosses the line at 20/1.

The cab drivers on the street far below are getting fatter on our titbits. They flock like crows around the concourse and eye us in their rear-view mirrors, sometimes asking what we do, going into work at the same time as cleaners. We play it down, don't want to give the wrong impression about the money we're making though we know we are overpaid. But that's what we cost, it's only the going rate and anyway there is no such thing as value for money. In one year you can make more than your dad made in twenty. The richest 5 per cent of the population owns 35 per cent of the wealth in this country. The poorest 5 owns nothing.

But 'enough' is a dirty word around here, for how could you ever have enough when there is always someone else who has more?

07:24 Iraq prepared for confrontation, says Latif Nasif Jassem, Iraqi Information Minister. Al's flag flutters on the top of his monitor. The overhead TV is airing Aziz again, intercut with some F 1-11s. Across the floor, the Grope's office is still empty. In the centre of the screen, the greenback flips and bounces. Finger on the money pulse. Someone's PC emits an urgent bleep to sound a stock reaching a critical point. The plunge on the graph could be a buy or a sell prompt, it all depends on who you are, what you want, who you talk to, what you had for breakfast. There is so much you can find out with a bit of keyboard control. Rubber in Jakarta. Civil disturbance in Seoul. T-Bills in Chicago. There is a rising hum to the floor and the throbbing returns to my left temple, sneaks round from the back of my skull.

Al flops down in his chair beside me and says biotechs are where it's at. 'This company is going to make dialysis a thing of the past, Phase III trials just started.' He side flips the report to land neatly on my desk. 'Do your clients a favour and just look at the chart, any day now the stock is going to break out.' I run an index finger along the title, even look down at the first page, as if boning up on renal failure could rescue me from this malaise. This is exactly what rescues Al from a head-on collision with his own shortcomings – a belief in what happens next. He is not about to be toppled by what's gone before. He is not about to have his future short-circuited by the past. I might do well to follow his lead.

I lie back in the chair and watch the tickertape roll left-to-right across the opposite wall, last night's New York close creating the illusion of momentum in my life. But wasn't that exactly what seduced me so early on? Not the money, but the possibility that life could in fact be as random as a stock chart, that in the next second you could be ricocheted from a trough to a peak and be utterly transformed? I could get up from my chair right now, switch off the screen and walk out into a different life. I could become a cokehead or a mountaineer, screw the guy beside me or even the girl across the way. Gain ten pounds, learn Chinese. I could do anything on a whim and the future could take shape out of the old accumulated past moments lining up right out of the *now*.

And how could you *not* fall in love with this world where there is so much happening, where everything can change in the next moment? With foreknowledge you forego the thrill, life is no more than a fixed match. So what would I have chosen to know in advance? Stephen's decision to cut me loose? But deep down I knew it was coming. I just hoped it could be delayed for as long as possible.

'Check it out, Geri,' says Al and I turn round to see him facing the wall behind us with little pieces of sellotape stuck to his right hand. He smoothes out the taped pages and we both stand back to admire the A3 cutout of General Norman Schwarzkopf in his fatigues. 'Got it from one of my old classmates at First Boston,' he says and picks up a newspaper caption from his desk and sticks it level with Schwarzkopf's nose: STORMIN' NORMAN SQUARES UP FOR WAR.

'Some bullshit feature in there,' he jerks his head at the *Sunday Times* lying open on his desk. 'Taking potshots at Schwarzkopf. I mean, you guys are supposed to be our ally, right?'

'Newsflash, Al. I'm Irish. And Ireland is neutral. We don't fight wars.'

'They just fight in pubs, Al,' Rob chips across the monitors. 'And blow people up.'

'You guys see that guy interviewing Stormin' Norman last night?' asks Al.

'Like watching a snuff movie,' says Rob and Al swivels around tetchily, the way he does whenever Rob cruises into his US political airspace.

'You don't know what you're talking about. As per usual,' says Al, chucking a tight paper ball in the bin behind Rob's head.

'Oh, and you do, right, mate?'

'Whatever.'

'So you've seen one then?'

'Maybe.' Al tilts his head face up to the ceiling, arms behind his head.

'I don't believe it.'

'He has? You HAVE?' Rob shoots out of his chair and, in a second, is crouched between the pair of us, doing a quick head scan of the trading floor. 'Come on mate, spill.'

Al taps a shiny right shoe under the desk.

'Come on, Al,' I plead. 'You can't just say that and not follow it up.'

'Get a move on, mate,' says Rob, 'it's two minutes to the morning meeting.'

Al lowers his arms and adjusts his cuffs. 'It was in my freshman year,' he grins down at Rob. 'That's first year at university to you, dickhead.'

'I don't believe it,' I lean closer.

'Hey, I'm not proud, you know, it was like my roomie's friend of a friend...'

'That's flatmate to you, Rob,' I say.

'Shut the fuck up, Geri. OK, OK. So? Al?'

'He paid like 300 bucks or something for this video, a really shitty copy. And we were wasted one night, so he puts this thing on and there's just the four of us...'

Al bends forward in the chair, elbows on knees, considering his spread-eagled hands.

'Yeah?'

'So we watched it. Or some of it. I can't remember.'

'And what happened?'

'And then I fell asleep.'

'What happened in the film, I mean?'

'A girl... a Mexican girl... that's where they, uh, get them. Y'know, smuggle them in or something, or do it there, I guess. It was pretty hard-core stuff, I mean, gangbang and she was a kid really. And then they did it.'

'What?'

'You know, held her down and beat the fuck out of her.' Al stares straight ahead like he sees something on his Reuters screen.

'Did she die?' I venture.

'What the hell d'you think, Geri? It was a snuff movie, not *Sleeping Beauty*.'

'Jesus CHRIST, Al,' I hiss. 'You actually watched this?'

'Hey, it's not like I wanted to, or paid any money or anything. You gotta remember we'd been tequila slamming since lunchtime after this ball game, I can hardly even remember.' He tugs at his sleeve. 'Like I said, it was one of those things.'

'I can't believe you even admit to it.'

'You asked, right? And hey, you guys, I don't want to hear this coming back.'

'All right, mate, all right. Be cool,' says Rob.

'So what about the guy who owned the tape?'

'Never saw him again. He was a fucking asshole anyways.'

Rob stands up, stripping his eyes away from Al for the first time, shaking his head and smiling. 'Gotta say, mate, I'm impressed. And there's me thinking you were just a swot.'

07:29

I JOIN THE WARM HERD OF BODIES bottlenecking at the entrance to the conference room where the heads of Strategy, Foreign Exchange and Commodities stand in a tight nodding cluster on the podium. All around me is the sweet smell of money in the morning – laundered shirts and expensive cologne. It's a record turnout what with this countdown to war and everyone wanting to see our battery of analysts flex their clairvoyant muscle, telling us what's going up, what's coming down, and how we can make a killing when the bombs start falling. The room is packed to capacity so the door has to stay open with the Asian desk crowding the threshold. I reverse into the forward surge of men behind me and duck sideways to the wall. Zanna stands to the left of the podium power cluster, but within easy touching distance. She's in profile, a curtain of blonde hair obscuring everything but her nose. Although she is ostensibly shuffling through some loose papers, I know that she is hyper-aware of her natural exclusion from the big boy's huddle. Ever since she joined Steiner's Research Department, Zanna has provided a welcome splash of colour against the tedious backdrop of suits that headline every morning meeting. Easily the most glamorous person to walk through the swing doors of the bank, she is a vision of graceful style whose two-year stint at *The Wall Street Journal* culminated in a front-page exposé about how Steiner's traders were being sent death threats by the Japanese yakuza because we were making grillions out of a program that calculated the index sixty-three seconds before the Tokyo Stock Exchange computer could. When Zanna's boss didn't give her the requisite column inches she demanded after her prize-winning article, she handed in her resignation, telling him the next time she saw him would be when she was firing him, *sunshine*. While I was yawning my way through my second year at college, Zanna was at Harvard Business School getting second place in the class of '83 (after Stephen of course), before being snapped up by Steiner's, who decided that the smart thing to do would be to hire the woman who had pulled their pants down on the front page of the *Journal*.

When Stephen introduced us I soon realised Zanna practises secret arts that no other woman working in the City knows: how to tie a scarf so it doesn't look like a dog collar, how to achieve that 'no make-up' look in under five minutes, how to sculpt hair into an effortless French plait. In short, Zanna knows how to present a structured package of feminine beauty and formidable intellect that is guaranteed to catapult her past the Cuban-heeled pack of Women Who Have Made It in the City, the lone wolverines who think that a slap of lipstick and a pair of tits will stop them being taken seriously and that being generally ungroomed in a dykish dark suit is the best way of cracking your head through the glass ceiling.

When I called round to admire her remodelled master bedroom before Christmas, she flung open the towering wardrobe doors to reveal a compartmentalised nerve centre of order: ghettoised cashmere jumpers alongside horizontal double height rails, a battery of drawers in descending widths, suits cascading into a row of individually bagged party frocks. I breathed in a trace of cedar, and looked down at the row of shoe bags that stretched across the base – Charles Jourdan, Salvatore Ferragamo – thinking this is a wardrobe that could streamline your whole life with the perky announcement that WHATEVER might happen, you would never be inappropriately dressed. Or find yourself at 5 a.m. on a winter morning, holding two stockings under a naked light bulb to check if they are both black, or effing and blinding your way through the cavernous darkness of an overstuffed wardrobe for that blue suit that seems to have vaporised.

English women, sighed Zanna, closing the wardrobe door, *do NOT understand grooming. Hair. Nails. Careers.*

Rosanna P. Vermont is a thirty-year-old Europhile Yank whose mother concordes between her antiques shop on the New Kings Road (where she spends a fortnight crying bravely on her daughter's shoulders and bemoaning the impossibility of getting a decent latte in this town) and her clapboard divorce settlement in the Hamptons. Zanna's father, meanwhile, spreads his middle-aged wings in a new pad on the Upper East Side, calling her to say, *Honey, haven't you spent enough time in Europe now? You could have anything you want at my firm, you know?* But what Daddy doesn't see, as he surveys his giant banking kingdom through a glass partition, is that his daughter wants the thrill of pioneering, of doing it her own way in a European banking system that's still in its infancy compared with what he is offering.

When he's not begging her to come home, he's begging her to send a birthday card to his new girlfriend who is old enough to be her younger sister and – to judge from the photo I saw, bears a remarkable resemblance to Zanna – although she has never mentioned this and I don't think it's necessarily constructive to make that kind of connection. I mean, you could argue that Zanna looks very like her mother, in which case it's just Daddy doing a normal guy thing and trading in his wife for a younger model. In the end, Zanna did, in fact, relent and send a card to the girlfriend, because *Daddy needs me to be inclusive.*

Zanna's favourite movie is *Glengarry Glenross.*

Her favourite sayings are:

Always be closing.

Never stand in a queue.

Repeat after me.

Most people do not see the kindliness in Rosanna P. Vermont, what they see is the chilly veneer. But I know her to be generous in gesture, which I realised only too well 174 days ago when she called me up after Stephen dumped me.

'Geri, are you there?' Her voice on the answerphone stopped me and my vodka refill halfway across my living room and I was convinced that she could somehow tell I was home. I stood there with the freezer-fresh bottle dripping in my hands, but I couldn't see a way of talking without sounding like I was cracking up, and I couldn't bear to see my distress reflected in Zanna's eyes. 'You're there, aren't you?' she said when she called again a few hours later. 'We're going out. We're going to get you through this.'

So we went out and got blasted, after she'd dragged me round Sloane Street, through a jungle of frantic females fingering anything black, shoving me into changing rooms with dresses that I would never have picked off the rails myself. 'Retail therapy. It gets you through the first wave.' I capitulated over the red and black Balenciaga, because it was easier than arguing, because the only way to move was forward and because Stephen wasn't the one sitting at home alone with his mouth impaled on a bottle of Absolut.

That night we went to the LA Café, brushing past swarms of girls in puffball skirts, and Zanna let me sit at the bar lining up the sea breezes and amusing myself and the barman by composing a Rule Book for Wannabe Female Bankers (subtitle: How to Get On Without Getting Fucked), reading my napkin scrawl aloud to both of them:

1. Don't even blink when someone says 'Cunt'. Better still, say it yourself.

2. There is NEVER a good reason to cry in the office.

3. Always remember that two women standing together on a trading floor can only be gossiping; therefore treat all female colleagues with total contempt.

4. Learn how to drink copiously. Know the point at which you are likely to keel over or shag someone you shouldn't.

5. Keep your sexual playground OUTSIDE your office unless you want your performance to become the topic of discussion over the bar.

6. Never get period pains in the office. Adjust your contraceptive pill cycle so that you menstruate at weekends.

7. If you absolutely MUST have a baby, avoid a pregnancy and arrange a secret adoption during your summer vacation.

When Zanna decided enough was enough, she hauled me out onto the street and hailed a cab, gripped me in a cheery hug. *Congratulations, Geri, you've done your grieving.* And sure enough when I woke the next morning and saw Rex curled up on my dress on the floor I realised it had been thirty-five hours since I had cried and that was progress.

One hundred and fifty-seven days ago she pulled me off the trading floor and into the loo and put her arm around my shoulders in a manner that resembled something approaching the distant kindness of strangers. *Never ever on the floor*, she said, dabbing at my cheeks. But people lose patience with a grieving that should be over and I soon became a project that did not proceed as planned.

So in late September Zanna pitched up at my door in loafers, jeans and a French nautical T-shirt like she was an advert for spring cleaning. A renovation of the heart. 'You should move, trade up, Geri.' She thrust a Savills brochure into my hand. 'South Ken is more happening. Kensington is full of Armenian widows droning on about their dead husbands.'

'What is happening to me, Zanna?'

'It's taking longer than I thought,' she admitted, a thoughtful sadness about the way she nodded her head.

'I will never give my heart again.'

'Bullshit. This is not a bereavement, Geri, this is a break-up.'

'Because I will have no heart to give.'

'It's never the same the second time. You will be better protected.'

'How?'

'I just think you endowed the relationship with more than was there.'

'You're saying I made it all up?'

'I'm saying you invested the relationship with way more than it had.'

She stood in the kitchen and watched me fiddling with the lid of the kettle. Rex slunk past her to settle on my bare feet.

'So everything I know is wrong.'

'It was a symptom, not a cause, of what's wrong with your life.'

'And what's that?'

'You haven't got a plan, Geri. You've got the world at your feet, but you act like you don't *want* it. You won't decide where you are going with your life. And Stephen, like the rest of us, knows what he wants.'

'And it's not me.'

'And it's not you.' Zanna patted my cheek. 'Repeat after me: he is never coming back.'

'He is never coming back.'

'It is so over.'

'It is so over.'

■ ■ ■ ■ ■

By November she had switched to a strategy of tough love, frustrated by my extended convalescence. 'Your breasts look starved,' she frowned over my shoulder at the mirror at Harvey Nicks where I stood encased in a pearl-boned bodice with thirty-five intricate hooks and eyes.

'This is not me,' I said to my reflection.

'That's good,' she nodded grimly. 'Because the old Geri is gone. This is the new one.'

I fingered the crepe puffball that stood stiff like black meringue. My bare feet seemed a long way down. 'What's she like, this new me?'

Zanna gripped my shoulders as if taking the measure of my skeleton. 'She knows what she wants and goes out and gets it. And she never looks back.'

I shrugged her off and she grabbed my arms. 'OK, so tell me your other great idea, Geri. Your other great plan.' Her thumbs pressed hard into the bone. 'That's right, you haven't got one. So quit wallowing, grow up. Don't be so female about it. Don't get stuck in the victim role.'

She sighed and released me so suddenly that I swayed a little and scrunched my toes on the carpet. 'You want to know the truth?' Zanna folded her arms. 'It was never going to work out with you and Stephen. I never thought it would. But you were the only one in the world who refused to see it' – and for a fleeting moment I wanted to smack her in the mouth right there in the changing room, rip the fucking crepe off my body and stuff it down her throat till she gagged. Instead I just smiled and croaked, 'Thanks.' She hugged me so fiercely that the bodice dug into my ribs and then said, 'Now go pay for that dress.'

The Grope shoulders his way through the crowd up onto the podium and the powercluster parts spontaneously to accommodate his presence. Back in October '87 when the markets crashed there was a morning just like this when he assembled the whole floor to say this would be something to tell our grandchildren about, *If you can keep your head when all about you are losing theirs*, and all of us shuffling to attention, none of the usual pushing and shoving at the back, the guys up front lip-chewing with folded arms and quite a few of us nodding at what the Grope said. Like we knew what was happening. Like we understood. Trooping back to the trading floor to man our posts, waiting for the FTSE to limp out of the box and drip blood all over the Topic screens.

We sat breathless in front of the flickering monitors, watching the Dow struggle to even reach an opening, shuddering through a spiral as the programs puked all over it. Watching a new little twitch in the Grope's temple as he stalked the floor, stopping to study each trader's position like he was in a hospital visiting casualties. *There is always a price at which we do business and the phones will always be answered. Not like some British banks I could mention.* The credit spreads blew out like volcanoes, the black hole that was Rob's mouth just after taking down some BBB+ bonds at 60 that he could only knock out a few minutes later at 45. *This market is disappearing up its own asshole.* So they flew in some fire-fighters from New York to show us how to behave in a crisis and they sat around squeezing little American footballs, mispronouncing the names of European companies and going *yeah yeah uh huh*, putting into practice risk-containment strategies they learnt at business school. Schlepping home in the October evening to watch the TV action-replay of our day, where other people in other banks sat staring at screens, everyone looking to everyone else for an answer.

Day 2, the Dow was off 22% when someone whispered *buying opportunity* in the morning meeting and the Grope looked like he was going to machine gun the whole room. Rumours of people jumping off buildings, chickens coming home to get axed, the day that God left the storm-ravaged City and everything spun out of control. *When the dust settles, someone is going to pay for this*, said Rob. Then the Red Adair hand-holders showed up at the office in their travel suits and shook our hands. *Good luck, you guys*, like we'd been in the trenches together, took their little leather footballs and jumped in a cab to get the Concorde back to their guaranteed promotions, leaving us with collapsed premiums on all their inherited hedge positions and Rob swearing down the phone to New York for months.

It all ended in a universal fight about who had predicted this, who understood it and who knew what to do. A big scramble to lay the blame. Saying things like: *The markets have a life of their own*, which really just means that nobody has an overview, nobody is in charge. Talk about how the index shouldn't be able to fall like that, blame it on the futures and those smartasses in Chicago, blame it on the champagne, blame it on the arbitrageurs, and then suddenly everything that was good before became bad. Strolling through the debris, picking up the pieces, reconstructing the business, putting toes back in the water and getting philosophical over margaritas about the excesses and how every cloud has a silver lining. Turn disaster into opportunity, seize the chance to get rid of the walking wounded who shouldn't have had jobs in the first place, get lean and mean down the gym, run a red pen through the expense accounts, cut out the dead wood. Only the fit will survive. Out there in the limbo world of non-banking are the souls of a lot of people we used to know.

But a year later we were liberated by the release of 'Wall Street' and the reconfirmation that greed is good and lunch is for wimps. The traders were flying in truckloads of Brooks Brothers' button-downs, dragging their girlfriends along to see how cool their jobs looked on a big screen, some even gekkoed their hair but couldn't carry it off like Michael Douglas. The book stores were swamped with block orders when *Bonfire of the Vanities* came out and the trading floor was elevated to an art form, 400 pages longer than anything most traders have ever read, but there it was in black and white: we were Masters of the Universe, we were making history while coining it, having a lot more than our fifteen minutes, and we would never die.

And then the floodgates opened and there was 'Liar's Poker' with real connections and Solly's just down the road, people who said they knew Michael Lewis and people we actually *knew* in the actual book, *no kidding, check it out*, and all the x-rated stuff that wasn't in the text.

I stand up on tippy toes and peek over Al's shoulder to see Zanna speed-scan the room but her professional half-smile takes in the whole audience and doesn't linger on me. Tucking her papers decisively under her arm, she touches the blue Hermès twist draped over her collarbone and takes a step towards the management huddle. I know she is desperate to have a word but I also know that she won't be given the chance. This is a day for big boys and heavy weapons and deep voices and the switch to a female frequency might just break the spell. The heavyweight cluster breaks apart and the Grope turns to survey the room, arranging his face into the shape of a beginning. The crowd babble fades to mute. We wait, all eyes on the Grope who nods to his right, 'Go ahead, Dick.'

'Well, I can tell you one thing. We're not expecting many sell orders in the oil market the next few days,' the Head of Commodities breaks the surface tension with a bit of humour.

'As you know, we've seen a steady decline from the $41 peak in October when Saddam threatened to start shooting missiles at Israel.' He rattles through a retrospective chart summary of where crude prices have traded, tapping a finger on the lingering end point of the line as the screen fades into the dull heartbeat of GOLD.

'Don't expect a rally, guys. Except amongst the Swiss, of course, who'll be busy stockpiling in their underground bunkers.' He grins to signal it's time for another laugh, before assuring us that the only safe haven will be the dollar. This is a cue to the Head of Foreign Exchange and the screen fades to two charts marked $/YEN and $/DM, both dotting into an upward slope. I lower my head into a discreet yawn, so close to Al's back that I have to be careful not to get lipstick on his shirt.

The Strategist stands up and rushes through a couple of dense diagrams of the leading indices, the long bond, the theoretical of a spiralling oil rise and is just getting into his stride when the Grope steps forward to deliver the crushing interjection – 'Thanks Jim' – signalling a return to the real world where phones are ringing and time is money. He flicks a button and the screen dies. He looks to the right and then to the left and says, 'Well, like I said in '87, this will be one to tell the grandchildren about.' But he doesn't do the Kipling quote.

'We all know there's gonna be a war and we all know who's gonna win. That leaves only one question: How long is it going to take? My hunch is short and sweet, in a few weeks' time Baghdad will be burning and this is all a blip. This is yesterday already.'

Al's head nods in front of me, and for a moment I believe that the Grope's glare is fixed on my exposed face.

'So I am here to tell you that life goes on. Now, some of you have been around longer than others and you will know that nothing gets in the way of Steiner's. This is a time for a clear head, a strong voice and a will to win. We will lose some money but we will make more. We will live to tell the tale. Out there in the desert are four hundred and fifteen thousand of the best ready to kick butt. Remember that when you go back to your desks. We're fighting a war on all fronts. And Steiner's will win.'

There is a momentary pause where I think that somebody might start clapping. All the earnest rookie faces I can see are alive with the thrill of history unfolding all round us but the rest of us, the hardcore platoon of Crash survivors, we know it's the same old story of damage limitation: watching your ass and living to tell the tale. The trades keep getting bigger and smarter and harder to unwind but just like before, there is traffic on the streets and people going to work, the western world flexing a collective muscle while deadlines expire all around us.

The Grope waves a hand and we troop out of the room. I turn my head to look for Zanna but I am swept along and swallowed by the shirts. Back out on the trading floor there's a new mobilised sternness on all the boys' faces, as if we were landing on the beaches. You need to kiss the cross around your neck and dodge the bullets, pick your way gingerly through the index minefield before a stock tick blows you to bits. Tonight, when darkness falls, the paramedics from Financial Control will sneak out to pick over the remains: whose trading book is haemorrhaging, who's already dead and who has managed to limp away intact.

We sit in the best entertainment time zone. In a few hours' time, the East Coast will be yawning its way into a fury, the Big Guns will be barking across the hoot-and-holler from New York, smooth, seductive, everyone crooning some market song, jargon jumping off their tongues with practised ease. You could listen for hours to the flow: the economists cataloguing the reasons why we don't know anything, the strategists reducing it all to a binary outcome, the analysts draping their punchlines in caveats and disclaimers, this whole torrent of soothsaying and disinformation funnelled down the throats of the sales force. And in the middle of it all, hunched over their keyboards, the traders' fingers hover over the button as they prepare to slap their necks on the block: bomb disposal and fuse ignition, the heart of the machine that is Steiner's & Co.

I am bent down beneath my desk trying to fish the pack of Silk Cut that I kicked under the pedestal when I hear the throat-clearing rrrrrhum that announces Pie Man's arrival.

'I – eh – have something for you,' he says in that breathy wheeze that always sounds like he has just hauled his weight up ten flights of stairs. 'It's really interesting.'

'I bet it's not,' I say because I already know for sure it won't be interesting at all.

He giggles, his laugh is a staccato gasp, a real head-turner until you get used to it.

'I'll bet it's some unsolved puzzle from one of your maths journals.'

Pie Man brings me these little offerings in the hope that they will muster my own enthusiasm for my numerical talent and although I almost always ignore him, he still refuses to accept that the object of his fascination is not mine. I consider staying put here underneath the desk until he goes away but it's dusty and hot from all the power cables and there are some nasty-looking substances stuck to the underside of the wood. His feet shuffle backwards as I crawl out and settle in the chair.

It is two years since Pie Man arrived on the floor to join the gaggle of rocket scientists who are going to catapult Steiner's into the next century. Structured Product Development is the name of this little centre of quantitative innovation that was the brainchild of our CEO Conrad Feinstein. It turns out that although Steiner's is making shedloads in the Jap warrant market, some of our competition is making *way* more. The problem is that our business is pretty much entirely based around customer flows while the smart money round at Bankers Trust and Salomon's is all proprietary. In fact, word is they are raking it in right now with Jap-structured derivatives designed by some clever Maths quants and when Feinstein realised this he told the Grope to go sort it. So the Grope went out and bought an MIT Maths professor (subsequently christened Dr Who by Rob) so tiny that he looks like a schoolboy in a swivel chair. Then Dr Who went out and hired a bunch of Maths post docs that you can still get pretty cheap from UK universities. They arrived and spored: the geeks are cloning and mushrooming and will eventually swallow us like the whale.

We call them SPUD. Rob also calls it the modelling department ever since he heard them discussing mathematical models and, on a slow day, he will rip out Page 3 and stick the topless poster onto the wall behind them, which always gets a laugh. Just before Christmas he ordered a Santa stripogram and Dr Who surprised us all by getting really into it. When she sat squirming on his lap, he flicked the little snowball tassels on her nipples and emptied out his stocking full of flavoured condoms. Through it all Pie Man sat motionless like he was paralysed but he managed to flee before Rob slipped Madame Claus a tenner to give him a feel.

'Take a look at page 43.' Pie Man slides a copy of the *New Scientist* into my line of vision. The cover is a circular whirl of silicone chips swirled into a conch shape arranged so that it vanishes into the distance. There is a pinkish smudge mark on the corner and what looks like sugar crystals stuck to the edge, probably from the biscuits that Pie Man consumes, his huge bulk hunched at his desk.

Pie Man eats constantly while he works and without breaking concentration, as if this refuelling is essential to the process. And he is getting bigger by the day, a steady swelling that has his trousers now barely hanging on below the bulge of his belly and shows a white triangle of hairy blubber when he tucks in his shirt at the back. He wedges his bulk into the swivel and rolls forward. His two-fingered hands paddle at the keyboard as he leans squinting into the screen. His eyes are getting smaller, receding into the swell of flesh underneath his lids. Each morning he stuffs a Tesco bag of goodies in his pedestal and throughout the day his hand rummages in the top drawer in blind selection: fig rolls and Kimberley Mikado, sponge fingers, Garibaldis with raisins embedded like dead flies, all the soft, cheap and chewy biscuits of childhood. He nibbles around the edges of jammy dodgers like a giant squirrel, small fragments showering the desk until all that remains is the red-clotted centre. But with other brands he'll often shove the whole biscuit in his mouth and crush it in one swift move, swallow and take another one right away. He swills Coke, eats crisps and his bin piles up with wrappers.

You are such a fucking slob, Pie Man, said Rob once, pointing to a river of dried mayo down the middle of his tie, so now he eats with the tie slung back over his shoulder, casting furtive glances around the floor as if checking for predators moving in for the kill. He smears his hand across his mouth and belches silently with a slight puff of his cheeks.

'OK, Geri, look, I'll show you,' Pie Man rustles the pages, leaning in so close I can smell the sweet scent of vanilla, cut with stale aftershave and a faint body odour. I push my chair back and turn downwind. 'The genius in the pram': he reads the centrefold headline aloud and points at the black and white photo of two babies lying side by side in a bassinet. 'You see, they've been doing studies in retardation. Trying to build a systematic cognitive profile of mathematically gifted individuals.' In the inset picture two girls of eight or nine stand either side of a blackboard with a long chalked proof. They are smiling and wearing checked pinafores. One holds a rag doll and has her hair in ribboned bunches. They are both ugly as sin. But Pie Man is off now, telling me how the latest research says that these kids have an 'intense drive to master', that specific tests are better predictors than IQ at showing math and verbal giftedness and that the amount of deliberate practice, blah blah blah. He jabs a pudgy finger on the text.

'And the article says—'

'Not interested.' I shake a cigarette from the pack on my desk and push the mag to one side. Pie Man rabbit-twitches his head. But he does not slink off to his desk, he just loiters with intent, fingering the pages. I know he wants to urge me towards a deliberate workout so that I can hone my skill, since research shows that training is what makes all the difference, the harder you work the brain muscle the more it will develop. He lingers by my desk trying to seduce me with puzzles and paradoxes, slipping volatility smiles and binomial trees and Monte Carlo simulations into conversation as if they were aphrodisiacs. I keep on telling him I'm not interested, I do not care but Pie Man does not hear the No. He suspects me of false modesty and continues to pester me with this stuff, refusing to accept that I do not want to explore my special talent.

In the early days I would occasionally perform – recite all the day's trades in Rob's book in the correct sequence or the FTSE closes backwards for the last ten days, or solve the equations that Pie Man would scribble down for our little audience. But I soon tired of being the freak show and refused to play. Pie Man tries to tempt me back, always sniffing around mathematical curiosities like a favourite dessert, always finding reasons to hang around my desk, wishing we could be mates or join in conversation about the hanging paradox over a pizza. A few weeks ago he came to tell me that he loved swimming and maybe I'd like to go to the new pool at the Tara Hotel in Kensington with him since he'd overheard me say to Al that I hardly ever swam anymore because it's so boring on your own.

'So what this latest research actually shows is that—'

'I don't give a shit.' I blow a funnel of smoke sideways at the photo of the two little girls, their eager little smiles.

'—what it suggests is that—'

'I DON'T FUCKING CARE, OK?'

The force of my lungs and the strip-throat burn astonishes me. For a brief moment the trading floor is a sea of faces turned in my direction while I struggle against the sudden threat of tears. I lean forward and stub out the cigarette. Pie Man has snatched up the mag and is clutching it in front of his crotch as if he's just been maimed. He takes a slow appeasing step backwards keeping his grey eyes wide and fixed in alarm on my face.

'Sorry, Geri, I didn't catch that,' Rob smirks and there is a ruffle of laughter. Pie Man is lumbering off down the line towards the safety of his desk with the panicked gait of a wounded beast.

I get up, walk away from the desk. I should say sorry, I know, I should make some gesture of reparation but for now I will just add that to the whole stinking heap of things that I should do with my life.

4

chinese wall

08:02

'GERI?' JULIE'S INQUIRY BOUNCES ROUND the empty loos. 'Are you in here?'

I hold my breath and wait and hope that she will have the decency to walk away but of course all she has to do is bend down and check for my legs. When Steiner's refurbed the trading floor two years ago, they didn't trust a British outfit to deliver their vision and so even the loos were done American-style, kitted out with half-doors that you could see over, and quarter inch gaps running down the sides. The idea was to make it difficult to snort coke in private, though no one in London had identified this as being a particularly pressing issue amongst the female employees. The secretaries were immediately up in arms and began conducting trials, one of them in a stall going, *OK OK, can you see me now* to the one on the other side, who would be looking through the gap in the door saying, *Clear as day, I mean it's just ridiculous*. The blokes thought it was a scream, the idea of girls looking at other girls in the loo, but it caused the closest thing to mutiny amongst the proles and quickly snowballed into a campaign that wouldn't go away. Thus the right to change tampons in private, the right to a secret shit, the right to anonymous crying and malingering finally got elevated up the management chain until one day there was a 'Men At Work' sign on the door and the gaps were filled with wide bristly strips of draught excluder. Dignity was restored.

'He wants to see you,' Julie pulls up outside my cubicle. 'Straight away.' I take out the Diazepam bottle, tip out another little tablet that might reinforce the hollow wall between what I am actually feeling and what lies beneath.

'You OK?'

I unlock the door and Julie snaps on the tap to hurry me up.

'Room 2101.' She hands me a paper towel.

'Why all the way up there?'

'Because that's where he is. You need to hurry now.'

'Sure. Let me rush to my own execution.' She trails me all the way out to the lift and even presses the button like she doesn't trust me not to plummet to Ground. I am staring at the lift doors feeling my future dissolve before me, ascending to the 21st, where we never get to go.

It feels like breaking and entering because the air in Corporate Finance is different, the carpet rich red and springy like walking on sponge. Climate control, panelled walls, impeccable soft furnishings, no trashy receptionists, an air pocket of soundproofing that strips the voice of individual register. No risqué canvases or distracting feminine forms, just hunting scenes in reassuring pastoral and large landscapes and a crystal fishbowl on a mahogany plinth.

But Julie has clearly given me the wrong number because the door to 2101 is ajar and there, standing just inside the threshold, is the unmistakable side profile of Anil Kapoor, Steiner's legendary Head of Investment Banking whose name is stamped all over some of Wall Street's greatest mergers and acquisitions. His photo graced the cover of *Fortune* in November, this near-mythical presence from the land of wizardry and omnipotence that is a cultural universe away from the inferno of the trading floor. This is the man who has broken every record for biggest, largest, longest – the highest-ranked, highest-paid, non-white in the industry, a mascot for the minorities and a PR coup for the board of Steiner's who spatter his face all over the annual report, together with as many blacks and Asians and females as they can rustle up in the back office to create the illusion of diversity in our human resources. Though rumour has it that Kapoor has no time for political correctness, apparently he didn't even have time to attend his mother's funeral when she inconveniently pegged it on the day Amco announced a 4.5 billion dollar merger with Amox, although, as Tom Castigliano explained it to me, Kapoor *would* have gone, except the funeral was in Bombay and that was like a continent too far. But he did take a weekend off later to scatter the ashes over some river, and did I know that Kapoor went a full nine days without sleep before that merger was done? *So what?* I said, *Keith Richards did that back in the Seventies.*

Stephen had clandestine talks with Kapoor a couple of years back. It was just before the Kit Kat deal though I only found out long afterwards. *I can't believe you didn't tell me*, I said. He didn't want to complicate things, he said, and had only met with Kapoor because he was such a big admirer, he had no real intention of jumping ship. *You really think I would shoot my mouth off?* He shrugged, as if to suggest there might be something about me that was leaky, unsafe. *Sometimes you just say things without thinking, Geri. Maybe it's an Irish thing.*

'Geri, come in,' says the Grope's voice from inside the room. Kapoor turns his head slowly and takes me in with a cursory scan and there is nothing soft or gentle in those brown irises, like polished stones set in pools of iced white. A slim brown hand with a flash of pale underside flicks upwards in a brief gesture and he glides away to the other side of the room. He is sleek, polished and buffed; the kind of impeccable grooming that Zanna so admires. And his movements are balletic. I could imagine him in a silk sari of godly blue, choreographing the seduction of a veiled nymph. The skin tone would have to be exactly right, the light flattering, the temperature controlled. Kapoor's is a marbled beauty, preserved and bejewelled, his reflection in a gilt mirror is a still life.

'Close the door and siddown.' The Grope points to a chair on the opposite side of the small oval table. Beside the Oriental apparition he is monochrome and flat like a yokel who's just pitched up in town. But I notice he is wearing a jacket, which he never does on the trading floor – he may be running a very profitable trading and sales division, but in Kapoor's universe, he is plant life.

'We have a situation.' A tingling anticipation has me immediately on ambush alert and I am already fiercely regretting last night's Absolut. This is most definitely not a conversation about my relocation: Kapoor just being in the same airspace suggests it's way more than I can even guess at, since he doesn't get out of bed for less 500 million.

'So tell me, Geri,' says the Grope. 'Does Vulkan Valve mean anything to you?'

'We were just talking about it on the desk this morning.'

'Why?' shoots Kapoor. It's clear this would be a bad time to mention that Al has been pitching Vulkan as a sales idea to clients all morning. So there might be an item missing from the Restricted List of company stocks that the sales force is banned from talking about. When Vulkan Valve's name is mentioned and the western world's chief rainmaker is in the room, the chances are there's a deal in the pipeline. Which means that the entire sales force is gagged, cannot breathe the company's name or do any business in the stock. But Al would normally be diligent about procedure and it's hard to miss the List since it is photocopied onto bright pink paper, the colour coding insisting that you notice it amongst the others that pile up on your desk.

'Why?' echoes the Grope.

'Oh, just because of this new MSTAR portable radar thing. It was all over *The Times* at the weekend.'

'So we know our salespeople read the papers,' the Grope grins, looking instantly relieved. Kapoor is already speaking into the internal phone in tones of soft menace.

'Were you pitching it?'

'No, no, I wasn't.'

'So what else do you know about Vulkan Valve?' the Grope continues.

'Very little. Electronics, defence, some hoo-ha about selling weapons to South Africa a while back. I've never done any business in the stock.'

'And what do you know about Felix Mann's interest in Vulkan?'

'We've never talked about it.'

The Grope leans in to face me. 'You mean you are not aware that he owns a chunk of the stock?'

I shake my head.

'So much for knowing your client,' he quips in a man-to-man with Kapoor who does not respond.

'I don't know all of Felix's positions,' I mumble in my defence. What I want to tell him is that it's all very well saying the golden rule of sales is Know Your Client, but if your client's portfolio is secret and he doesn't feel like telling you he could own a herd of zebra and you wouldn't have a fucking clue. I would also like to bellow out the words 'Cargo International' so we could take a nice little trip down memory lane and remind someone what it feels like to be a tortoise.

'OK, Geri, here's the score,' the Grope continues. 'Felix Mann owns 151 million shares of Vulkan Valve, which means your client owns 13% of the company.' He waits for a reaction to this announcement though I am not sure what he expects me to do.

'And we have a very sensitive situation. But in order to talk about it we have to bring you over the wall.'

Kapoor's wince is almost imperceptible, as if he's been pricked by a sharp object. This is, I know, a reflex response to the act of disclosure – Karpoor's concern is exactly what Stephen's always was: I am a salesperson and therefore a liability. I could shoot my mouth off at any moment. The Chinese wall between Investment Banking and the trading floor is in reality as porous as a sponge.

'The consequences—'

'I understand.' Hung drawn and quartered.

Kapoor places a flat hand on the table and begins to speak. 'The ownership structure of Vulkan Valve is as follows: Felix Mann is the largest shareholder with 13%. The board of Vulkan owns 10%. And now an Interested Party has come to Steiner's because they see an opportunity in Vulkan Valve. Our Interested Party knows that Vulkan's board will fiercely resist any attempt at takeover. And Felix Mann's intentions are, of course, unknown.'

'I have told Anil—' the Grope begins in but Kapoor cuts him dead.

'Our Interested Party has been made aware of your—' he pauses, eyelids flutter '—special relationship with Felix Mann.'

'We want you to find out what Felix wants to do with his 13%,' says the Grope, rising from his chair; he's been restless all the way through and is standing up now, with hands in pockets, staring down at me from his full height.

'So,' I venture, 'you want me to get Felix to talk to your Interested Party because they're going make a bid for Vulkan?'

Kapoor flinches at the vulgarity of articulation. He is clearly full of misgivings about this whole venture and the Grope's eager-beaver eye bulge tells me this is all his big idea. He has pitched me and my special relationship in a bid to turbo-charge his career and take it to the next level. And Kapoor doesn't like this one little bit because it means trusting me with inside information. But greed is a great motivator and how else will they find out what they need to know?

'Has your Interested Party spoken to Felix?'

The Grope eye's pop at this egg suck.

'Our client would be delighted to speak to him,' says Kapoor through gritted teeth. 'But Felix Mann refuses to enter into any kind of dialogue. He refuses to return our calls. He has declined, through his secretary, all invitations to meet with or talk to the Interested Party. We have made a number of representations via Tom Castigliano in Hong Kong. We understand that Mr Mann also refuses to speak to the board of Vulkan Valve, although we cannot be sure of that.' He tilts his head towards the ceiling. 'We do not know if Felix Mann will accept or refuse a bid.'

'Felix is pretty difficult about seeing people.'

'Apart, of course, from you.' His silken voice has a steely edge. The hawk eyes blink.

'He never consults anyone. He doesn't really take input. He just does what he does.'

'Must make for a very challenging sales role,' Kapoor murmurs and there is the faintest trace of a smirk on his banker's lips, reminding me no matter how big the big guys get they just can't resist taking potshots at the little guys. They have never really left the playground, and the thrill of inflicting humiliation is just as exciting as it was all those years ago when they licked their first bloodied lip, lying on the tarmac in the shadow of the school bully who spits in your mouth to raise a laugh from his rubbernecking acolytes. The dry taste of that blood never leaves you, the roaring in your ears becomes a burning flame in your heart that erupts in your chest into a volcano of furious energy and you spring to your feet to a gasp from the crowd and as he swaggers away, you leap onto his back and topple him into the dust, you are punching and thrashing, you will tear him limb from limb and it takes three teachers to pull you off in the end. You stand panting and bare-chested in the playground above his blubbing mess, while the crowd shrinks back from the apparition before them and you savour the narcotic of power and you know that you have found the meaning of life: this is just what you need and you will never bite the dust for anyone again.

'But Felix Mann will talk to *you*, Geri,' the Grope flops back into his chair. 'So we need to get you back out to Hong Kong so you can pay him a visit.' He slaps his hand on the table. 'We want you to get a simple answer to a simple question.'

'Felix only ever says what he wants to say.'

'Oh, you can do better than that,' the Grope flashes the full dental suite. 'We need to know what he thinks. You just work your magic and we take it from there.'

'Our Interested Party would of course prefer to proceed with some foreknowledge,' says Kapoor, 'so this kind of intelligence is critical.' The Grope leans back nodding. 'You realise that you are now an insider and all that that involves?' Kapoor continues. I nod on cue. 'So you may not discuss this with anyone inside or outside the firm.'

'Felix may want to know more.'

'No more information,' Kapoor raises a warning finger. 'Refer him to me. Think of yourself as a secretary who is taking a phone message. I'm sure you can manage that.'

'Right, so it's what – like 5 p.m. in Hong Kong now?' The Grope is on his feet again, his hands working his pockets like he's adjusting his balls.

'Five twenty-two.'

They both stare at the phone on the table. I dial the number. Picture Felix raising his head, considering.

'Geraldine.'

'Felix.'

'You didn't call me at our usual time.'

'Sorry, Felix. Something came up.' The Grope stares at my mouth like he's lip-reading. Kapoor swallows shallowly like there is a sour taste in his mouth.

'You are not at your desk?'

'No.'

'You are in a meeting room.'

'How did you know?'

'A quality of stillness. No background noise.'

'Felix, I need to come and see you. '

'What an unexpected surprise.'

'Tomorrow afternoon?'

'I look forward to it.'

'Thanks, Felix. I'll let you know the time when I get a flight.'

'And Geraldine?'

'Yes?'

'Do give Mr Kapoor my regards.' The line goes dead but I can hear the smile in the dial tone.

'So you're all set?' says the Grope.

I nod, put down the phone.

'He made a remark,' says Kapoor.

'He could tell I was in a meeting.'

'And there was something else?'

'He said to give you his regards.'

A faint tinge of pink smears his cheek, a Duchenne spasm tightens his jaw.

'What?' the Grope's head snaps up. Anil Kapoor eyes me, some sort of indecipherable message etched on his brow. And then he slips out of the door almost as if he was never there.

'OK,' I move to rise from my chair.

'Not so fast, Geri,' the Grope raises a palm. 'You tell me how the *fuck* Felix Mann knew that Kapoor was in this room?' He shakes his head like a wet dog.

'He guesses stuff. Can I go back to the floor now?'

'No,' he says. 'Our Interested Party wants to meet you.'

I wait outside in the corridor like a naughty schoolgirl. The Grope glares at a tapestry wall hanging as if he finds something offensive in its elaborate weave. When the door to the conference room opens he barges in front, making a wrist-flicking tugging motion as if he has me on a leash. And there, in the middle of a roomful of suits, grinning like a toothy game show host is a man with a huge white Stetson on his head. It is Max Lester II, aka Max-a-Billion, the instantly recognisable CEO of Texas Pistons, and my second celebrity face-to-face of the morning. He looks exactly like he did in a recent photo shoot at the Bush family ranch with a spaniel darting madly round his feet. So *this* is our Interested Party. Texas Pistons is cash rich and hungry for growth. I can see the headlines now: *Yanks take out British guns.* And Vulkan Valve is the perfect target.

'This her?' he goes to no one in particular and the Grope makes a little hand flourish in my direction as if he's introducing an exotic pet. I step forward gamely while Max-a-Billion checks out my tits.

'Geri Molloy,' I stick out my hand. 'Good to meet you.'

'Well, hello there.' He clasps it in both of his and peers down at me from beneath his brim. His scent is hotel-citric, his skin is curiously waxy as if he is wearing stage make-up.

'So what's your secret, Geri Molloy?' He lets my hand fall and walks over to a big white couch behind which stands a posse of obvious Texans grinning like apes.

'C'mere,' he flops down and smacks the space beside him.

Max is well known as a giant playboy round town, is great pals with Charlton Heston and so evangelical about the right to bear arms that he has launched a nationwide series of Babes 'n' Bullets weekends where women can fondle magnums and take turns shooting cardboard rapists in the balls. The Grope urges me forward with a hideous smile. Kapoor stands over to the side with a princely aloofness.

'You got all the hotshots on your trail. Must be quite a little charmer.' He guffaws, his wattle redneck puffing in and out. The atmosphere is part locker room, the only thing missing is that he doesn't pull me onto his lap.

'Geri Molloy,' Max-a-Billion repeats, nodding his Stetson as if he is testing the name for size. Stares steadily up at me with black eyes that he believes can burn through to the true core. I have seen it before, these men who place all trust in their own judgements.

'Siddown here,' he belts the cushion beside him. I sit at the furthest reach. Everyone else in the room remains standing, apart from a few of Kapoor's boys who are huddled over some paperwork at the far end of a roomful of guys who are all, of course, convinced that I am only here because I am shagging my biggest client.

'Let's cosy,' he says and for a moment I think he might grab me and mash my face in his groin.

'So ole Kappor here told you the story? Told you what I need?'

'Yes.'

'Got the key to Felix Mann's heart? You gonna work your special magic on this fella?' The Grope stands over at a diagonal like a henchman, arms folded across his chest. 'You gonna find out what Felix wants to do with his 13%?'

'I'll do my best.'

'She'll do her best, you boys hear that?' he bellows and the grinning circle chuckles on cue like quiet hyenas. Kapoor is inspecting his shoes as if he has just trodden in dogshit. 'And tell me, Miss Molloy, just how *good* is your best?'

'It's real good,' I say and Max-a-Billion slaps his thigh.

'It's real good,' he honks, 'it's real good,' and the Grope is grinning wildly and the whole room is an orchestra of merriment. 'You hear that, Ae-Neel?' He throws a glance over at Kapoor who is locked in a rigor mortis on the far side of the room. 'Nah, he's got no sense a humour.'

Max-a-Billion leans back, rests his arm along the back of the couch, his fingers almost touching my hair like we were in a cinema. I have cheek strain from holding this polite smile. 'So where you from, Geri Molloy?'

'Ireland.'

'Figures. Smart and hungry.' He nods, looking me up and down and then whips his Stetson round. 'What's the matter with you boys, whyn't you offer the lady a drink?'

A flurry as two lackeys step forward, one pulls back. 'Whadya say? Let's have us a cocktail right here.' One of them sneaks a glance at the wall clock. 'I've been up for two days straight and I don't give a goddam what time of day it is. Wild turkey for me. And for Miss Molloy?'

And I think, fuck the Perrier. The client is always right. 'Vodka. On the rocks.'

Max-a-Billion taps my shoulder pad with a finger. ''Cos it is *Miss* Molloy, am I right?'

I nod. I see there is a clear tendency towards roughness in the yellow tint of his pale iris. I can easily imagine Max with his trousers round his ankles and some plump young blonde, a little too much pressure on the trachea. Or perhaps I am wrong, perhaps Max likes to receive, to be anointed with pain. A masked Amazon spilling out of a rubber corset with gashed red lips and a coiled whip by her side. She makes Max undress in front of her, strip down to his vest and boxer shorts and steps closer in her stilettos. She meets his watery gaze. His lips tremble pinkly and she jabs his chest with the whip handle. Leans closer, spits in his face and he mouths a mottle of webbed saliva. He moans and she slides his shorts down with the whip, prods him hard in the mid point of his belly and then barks BEND OVER, pointing to the bed behind her. Max-a-Billion spreads his hands wide, she lashes his wobbling buttocks with the whip and he jerks forward with a muffled scream as a pink welt blooms on the pale flesh.

'You got yourself a good man, Geri Molloy?' My lips quiver. If Stephen could see me now, he would consider all this to be in extremely poor taste. Like Kapoor, who has managed to slink away to the farthest desk now where he is in quiet communion with a spreadsheet.

'Or are you savin' yourself up till the right one comes along?' He winks, he actually winks beneath the Stetson.

I take the tumbler, heavy, sparkling, two inches of solid glass at the base. Max-a-Billion leans in so that the brim practically touches my forehead. I wonder if he has thought about Pissed On as a nickname.

'Bottoms up,' he clinks and knocks it back. I follow suit.

'Atta girl.' And I imagine this as the opening round of a drinking competition that will have us slugging it out until Max starts chasing me round the room. But he waves away the man with the tray and stands up. I rise on cue. He ushers me forwards and I'm half-expecting him to slap my bottom as I walk ahead. Instead he drapes a heavy arm around my shoulders and walks me to the exit.

'You an' me might just get together sometime after this is all done,' he says. His eyes are little slits of light beneath the Stetson and he stands stroking my arm on the threshold. 'You do real good now, Geri Molloy.

You do real good.' He doffs his hat, turns back into the room and an invisible hand closes the door behind him.

The spotlit corridor stretches out in front of me like an empty runway. It is the flight instinct I feel tugging at my gut, the need to escape somewhere safe and dark and quiet and far away from men who would weave me into the webs of their own design. I could just tip over and sprawl here on the carpet, let my lids shutter down, will my heart to sleep on the velvet and wake in a white room with kindly nurses patting my hand and telling me I am lovely and I should not worry about a single thing, that this life of mine has been put in suspended animation while I catch up with it and decide whether or not I want it back.

I hurry away before the door opens again and the Grope comes to hunt me down. I am now the centrepiece of his bid for stardom so he will want to keep me close. Doubt snaps at my heels and I am feeling the chill. The Grope, Felix and Stephen like the three fucking fates, my life story scripted by three men, and me the willing pawn.

'A simple answer to a simple question.' The very phrase makes me want to howl with despair, for this is just the kind of cat-and-mouse that Felix enjoys. A trade for a trade. All the cards dealt to him and me sitting there empty-handed with nothing to offer apart from myself.

5

the smile curve

08:57

ZANNA STANDS BY THE WINDOW of her 12th floor office, talking
into the phone in her reassuring client voice. She makes a little gap
sign between index finger and thumb so I slink into a chair and survey
her shelves, the tombstone display of deals that she has worked on
and above them the framed photo gallery CV: Zanna marlin fishing in
khaki shorts and a green visor cap with Daddy and the toothy CFO of
AIG, Zanna in a white visor teeing-off at Gleneagles with the Finance
Director of News Corp looking on admiringly, Zanna in last year's
favourite Chanel sunglasses, hugging her IVF nieces in twin sailor suits
on a yacht off Cape Cod Bay.

She sits down at her desk and runs a hand over the glass peak of a
fist-sized sun-trapping iceberg that her mother commissioned from a
reclusive Swedish designer who turns down 99 per cent of the offers he
gets. She replaces the receiver and makes a note in an open file, holding
up a silencing palm.

'Come out for a coffee,' I say.

'Hello?' She points to the clock. 'I can't believe you're not snowed
under down there. Anyway, I've got a conference call in five minutes,'
and she starts yakking on about how the looming war is inconveniencing

the European road show she's doing with some big-wheel CEOs.

'I'm going to Hong Kong.'

'So you said yes!' She pushes back her chair and leaps up. 'Oh Geri, congratulations!'

'No, what I meant is the Grope's sending me out to see Felix about a piece of business.'

'So what about the relocate? You haven't said yes?'

'I thought the Grope had called me in to talk about it but it turned out he wants me to go see Felix about this other thing.'

'So you didn't discuss it at all?'

'No.'

'What did Felix say this morning?'

'There wasn't really time to talk about it.'

'So when are you going?'

'This afternoon. Julie's trying to book me on the 14:05 flight.'

She sighs, casts off the celebratory mode and folds her arms tightly. 'Don't you think that this proves just how much you need to be in Hong Kong, seeing as you've only just come back?' Zanna is at her exasperated best now, tucking her hair impatiently behind her ear. 'And when you've met with Felix and done your business he's going to ask you if you're saying yes to the relocate? So what are you going to say?'

I shrug and this immediately infuriates her. 'You want to risk losing all his business? You got another life plan I don't know about?' She is warming up to a lecture I do not care to hear, the one where she tells me I need to pull myself together and step into the adult world. Of course, Zanna herself couldn't wait to get out of the playground and start taking charge. She has told me how she learnt to read the time at nursery so that she could check her mother's erratic pick-up after long lunches with her girlfriends against the big clock on the nursery wall. She interviewed teachers and parents, did her own research and compiled a shortlist of target colleges before she even started second grade. She timetabled her teen years, methodically ticking off a list of essential skills to master – tennis, sailing, skiing (although not boarding), snorkelling, waterskiing, riding (but not show-jumping, there wasn't time), conversational French, flawless make-up, effortless teriyaki.

'Geri, you're a wreck,' she sighs, pats my cheek. 'You can't keep drifting like this. I mean, look around you.' She gestures wide. 'We all know where we're headed. Even bone-headed traders like *Rob* have got their sights locked on a personal destiny. You need to get a future. This is not playtime, this is your life. I mean, you don't even care about the money like you should. You don't even enjoy spending it.'

'You know Kierkegaard once wrote a piece called "The Unhappiest"?'

'Ever met a happy philosopher?'

'I'm agreeing with you. I mean that was his advice. The happiest were those who lived in the present. Kierkegaard said—'

'*Stop!* Don't turn this into an existential crisis. That would be too dull. Remember what I told you last night. You've got to face up to the real reason why you don't want to go to Hong Kong.'

A bird wheels wildly in the window behind her. She rubs my upper arm briskly and then squeezes it, pinching the bone. 'And go eat something, will you?'

'I'm out of here.' I turn away from her, wave in the air and head off down the corridor.

'Ring me when you get back,' she calls out. 'And good luck. Do the right thing.' By which she means let go. Stop waiting for Stephen. But Zanna does not know how bad things are. She does not know the extent of my shame. How I can lie on the bed in the darkness and trace a finger along my collarbone, let my hand slip down, imagining it is his touch, soft, warm, barely slipping down to my breast and already an urgent pulse between my legs as I press my thighs hard together and apart, and thrust upwards, my fingers sliding easily into my own hot wet grip but Stephen flees at this point and my fingers are a poor imitation, bringing only an empty coming that leaves me hollowed out. And I have reached the ultimate humiliation in my own bed, jerking off to the remembered touch of a man who has chosen the most unequivocal departure.

■ ■ ■ ■ ■

Jesus Christ, am I ever going to cut loose?

'Sorry for shouting at you earlier,' I stop by Pie Man's desk. 'But you caught me at a bad time.'

'No problem.' He nods, the flesh wobbling around his chin. 'I just thought you'd find that article interesting.'

'I know, I will read it.'

'I didn't mean to badger you. Just, it's very relevant to your – eh – your talent.'

'I've just been really tired. All the travelling.' He bobs his big pale head and smoothes his hands unseeing across the desk, knocking a pack of Marlboro to the floor.

'Didn't know you smoked,' I bend to pick them up.

'Oh, no, I don't. Someone left them here and—' Pie Man watches me open the pack and fish out the lighter inside. 'They'll do,' I exhale.

One of his geek mates across the way looks up, staring straight through me at some calculations on his inner eye. The desks here on SPUD look curiously naked because they don't have Reuters or Bloomberg and they don't have phone boards, instead they have the yellow plastic phones that mark you out as a non-producer. Rob will make a big play out of the fact that the geeks don't have equipment and he occasionally wanders down and picks up a handset and bangs it hard against the desk then holds it to his ear and goes *Hello, hello, is that you, Mum?* while Dr Who makes a great show of pretending not to notice.

Pie Man twiddles with a stubby little pencil. His own desk is littered with pages of his even and beautiful script, almost calligraphic, as if the calculations are an aesthetic homage, the numbers flowing left to right, horizontal, vertical, in perfect alignment.

'It's like artwork,' I pick up a page.

'Oh, that's just an algorithm for—'

'Yeah, I know, I meant your handwriting. It's beautiful.'

'Oh,' he blushes, looks down and sticks his little stub in the sharpener.

'How come you always write in pencil when you never rub out?'

'I like to leave the full trail, to see how I got to a point. If I have all the steps then I can trace it back.'

And he raises his head, glances at me briefly full face. I think of Piggy in *Lord of the Flies*, or Billy Bunter, but there is a razor edge to Pie Man. Beneath the blubbery lids, his eyes are a sharp blue. Youthfully clear, though his age is hard to decipher since the swollen flesh disguises all clues. He looks away, brushes at some crumbs on his sleeve. Soon he will be off to the canteen, shoulders hunched beneath the monstrous craving that propels him forwards up the stairs. Sometimes he returns with three pre-packaged sandwiches that he eats methodically, large slashing bites with his head angled sideways. I have seen him masticate even when his mouth is empty as if in involuntary reflex response to the thought of food. And I wonder how these habits developed unchecked into adulthood, if Pie Man's mum and dad are like him, the three of them weighed down by the burden of a ravenous hunger, slumped at a kitchen table groaning with food. Perhaps the impulse that tells you are replete can malfunction, smothered by an avalanche of food that keeps slipping down your gullet.

'Oh Jesus, I am such a fucking idiot.'

'What's the matter?' Pie Man looks up alarmed.

'I completely forgot about Rex.'

'What?'

'I've just remembered my dog walker won't be able to take him tonight because she does these stupid Shih Tzus in Chiswick on Mondays. And I have to catch a plane.' I turn away towards my desk. '*Fuck.*'

'Wait, wait, maybe I could help.'

'You know a dog sitter?'

'No, but—'

''Cos Rex hates kennels.'

'No, I mean, what about me?'

'What about you?'

'I mean I could look after Rex for you.'

'Thanks anyway, that's kind, but—'

'He knows me.'

'No he doesn't.'

'Yes he does. Remember that time I bumped into you in the park? I even threw his ball.'

And I do recall a dingy Sunday morning, not long after Stephen, and Venice, when Pie Man suddenly appeared by the Round Pound. He stood there inside a massive green anorak like a parachute had collapsed around him, hurling the tennis ball over arm with a surprisingly long bowl, Rex barrelling after it.

'Remember I told you I used to have a dog when I was growing up?'

'Denis. The black and tan mongrel who ate worms.'

'That's right,' he nods happily.

I park my butt back on the edge of his desk and Pie Man scrabbles to move a jumble of papers to one side. 'You only met Rex for a few minutes once.'

'You said he liked me.' And it's true, Rex did like him but of course Rex likes everyone who tickles his tummy and scratches his head although I don't say that; I look at Pie Man's earnest face while I'm formulating a no, then I think well it's not as if I have many options – and it's not as though he'll go out clubbing and leave Rex locked up indoors. In fact, Rex would love Pie Man, plus they have interests in common like eating and lying on couches.

'I wouldn't be back till Wednesday morning.' I am still scrambling for another last minute non-kennel option but there are none because there are no other single women in the City stupid enough to own a dog.

'That's OK. No problem. Really.'

'I guess I could get Lisa to drop him over to your place later only you'd have to leave work early.'

'I can work at home. I sometimes do, so it wouldn't be—'

'Are you really sure about all this?'

'Yes, yes. It would be great to have him.'

'I don't know. Maybe I should do the kennel. Maybe he'd be OK this time.'

'No, don't, he'd hate it. I'll look after him really well. I won't go out or anything.'

'Well, OK then. Thanks a lot. You're a lifesaver.' And Pie Man beams like he's won a prize. He pushes back the chair and stands up as if this adds extra weight to his commitment. Smoothes his hands over his stomach, hitches his trousers. He is all business now.

'So where are you going?'

'Hong Kong.'

'But you just came back.'

'I know. Just can't get enough of the place. So give me your number and your address and I'll give it to Lisa.' He writes on his pad with his little pencil.

'Hot date, Pie Man?' Rob sticks his head over my shoulder.

'Oh, fuck off, Rob,' I say.

'Remember the Daleks, boys,' Rob say. 'Would have taken over the whole fucking universe if only the designers had given them legs.' But no one in the SPUD hub is listening. Rob's wit is not theirs. Anyway, mostly they ignore all of us, they think we're like show dogs at Crufts, all posture and veneer, and this is true. But in this business of peacocks, if you're not showing your tail you're invisible.

'That's one hell of a tie you got there, Pie Man.' Rob gives it a little tug. Livid squares of purple and orange checkerboard like a howl for the Seventies. 'But seriously now, I've got an important scientific question for you.' Rob gives a mischievous smirk and squeezes his arm around my waist. 'Let's put your PhD in astrophysics to use.'

I shrug him off. 'Actually it's Maths.' I know this because I saw Pie Man's CV lying on his desk one day. His thesis was 'Binomial Modelling of Stock Market Returns: Estimating the Probability of Various Outcomes of Future Prices on the Stock Market'.

'So riddle me this,' Rob continues. Pie Man stiffens, fingers the pencil. 'Why would being strangled give someone a better orgasm?'

Pie Man blushes and lip chews, fingers a thumbnail in his ear, all the textbook litany of tics, and I wonder if he would trade it all – the whole giant IQ, the whole big brain thing – just for one day to feel what it's like to be Rob, to be stroking the silken inner thigh of some slender arm candy, hovering in a perfume sweat cloud above Laila in the back office or Claudia in Fixed Income or Annabel in Private Clients or any one of Rob's other ex-fucks.

'Come on, mate.' Rob's neat torso bounces athletically in a series of desk level press-ups. 'You're the scientist. There must be a biological explanation.'

'Well,' Pie Man does the coughing thing again, 'oxygen deprivation.'

'Yeah, we know all about that round here, don't we?' Rob nods his head at Al who is doing his sales march around the corner perimeter, the cord stretched taut behind him. But Al ignores him; he is busy pitching something that, luckily, does not sound like Vulkan or MSTAR, though of course my lips are sealed: I cannot say anything. 'Come on then, let's hear it.'

'Possibly because,' continues Pie Man, 'oxygen deprivation causes increased blood flow to – eh – to certain parts of the—' and he flicks a sideways glance at me.

'Don't worry about Geri, she's a big girl.'

'Increased blood flow to the – eh – organ.'

'Wahey. Thank you, my man.' Rob backslaps him.

'Julie's looking for you about some travel.' Al saunters towards us with his Columbia water bottle and nods at me.

'You off again, G?' asks Rob.

'Back to Hong Kong.'

'What's up?'

'Need to know basis.'

'So you taking Pie Man with you to carry the bags?' Rob nudges Pie Man's shoulder.

'Actually he's offered to look after Rex for me,' I smile inclusively.

'Well, well, so you're coming up in the world now, Pie Man. Dog-sitting for old G while she jets off to see the Cat?'

Pie Man nods uncertainly.

'So what's cooking at SPUD then?' Rob picks up a page from the desk. 'What's this? A blueprint for a new rocket?' He taps at what look like semi-circles with scribbles but are actually volatility curves.

'You wouldn't understand it, Rob,' I say. Pie Man watches anxiously as Rob lets the page drift downwards.

'Seriously though. Tell us, how is the power plant at SPUD? Have you built the model that's going to make our fortunes?'

Pie Man looks from Rob to Al to me and smiles, a bland spread of the lips as if he is mimicking someone else's rules of discourse. 'We're working on a new project.'

'Oh yeah, what's that?' asks Al.

'We're, eh, looking at convertible bonds.' He casts a quick eye at Rob.

'My babies!' says Rob. 'You need to get me involved.'

'Yeah,' I say, ''cos Rob's got a PhD in maths so he'd be a big help to you all.' Al snorts into his water bottle.

'So tell me this, G,' says Rob, 'how come you're slumming it down with us at the coalface when you could be breathing in all this pure mathematical air? Is it 'cos you want to be where the real money is, by any chance?'

'Geri could easily be the best in our quant group,' Pie Man blurts out.

'Only she doesn't really have the figure for it,' Rob winks at Pie Man's belly. 'Joking apart though, tell us what you're up to with my convertibles.' But Pie Man hesitates, he's wary of ambush tactics. Sometimes

Rob nabs him on his way, back grabs a bag of Cheese 'n' Onion and waggles it, *Now, that's not going to help you get the girls, is it, mate?*

'So tell us then.'

'We're building a pricing model. There's nothing any good out there.'

'You mean some Black and Scholes options thing.'

'No, no, something much more sophisticated than that. Black and Scholes is basically primitive.' Pie Man hurls all caution to the wind and begins to elaborate on the finer points of theoretical value, his enthusiasm growing so that he forgets his audience and launches into a mini-lecture on volatility estimation and binomial pricing.

A little string of muscle tightens in Rob's neck, the same one that is held taut when he takes down a big position or when the Grope finger-signals him into the office. Convertibles are his passion and his meal ticket and I know it bothers him enormously that he didn't know that SPUD were building a model and that the Grope must have sanctioned this project, and no one even thought to tell Rob or came to pick his brain because he left school at sixteen and never went to college and everyone in SPUD thinks he is a moron. Or at the very least a dinosaur.

But SPUD *is* the future foretold because one day the geeks will rule our world. And this is what Rob cannot see, standing there tight-lipped and simmering as he tries to keep up with Pie Man's lecture. SPUD is our very own little Silicon Valley, puttering away like a nuclear reactor. Their mission is to take Steiner's into the twenty-first century of derivatives power by designing models so clever that we will make bucket loads by just looking at a screen. They will be scanning the financial horizons for value and opportunity. Their quantitative model will transform our lives, change everything, tell the market what value really is and we will all become slaves to the geeks who built it and people like Rob and Al will be rendered obsolete because the model will eventually do us out of a job. This is why Pie Man sits at his desk late into the night. I see him the odd time when I've stumbled in drunk at midnight in search of my keys and he is beavering away with algorithms that no one here can understand but which will become the norm. I get it because I can do the maths and Pie Man is right – I could get involved, I could even be the best but I do not care. And maybe that's my problem.

Rob is rigid now, his lips grey, he senses there is a whole wide world of value out there from which he will be forever excluded.

He will never make it to the next level.

He reaches out and lifts Pie Man's free hand and turns it over shaking his head at the grubby inside of his cuffs. 'So basically,' he interrupts, 'what you're saying is you and Dr Who are going to build a computer system that is going to tell me what my convertible bonds are worth?'

'Well, yes.' Pie Man blinks as if Rob's statement of hollow fact is just a mundane confirmation.

Rob drops Pie Man's hand. 'Well, what if I said I already know what every single convertible bond is worth. It's worth what the market is prepared to pay. So we don't need some mathematical model to calculate any theoretical value. We just need shit-hot traders who know what the fuck they're doing.'

Pie Man levers himself up to his full height and stands there above us all, looking curiously unaffected by Rob's contempt as if he possesses some transcendental insight that has him operating on a higher plane.

'In a few years time, it will be all technical trading,' he says, looking down at Rob and speaking slowly as if he is addressing an imbecile. 'And people like you won't be able to get a job in this place. Just watch what technology is going to do to your careers. In fact, none of you will survive. Your kind of traders with your finger in the air, making up prices like you were on a fruit and veg stall. You think it's all supply and demand and some sort of intuition, some sort of special touch. You don't even *understand* the instruments you trade.' Pie Man sweeps a huge arm around the trading floor, his eyes glittering. 'Look at Joe Palmer and his team over there on the warrant desk – they're just bull market traders. You think they know anything about option theory? You think they even understand volatility?'

'They don't need to,' snaps Rob, 'because they made fucking more than a hundred and twenty million dollars last year.'

'And do you know how much more they are leaving on the table because of all that they don't understand? Double or triple that. *This* is where the smart money is going to be,' Pie Man thumps the top of his computer. 'You're all stuck in the Dark Ages with your trading books and your market feel. It's like putting monkeys behind the wheel of a car. In the future the quants will be running the show because this business is changing by the second. We are building pricing models for proprietary trading in derivatives so Steiner's can start taking principal risk in size. The real juice is all in equity right now where you can make easy money. Out of pretty stupid people who understand nothing.' He is flushed and triumphant, a lick of sweat above his lips.

'So the geeks will inherit the earth,' Rob pokes Pie Man's belly. It's a face-off between past and future. 'And you'll be earning the big bucks. Need to get in fucking shape then, mate.' He jabs again, a little harder this time and Pie Man seems to wobble.

'Word is there'll be no geeks in the closet,' says Al. 'They'll all be out visiting customers.'

Pie Man winces with a nervous giggle that comes out like a subdued shriek. Rob and Al stand sleek and tall side by side staring up at this vision of their redundancy and the apocalyptic vision of markets run by fat boys with mathematical models. The future is no longer theirs. And SPUD will have the last laugh.

Rob smiles. 'So tell us then, Pie Man, how's the swimming?'

I kick Rob's ankle to pre-empt the stage-managed humiliation that is surely coming, but he doesn't miss a beat. Pie Man frowns, perplexed.

'I hear you're a big man for the pool?' says Rob. I slither off the desk and stab the heel of my shoe on his again, but he doesn't flinch. And of course I know where this is headed and it's all my fault for getting a cheap laugh, for telling Rob and Al that Pie Man invited me to go swimming in the new pool at the Tara Hotel.

'What d'you mean?' Pie Man is puzzled now, his blubber neck ripe for the slash.

'I hear you might be starting a swimming team.' Al snorts on his bottle.

'Just shut up, Rob.' I prod him again but my heel wobbles and I nearly tip over.

'Steady on, G, you'll be on your face in a minute.' And I can tell by the crease lines tightened about his jaw that Rob will go all the way with this one. 'We should go down the pool some time, mate. Just you and me, Pie Man, a few lengths.'

Al is shaking his head, face pink with the effort of holding back his laughter. Pie Man is less certain now about the merriment and is nervously flipping the pencil, a smile ghosting his face.

'But maybe you prefer going with the girls?'

Al can no longer hold it. 'Oh man, oh man,' he goes and takes a swig of his water and then snorts the whole fucking spray right in front of him and Rob explodes just as Pie Man's face crumples into knowingness. His eyes swivel towards me, something forming out of all this confusion in his face, the colour rising for sure, a pink blotch on one cheek.

'Best way to check out the merchandise, eh? Geri in a hot bikini,' and Rob winks at Pie Man who is standing now utterly still, staring at me and the look that is always soft is hardening into something I cannot name. And I look away. Focus my attention on Rob's idiot face.

'You are an asshole.' I tell him. 'Of the highest order.'

'Yeah, he's an asshole,' gasps Al, his face creased and red. He is beyond laughing now.

Pie Man slams his chair against the desk and picks up the satchel that was lying on the floor like a faithful dog.

'Oh, come on, Pie Man.' Rob's arms encircle me from behind. 'You know me, just having a laugh.' I push him away but Pie Man is gone, barging through the double doors.

'You're such a wanker, Rob.'

'Ah, but you love me all the same,' says Rob and heads off to his desk.

Fuck buddy, Zanna said when I made the mistake of telling her that I'd slept with Rob in October. *That's exactly what he is. And believe me, you need a serious upgrade.* Their antipathy is mutual and entrenched. Like a chalk screech on board, their first meeting at the Lamb some years back. An airy contempt in Zanna's blood-thinning smile. Rob doesn't have Background: *he is not even a graduate, for Chrissake* – although he did spend a good amount of time hanging around Essex Uni trying to get laid. In Zanna's eyes he is a peasant, he has a thing for dirty jokes, does not know his way around the vineyards of the Loire, hasn't been to Cowes. He could not show her the good cultured European time that she would expect although she admits he could probably show her a good fuck. But it wouldn't be a career-enhancing fuck and if Zanna is going for a bit of rough she only does so in an unrelated sector. Childishness in males leaves her cold, she is not interested in horsing around. *You could at least have found someone who doesn't work at the same firm. Jesus.* But I'd rolled out of the bar one Friday night, insisting on Rob's place for a drink.

Madonna sliding out of the speakers, the coffee table bobbing on some unstable horizon when I sank back into the couch, closed my eyes on a double-vision sea of black and white, then Rob was framed in the threshold of the kitchen, shoulder leaning into the doorpost, arms crossed above jeans and bare feet. I held out my empty glass and moved into the hallway with the vague intention of going to the loo but was roadblocked by my passing reflection illuminated from below in the warm glow of a table lamp, seduced by my own tiredness, encouraged by my increased heartbeat that seemed to have fallen in step with 'Like A Prayer'. Ran a palm over my right nipple, blood rushing to key zones so that the hidden lips between my legs swell, and I swayed back into the living room where Rob's head was embedded in the couch leather. Watching me come closer and lowering myself onto him, splayed against the pit of his stomach. His hands on my skirted hips. His head level with my breasts, his face disappearing out of view with that concentrated expression that men have on the brink of pleasure.

We didn't even make it to the bedroom. The long-haired animal rug was scratchy and smelled of chemical cleaner. Rob came professionally on cue and afterwards he was careful not to flop his full weight onto me and I wondered why it is that I always get fucked from behind, if it's something intolerable about my face?

He rolled sideways, propped himself on his elbow beside me and surprised me by stroking my shoulder in slow repeated movements. I took his hand, slid it down between my thighs but as soon as his finger began its tentative exploration, I knew that no one could find the right touch, we were wasting time with the false promise of something that wasn't going to happen. *I need to take a shower*, I said, though what I really wanted was to hit something very hard. Instead I washed my hair, face, neck, I scrubbed my skin until I felt some purpose return and I stood naked in the mirror, my face almost human against all the sharp edges of ceramic and glass and steel, the sour taste of another night's drinking in my mouth. *I have to go.* He was standing up and fretful when I came back, wet hair dripping.

I don't want to – he swept an open palm through the space between us, testing the shattered boundary between friends and lovers. *What*? I opened the door. *Wreck our beautiful working relationship?*

09:48

'YOU'RE ON THE 14:05 BA FROM HEATHROW.' Julie places the travel wallet on my desk. 'Your car's booked for 10:30 so you have time to pick up your stuff on the way. And come by before you leave – the boss wants to see you.'

'OK.'

'Don't forget.'

'Yeah yeah, I won't forget.'

'Life in the fast lane, Geri.' Al smiles wistfully.

'Not all it's cracked up to be.'

'Wouldn't mind trying it for size myself.' He mutters and turns back to his desk, flips open a research report. He is rattled, but it is just the usual mortality rush. He's thinking of last week's sales run and the numbers that tell us what we are worth. And Al is at the margin, he is not living up to expectations and his unarticulated anxieties threaten to drag him low. I have a hunch that the memory of the humiliating fourteenth in the class of '85 still haunts him, the double whammy of non-inclusion in the best fraternity and the failure to bag the internship at Goldman's, his father's struggle to contain his disappointment at the graduation ceremony. *The next generation? They don't appreciate what hard work is for. They'll only ever let you down.* All those carefully scheduled 6.30 p.m. dinners in the Oak Room on the Friday before term, *Alexander, there's a lot at stake here.* Al nodding earnestly, not daring to shift his gaze from his father's face to the irrelevance of the menu, wiping sweaty palms on his trouser leg. *Yes, sir, I'll do my best,* the vision of an alternative fading before his eyes. In drunken conversations at school with other inheritors of the mantle, Al would have made tentative quips about the burden of paternal expectation, how the old man was like so focused, but you could only share so much with another guy who knew that your sudden death would shunt him up a place in class. So much easier, Al may have mused in the cab home, for the second-generation aspirants whose parental ambitions have just been transplanted: for them, it was a result, just getting through Admissions. Al was stuck at the front of a long line of Van Velzens that snaked back to Ellis Island, weighed down by the hopes of the first weary shoe that ever set foot on this soil, on a journey that would one day end in vindication and triumph when the unrecognisable descendant's photo enters the Hallowed Walls of the Alumni.

Meanwhile, surrounded by mementos while his real life carries on in exile, Al remains a tourist in our town. He will never take root here although he has studiously embraced the familiarisation programme that includes Covent Garden, Stratford on Avon, Sunday lunch at Simpson's, a tournament at Wentworth, three days at Lords, fish and chips, strawberries at Wimbledon. But I know he is secretly pining for peanut butter jelly and pretzels, top-loading washing machines and giant refrigerators, and yellow cabs with plastic on the seats. It's the little details that grind him down and mark him out as a transient in his own life. Still Al does his time in the hope that this European tour of duty might catapult him to the advantage over his peers that he couldn't quite manage at school. In career years there has been some slippage, and lately he's been reading about his classmates in the *Wall Street Journal* and he is anxiously measuring the widening gulf.

Each time Al comes back from a trip home he brings goody bags into the office: Oreos and bags of pretzels, Hershey's Kisses which we all despise because they taste like sick, but the M&Ms are a big hit. He is always a little mournful for the first few days and spends more time than usual on the US stock desk hanging out with the other expats. Two of them are from Minnesota and were crazy about ice-fishing and they all shared a mews in Glebe Place where we did once have a great party at Christmas. They'd filled the bath with ice and beer bottles and by the end of the night we were having head-dunking competitions in the meltwater. The Minnesota ice fishers could keep their heads in for a full minute and come up white-faced and smiling, have a tequila and do it all over again. The rest of us surfaced after three seconds screaming and dripping all over the bathroom floor and down the stairs and out into a chill night where my jaw ached and we staggered around with teeth chattering, trying to hail a cab with Rob going *Fuck this, I am DYING.*

■ ■ ■ ■ ■

'Hey Al,' shouts Rob, 'female line two.'

'Who?'

'Just kidding,' says Rob and Al shows him the finger. He is wary of unidentified callers ever since the golf tournament in the Bahamas where he met a half-Swede called Annika who had jacked in her job at a gator sanctuary in the Everglades to cure her depression by swimming with dolphins. Al assumed that she was part of the control group and not one of the patients who clustered together on the dockside like cripples at Lourdes under the supervision of psychologists from Cornell. Then one night Annika got hammered on margaritas in the beach bar and ran away across the dunes, stripping off her clothes in the dark like that scene from *Jaws*, and Al had a real job getting her out of the water because she was kicking and screaming that she just wanted to die. Al couldn't find her clothes on the beach so she had to travel naked in the ambulance, and naturally the paramedics were throwing him filthy looks like he was some kind of pervert rather than the guy who actually saved her life. Al took an earlier flight home but Annika managed to check herself out of the hospital in time to catch him as he was heading for the departure gates and even tried to break through security, and for a while there he was worried she was going to show at Reception one day, although he was pretty sure she wouldn't remember he worked at Steiner's.

'Speaking of dolphins,' Rob leans across the monitor.

'Which we weren't,' Al hangs up the phone.

'You know those penguins, the really big ones that stand up?'

'They all stand up, Rob,' I say. 'That's what they do.'

'You mean the Emperor penguins,' says Al.

'You know what those Antarctic explorers used to do with them?'

'Eat them.'

'What else?'

'Use the blubber to make oil,' says Al.

'What else?'

'Oh, I don't know, Rob, use them as goalposts?'

'They used to shag them.'

'Jesus, Rob.' I shake my head.

Al nods thoughtfully at his screen. 'Yeah, I can see that.'

'What do you mean you can see that?' I turn to him.

'You could sort of imagine them looking like women.'

'Two legs,' Rob grins. 'That little waddle...'

'How the fuck do penguins look like women if they're covered in feathers and they have beaks?'

'Hey, Geri,' Al raises both palms. 'I'm just saying I imagine that's what those guys were thinking of when they looked at the penguins after six months in the snow at minus 40.'

'So you would have sex with a penguin?'

'That is not what I said, I said—'

'Besti – AL – ity,' Rob whispers dramatically.

'Fuck you.'

'Remember *Midnight Express*, mate.'

'There were no penguins in that movie.'

'So what exactly is your point, Rob?' Al thumps his keyboard.

Rob shrugs, shakes his head. 'One minute a bloke is straight, next thing you know he's an arsebandit.'

'That's because he was in prison,' I say.

'Exactly my point,' Rob slaps the top of the monitor. 'There's our Al doing his nut in minus 40 for six months when this cute little penguin comes waddling out of a blizzard. So what does he do?'

Al is tensed now, head bent low over the notebook, pen twitching between his fingers. Rob winks at me. 'You're sick,' I pull a face and he turns away, still grinning, hands in pockets, and walks over to Futures.

10:23

'LISA CALLED ME ALREADY,' Pie Man stands up when I stop at his desk. 'And it's all sorted, she's bringing Rex over at five so I'll—'

'And you're sure.'

'Yeah yeah. It'll be fine.'

Julie is hovering by SPUD to make sure I see the Grope before I leave.

'So I'll call you from Hong Kong.'

'Don't worry, he'll be happy with me.' And Pie Man reaches out to touch my shoulder but his touch falters and instead of a cheery pat it feels like he is wiping something off his hand.

'Thanks, you're a star.' I am backing away. Down the row of desks Rob gives me the thumbs up; he has a phone to his ear and Bud Light standing by like a pointer ready to run some ticket over to Ops.

'He's waiting,' Julie reminds me and I follow her across the floor.

The Grope is standing up staring at the wall-mounted TV screen where the silent CNN headline reads Tariq Aziz repeats Iraq will attach Israel in the event of any attack on Iraqi territory.

'So you're all set?' he turns towards me.

'Sure.' Like there's an option.

'Hook up with Tom Castigliano when you get over there. He's fully briefed.' And he moves over to his desk, slides into his chair and I take up position on the other side.

'What you need to know is that we want this thing wrapped up before the first shot is fired in Baghdad,' he says. 'And the UN deadline expires Wednesday at midnight EST.'

'I don't know if Felix will play ball.'

'My instinct tells me Felix will go for it. I gotta good feeling about this, Geri. He's sat on his chunk of Vulkan Value for a lifetime now, this bid from Texas Pistons is a late Christmas present. So what if he won't see us or the Vulkan board and won't say what he's going to do? That's just 'cos he gets off on jerking people around. This will be a landmark transaction for Steiner's. We are not going to lose out.'

He looks at me, pauses, and then continues. 'And I have personally assured Kapoor that you can get a simple answer to a simple question.'

Oh boy.

But the Grope is lost now in contemplation of some glorious vision of the future. 'I told him we are going to go out and get Felix to play ball.' He raps the table and grins. He's going for the big one, he has picked this career moment to risk his all. He's already rehearsing the legend of how Goldman's were ready to snatch the deal from under our noses and he saved the day, a subtle insinuation that the great Kapoor was really dithering like a Jessie and how it was the Grope who changed the course of history right on the brink of a war. He is living the dream; he is starring in his own movie and it isn't going to end with his ass in a sling again, it's going to end with the story slipping into the chronicles of deal mythology and the Grope's big balls slapped right down on the table for everyone to see.

'So you've been with Steiner's now for how long? Five, six years?' I nod and study the concertina of creases along the arms of his shirt. 'We plucked you from obscurity and gave you a life you'd never dreamed of. Opportunity. Possibility. You know, I remember your first day. Your hunger, your desire to be something. Whatever it was driving you – past or future – you had it. And I watched you grow from greenhorn to the biggest producer on the floor. Smart. Focused. Driven.' He sighs and raises his head with a contemptuous jut of the chin. 'Until now.'

He grips the chair and rolls it back to thud softly against the window shelf. 'Oh, I've seen it happen before, and to better people than you, Geri. Don't think I haven't noticed. When you've been around as long as I have, you can spot the early warning signs. A kind of sloppiness sets in. Sharp edges going blunt. Sometimes it's the booze or the women or the dope and sometimes it's just complacency. The golden goose gets axed while you're asleep at the wheel. Sometimes it's loss of faith, like losing your swing.' He flexes his arms and air swings straight-armed and we watch the imaginary ball fly up and out through the window, soar across the City with thousands of other admiring heads following its trailblaze into space. 'Burnout is ugly, Geri. And expensive. The rot sets in and eats away. One day a rising star, the next a piece of trash. Some people just can't cut it.'

He gives me one of those searching looks as if he was scanning my neural pathways. I am sweating slightly and a display of sentient life would be very timely now.

'You still hungry?' and for a crazy moment I actually picture a croissant, an image of standing at Nalia's deli counter resting a hand on the glass dome.

'Yes. I'm still hungry.' I rise from the chair. 'I'm still hungry.' I repeat the words, for this is what Zanna knows so well about me: when you're raised a Catholic you understand the persuasive power of incantation. Silent prayer just doesn't pull the same punch. 'I'm still hungry,' and as I speak I can actually feel my tummy rumbling – for a croissant or the deal or the hunt for the coat-tails of the life I built.

The Grope nods approvingly and stands up tall behind his desk, hands in pockets now, looking out at the trading floor. Perhaps he is searching for the right sporting metaphor that will encapsulate this moment, something about the longest shot, the highest peak, the fastest run, something to spark me into the zone, some keepsake I can take with me on the plane.

My gaze drifts over to the CNN screen where the picture has shifted to the inside of an Apache helicopter and I sense some sneaking foreboding creeping up on me, a bad feeling about the frontline.

'What about the whole war thing?' I ask and he snaps his gaze back at me.

'There's four hundred thousand US troops out there just itching to barbecue Saddam's ass. This war will all be wrapped up in no time, you'll see, and Max Lester's not the kind of guy who gets spooked by something that's going to be over in a few weeks.'

He leans forward and places both knuckles on the desk. 'Take it from me, this stuff your newspapers write over here, Bush the wimp? They're wide of the mark. When I was a kid at Andover—'

'Andover?'

'Philips Academy, Andover,' he snaps. 'It's what you'd call the American Eton. Course George Bush was there way before my time but our tutor told the story about Stimson's visit to the school and how it set him on the road to greatness.'

'Stimson?'

'Stimson was the Secretary of War in Roosevelt's cabinet. Visited Philips in the summer of 1940 when George Bush was just sixteen. Delivered a vision of America's destiny. Subject? World leadership, the great battle between liberty and the enemies of liberty.' He frowns at the tombstones in the display cabinet and the listless Stars and Stripes and then suddenly jerks his head back to stare angrily at me.

'You know he flew fifty-eight combat missions, got shot down, spent thirty-four minutes in the Pacific before he was rescued by a destroyer.'

'Stimson?'

'BUSH,' he whacks the desk.

'Oh, right.'

'Does that sound like a wimp? Does that sound like the kind of guy who walks away from a tough job?'

'No, absolutely not.' I straighten up and uncross my legs.

'This deal is going to put us on the map, Geri.' He turns his head in slow consideration until his glare lights on my face. He is weighing every word. 'Texas Piston v Vulkan Valve,' he whispers with schoolboy daring and scrolls his hand through the air as if he was writing the imaginary tombstone that's going to put us right up there in the league tables. He flashes a triumphant leer towards the corner of the room and the glass cabinet. He folds his arms behind his head, running a tongue over his gleaming incisors, savouring the sweet taste of antici-pated victory. 'But,' he snaps out of his reverie, 'we're in a race against time here so just get out to Hong Kong and work your magic. All you gotta do is get a simple answer to a simple question.'

'Sure. Great.' I say, standing.

He flashes his teeth reassured, bestows a paternal nod. 'I'm counting on you, Geri. You can deliver on this.'

Faustino returns with my double Absolut and an espresso. This is not the first time I have shown up here hours before the lunchtime avalanche. The café bar is pristine and quiet but for the low rumble of jazz, the waitresses clinking in the wings, the glasses gleaming behind the bar. Technically speaking Faustino should not be serving booze at this time, but he is from Bilbao so he picks and chooses which English protocol is worthy of his embrace. He gives short professional shift to most of the traders, including Rob, a tilt to his magnificent chin when he takes their cash. They shrivel in their smart cut suits before his imperious good looks. Faustino likes me because I am not English or American and also because I told him that there are lots of people on the west coast of Ireland with jet black hair which is said to be because of the Spanish Armada. He has a deep respect for history and tradition and has confided in me that he does not approve of the new Guggenheim that is coming to Bilbao one little bit.

'Ever been to Hong Kong, Faustino?' He looks over my head into the middle distance and shakes his head.

'So if somebody asked you to go and live there, would you go?'

'Hwat peoples ask?' he frowns.

'Oh, say your boss, your client. All the people who own you.'

He takes a deep breath, holds it as if testing his lung capacity. 'No peoples hown Faustino.'

'So you would say no.'

'Hi go home to Bilbao,' he taps his chest. 'Hi promise.'

'Who did you promise? Your girlfriend?' I picture a sultry barefoot vixen standing outside a dusty casa.

'Mama. Hi promise my mama.'

'That's great Faustino. You promised your mum.'

'For sure.' He picks up the white napkin and snaps it like a whip. 'Familia, no?'

'Yeah right, familia.'

The door swings behind me. Faustino places a double espresso in front of me, watches over like a granny while I drink it. 'You hwan more?'

'I'm going to the airport,' I point to the silver Merc idling out beyond the concourse. 'I'm going to Hong Kong.' He nods in grave commiseration.

There is a spreading puddle by Rex's bowl as he slops in that chaotic way he has of drinking water. He is delighted at my unexpected daytime return and the little play we've had out in the courtyard. He trots over to his bed in the hall, flops down on a squeaky toy and stares up at me. 'Good boy,' I say and he grunts, settles his head on his paws. He has seen the suit carrier on the bed, he knows I am going to leave him, and I am hijacked by these sudden tears. I mean, how would a Labrador exist in Hong Kong, let alone like it? Even the plane journey would be a trauma.

'Look,' I tell him, 'you're going to stay with Pie Man, so lots of food. And I'll bet he'll let you sleep on the couch.' Rex closes his eyes. He knows all about abandonment. *You should've got a cat, Geri*, said Rob. *They couldn't give a shit if you're never there. They don't get attached to you.* Zanna too has been hassling me. *Just find a home for him,* she said the other night when I mentioned Rex as another reason why I couldn't relocate to Hong Kong. *You never liked him anyway,* I told her and at least she had the good grace not to disagree. Rex could sense it even when he was a puppy, some invisible force field that has always kept him from jumping up at her like he does with everyone else; he knew his place. *He is your surrogate child. Dogs are meant for ranches and farms. Rex should be living in Richmond or Wandsworth or somewhere, with a stay-at-home mum, kids, garden, the whole deal. You should be out in the world, not spending quality time with your pet.*

The fridge contents stare glumly back at me: balsamic dressing and cocktail cherries of a certain age. The vodka and a Sapporo, which I like to keep because the can has a military style.

14.3 days out of each month, I say now into the open fridge, *is how often we've been in the same country so far this year,* which is exactly what I said when Stephen once yawned that we saw each other all the time. He was reading *Companies News* while I looked for eggs to make pancakes, because they reminded him of home weekends from school. Rex was stretched out in a sun spot on the floor by his bare feet. When I replay these exchanges now I hear them as if through a voice distorter where all the frequencies have been adjusted, like fiddling with an equaliser, the bass boosted and ominous and the words heavy with a foreboding I had never previously heard. A remix of a favourite song where you hear the imperfections, the flatness of the high note, the muffle of a guitar string when the finger touches the fret, a certain looseness about the timing.

I meet a washed-out starved looking version of myself in the bathroom mirror. Even my freckles seem to be fading. *Thirty-two,* I told Stephen as he stroked the side of my face in the early dawn of our first morning together. *They're very endearing,* he smiled. But that was long before a lopsided asymmetry crept into the photos, contaminating every shot we took, not that there was time for many pictures in the hurried exhaustion of our time together. Once in an uncharacteristic wash of spontaneity, Stephen stopped a passer-by in the Tuileries and we posed in the biting February cold. I was leaning into the arm that Stephen raised to pull me close, but in the seconds between the opening and closing of the shutter, it looks as if I am clinging desperately to his chest, my mouth gaping on some unrecorded afterthought, half my face obscured by a thick lock of hair. Stephen's arm is slipping away out of view and he is smiling straight into the lens, meeting his separate future head on. The five-year documentary of our coupledom, a handful of memories re-shot through the filter of breakdown. Hyde Park, framed in a late summer afternoon, Rex puppy-playing on the grass between us, and with the skinned finality of hindsight, Stephen's wide smile seems taunting and mine naïve, both of us framed in a memorial to the sham we were becoming.

In the early days when Stephen still found my personality intriguing, I would rest my head on his naked chest while he toyed with my numbers thing, trying to define its boundaries. Those days before he stumbled on the outer limits of our relationship, before the rain came through our waterproofed park walks and Rex seemed to smell and I stopped buying new lingerie every weekend and we were both able to fall asleep in the same bed without touching. Negotiating our way out of the skipping couple advert, where the walk-by suggestion of his scent on some other guy could make me wet between the legs, sliding down the waterfall of passion that was supposed to ripple out into a mature and enduring intimacy. If I hadn't missed a few signposts along the way.

There are ring marks on the bottom shelf of my bathroom cabinet where Stephen used to store his customised Penhaligon's, and I am still finding things: Day 123 and the shock of a black tie at the bottom of a drawer had me standing again in between Stephen and the mirror, his chin tilted upwards in studied concentration while expert fingers knotted the silk strip round his neck. *I suppose you learnt how to do that when you were five,* I smiled. *Eight actually,* he said, in that manner I would now call self-congratulatory. I stood transfixed by the taunting reflection of his competence, the perfection of our public coupling unzipped to reveal a hideous bubbling beneath its shallow surface. What is he doing with me? I thought, retreating from the mirror with the loose bundle of answers unravelling in my arms.

■ ■ ■ ■ ■

The phone trills.

'Oh, I was expecting the machine.' I picture Aunt Joan in her hallway gloom, standing rod-backed like it's a deportment class, like she's still carrying the book on her head. 'Your office told me you were off on some trip.'

'I'm just about to leave for the airport.'

'I was going to leave a message, so.'

'Well, I can always hang up and you can leave one if you'd prefer.'

My smart remark is met with dignified silence. No matter how many resolutions we always find a way to fail at the first conversational hurdle.

'Sorry. So what's the message?'

There is an audible sigh. 'Your mother's had a turn.'

'What is it now?'

'Ah, she won't eat a thing.'

'So what's new?'

'Your dad is worried. I wouldn't call, only you know what he's like, not wanting to upset you.'

'He's used to it.' I can hear the dental edge in my aunt's voice, the niece who is always off gallivanting around the globe instead of hand-holding by her mother's bedside.

'She hasn't had a bite since Saturday.'

It is only three weeks since Christmas morning when I lay in my old bed listening to the sound of radio hymns down below in the kitchen and Aunt Joan opening presses and rattling cutlery, her practised moves about the place that is a second home to her, reminding me of whose space she is trying to fill. *In God's name, what would a person be doing in an office at that hour of the morning*, she said when I mentioned my usual 7 a.m. work start in passing. *So is it like they show on TV when all the men are in their shirtsleeves waving their arms and shouting?*

I said, *Yeah sometimes,* then she was quiet for a bit, turning the cup on the saucer.

Not many girls then, I suppose. She looked down into the bowl of her teacup, I flipped the lid on my cigarette pack.

And what's wrong with that?

And she said, *Nothing*, and stood up from the table trailing the unexplained remark behind her while a sudden rage at my mother rose in my sleep-filled mouth. *She* should be here, fussing over porridge, patting my cheek like a TV mum, telling me I don't eat enough, telling me I look a bit worn out and should have a lie down. She should be here, not holed up in the hospital a mile down the road, behind a heavy screen of medication, letting herself go, shuffling around in terrycloth, no longer caring about appearances for one who was always so fussy when we were small. *Comb you hair, now, Kieran and straighten out that dress, Geraldine. George, let me do that tie for you. And mind your good shoes now, Geraldine, don't be scraping them on the gravel.* Kieran up front, me in the middle and my parents bringing up the rear. Picking at the front garden hedges on the way along the road, Mum telling me off for damaging the plants. *Hello there, how are you, grand morning* at least ten times before we even get to the church. Grey stone pile at the crest of the hill, the slow tide of cars in the park ebbing and flowing in the window between ten and eleven o'clock mass. And afterwards in the car park I would swing around with the other girls, admiring each other's Sunday dresses, all of us enveloped in one big state of grace, having just eaten the Body of Christ. Dads lurked in the near distance, exchanging the odd word, while our mothers chatted over kicking babies in rocking prams and the occasional dog slunk past. And then off into the car with the hour's drive to Granny's. My mother fiddling with the radio, Kieran reading his stories while I counted receding pylons set against the grey and the car settled into a stillness, none of us knowing or guessing or having any idea of the shadows gathering up ahead – of what was to come, and how there would be no going back.

'Anyhow, there it is.' Aunt Joan sighed again.

'What d'you want me to do? I'm just about to leave for the airport.'

'You could call your father now and again, Geraldine.'

'It's just attention-seeking. She'll get over it, just like before. Or they'll have to do the tube thing.'

'She's after losing a lot of weight.'

'That's what happens when you don't eat. Anyway, you know what I think. The mistake was putting her in there in the first place.'

'Ah, well now, that was all a long time ago and you were only a girl.'

'She never should have stayed there, drugged up to the eyeballs.'

'Easy to be wise in hindsight.'

'I've got to go. The car's outside.'

'Always on the move. Where to this time?'

'Hong Kong.'

'Oh, it's well for some.'

'It's my *job*.'

'So you'll call your dad.'

'Yes.' Though the truth is that I won't.

In her silence I hear the tumultuous roar of all the things Aunt Joan longs to say: how I have a heart of stone, how selfish I am, how my father suffers in silence, how I rarely visit and hardly ever call, et cetera et cetera. All the accusations I read each time I look her in the eye, the struggle to keep them in. *A terrible extravagance,* she said as I packed up the dripping boot of the hire car on St Stephen's Day. *So I should have taken an airport bus?* I snapped and we were toppled as usual at the final hurdle. I stooped to kiss her dry cheek and she raised a hand to pat my head but got my neck instead. *Drive carefully now, dear.*

6

fill or kill

tuesday 15 january 1991
13:35
hong kong

I WAKE INTO A WALL OF HUMIDITY, the hotel balcony doors open so that the curtains billow lightly over my bed. A band of pain shrinkwraps my forehead while Baker and Aziz, the double act, walk left to right across the silent screen for the hundredth time. I hit the volume button and the CNN anchorwoman looks straight into the camera and says: John Holliman joins us live from Baghdad. John, now that President Bush has secured Congress's approval for the use of force to end the Iraqi occupation of Kuwait, do you think it's just a matter of days before we see military action?

John nods enthusiastically and reminds us all that we are just 48 hours away from the UN deadline for Saddam to pull out. The scrolling ticker on the bottom of the screen confirms yesterday's market closes that I already know. I play with the white paper cap on the juice glass wondering if a shot of vodka would make it more palatable.

John says something about Apache helicopters and I switch over to a local station where a game-show host is holding a microphone very close to a young girl's mouth. I press mute and walk into the bathroom. Maybe I should eat something. Maybe I'll feel more motivated when I get into the office or maybe I just couldn't give a shit about anything.

In the centre of my stomach I feel a sudden wrench and lean over just in time to puke a rancid slime into the bidet. I stagger back against the wall and slide down to sit on the floor, trying not to contract the raw muscles of my throat until the heaving subsides into a sobbing hiccup. I don't remember anything about the flight here except drinking on the plane with some guy relocating to Sydney for a job with FOX, some half-hearted argument about the war, an observation about how years of business travel has killed off any desire to see the world, the jaded airport lounges, the kerosene folded into your clothes, the stagnant cabin air, the petrified mucous membranes, the microwaved stink of bread rolls, the background roar, the sameness of your world. Looking at my watch, I calculate that I have napped for twenty-four minutes, which makes a steadily shrinking average of 302 minutes in each twenty-four-hour cycle since I started counting 180 days ago and I forecast that, at this accelerating rate of sleep decay, I will be constantly awake by the 1st of April.

Don't you ever sleep? Stephen would mumble when I slipped into bed at 2 a.m. and lay beside him, remembering how when I was a child, the night used to make everything possible, all desires and imaginings unleashed like caged animals to roam around my childhood bedroom, demanding that I stay awake. I used to sleepwalk through schoolday afternoons in Double Chemistry, the tedious blackboarding of molecular structures that I had already built in my head, immersed in daydreams of being an astronaut on a pre-moon flight training, cocooned in a chewing-gum-white suit, a tricolour emblazoned below the stars and stripes, my hair cut short for the Mission, the controller talking to me through a radio mike. A self-contained unit in a sealed pod, the only last-minute question I have is how do I go to the loo, but I am too shy to ask, don't want them to think I am concerned about such trivia. It is, after all, such a wonderful and weightless suit and I can already see the photo on the front page of the *Irish Times*. The Controller runs through some last-minute detail about record-keeping and the search-and-rescue sequence in the sea. But I am keen to be off and making history for Ireland, to find some as yet undiscovered organism on the moon. I have spent my final earthbound night talking to my parents across a fence (no closer than fifteen feet in case I contract some hibernating virus and take it with me into space, jeopardising my health, the Mission, and the entire Universe). My mother clutches a tissue and says how lovely I look in my suit and to be sure and ring as soon as I arrive. On the TV broadcast I appear to be waving specifically at her while my dad grapples with his lifelong struggle to find something meaningful to say. Kieran shouts that he can't wait till I get back and don't forget his moon rock. I want desperately to touch my brother's fingers through the wire, to bring him with me, to share the capsule hours.

There is a faint tinkle outside as if a trolley is passing. I go back into the bedroom and press the TV remote. A shrill Cantonese shrieks from the studio audience so I return to CNN. As I step into the shower, John's voice echoes off the tiled walls. The French have given up a last-ditch attempt to negotiate a way out and here in Baghdad they're preparing for war.

I stare at the curve of the bedside phone – I should fulfil my promise to Aunt Joan and call my father, offer hollow support down the line. I picture him crossing the chequered lino in the hall, but I am not ready to summon up the past. The day after Christmas I found him bent double on the nearside of my rental car.

Was this on it when you picked it up? He tapped a scratch on the wheel arch.

I didn't check. I stubbed out my cigarette on the sodden footpath. *Sure they'll charge you for that if you can't prove it, Geraldine,* he shook his head at the waste, the squandering. *It's only money,* I shrugged.

He leaned a hand on his knee and straightened up, *Lord above, it's easy come easy go with you.*

Oh, pack it in, Dad, I looked up at the greyness that pressed down on us.

Did you call your mother to say goodbye?

I shook my head. *What's the point in calling when all she does is hold the phone and won't say anything?* And I turned towards him just in time to catch his face fold into that familiar look of resigned acceptance of the bad things life has thrown his way and the heartless disappointment of a daughter who has never been sufficient compensation for the losses he has sustained. And I longed, as so often before, to just push him over, a good sharp bang to the head on the drive might get him to focus on all that is in front of him instead of all that is behind. Instead we hugged weakly and I sank into the car seat, slammed the door, fumbling with the keys, head down so he wouldn't see the stupid tears that were welling. I pulled out and waved blindly, heading down the road with the Mullens' half-Alsatian tracking my front wheel at a trot. I watched him break into a run until he stopped, suddenly hitting the outer limit of his world at the corner to the main road.

As I rounded the junction he was standing perfectly still, staring straight after me, his dappled body receding in my rear-view mirror until he turned and padded home. And I vowed as I do every year: last time I go back for Christmas. Last time I stand in the crowded departure lounge at Heathrow with all the scattered children of Eire – vets in Canada, doctors in Ethiopia, barmen in Boston, nurses in New York, drop-outs in Thailand, bankers in London, all of us headed back to the transit lounge that is Ireland and all that we had fled.

Even on maximum pressure the water makes no impact so I tilt my head backwards, imagine I am walking in the park with Rex, a downpour streaming over my face. In the partly steamed mirror I see my own mortality wrapped in a thick white towel. 'A simple answer to a simple question, Geri,' I tell my reflected face, 'that's all.' I wait for the familiar wash of a reassuring professionalism but the wave thrashes and pools around my feet. I need to shift this dead weight and kick-start my way out of this malaise into the real world where business needs to be done. I should have a drink. I should have something else but I forgot the Diazepam.

A high-frequency scream crescendos in my ear, like the shrill insistence of a distant alarm clock counting out some non-specific warning as I fumble for a detonator switch. Maybe I have tinnitus. Maybe this tightness in my chest is some form of adult asthma; maybe my body is crumbling and as I reach for the toothbrush I wobble on my heels as if my capacity to balance is slipping away. Come on, Geri, it's a day like any other. Back in my prehistory there used to be an engaging staccato of variety, the possibility of a day not going as planned. But now I have a nose for human targets with a definable range of manipulable needs. I know the sales routine so well that I can switch to autopilot and still effect an upbeat delivery. Trading favour for favour, that's why I exist, and let's face it, it's not really anybody's money. I am a heat-seeking missile, sniffing out the millions that need to find a way home to Steiner's, laying mines for the second-rate competition. I come from a long line of white-shoe firms, we don't do shit deals. Favour for favour.

A simple answer to a simple question. This special mission should be a cakewalk, I can do it with my eyes closed. This jangled brittleness is just the distortion of fatigue. The sabre rattling in the Middle East is just white noise. I try to visualise how it will go: I will follow Felix's lead to the boardroom, where he will order me some green tea. He will express his regret that my trip is too short for dinner at some newly discovered restaurant so that he can watch me struggle with local delicacies that he knows I despise. He will ask me what I read on the plane and I will say Descartes' *Meditations* and he will smile faintly, *Ah yes, the demon of deception*. If he asks me to comment on the downfall of Cartesianism, my answer will be four sentences long and directly to the point.

And then I will tell him why I am here. I picture myself departing an hour later, mission accomplished, with a confident smile and the simple question answered. Then I will call the Grope, pause for effect and tell him I've got what he wants.

There's a moment of dressing confusion when I wonder if my clothes belong to someone else: the linen skirt hangs insipidly around my hips, the shirt's soft lilac reflects an embedded blue in my skin and the slingback slips off my right ankle as I close the door behind me and step onto the deep pile of blue and rust. The lift doors chime open onto two suits, who break off from their conversation to acknowledge this exiled camaraderie between white briefcases far from home at such a precarious moment in history. Perhaps we are crusaders, or maybe there was just no one begging us to stay.

I stand on the steps of the Mandarin Hotel adjusting to the humidity and the sweet smell of harbour-side decay, change my mind about the cab and swing left in the direction of the office, already exhausted. This is predictable, although I don't really believe in jet lag. Down a side alley, beneath the spattered shade of a disintegrating candy-striped awning, a man sits motionless under a stained cape while a barber's scissors hack furiously along the flat plane of his skull. A tiny bundle of slippered old woman spits noisily on the ground beside them as she rustles in the rips of a plastic bag. Above their heads, air-con units clutter the alley walls like giant bird boxes, exhaling into the breathless stink. And beyond, the neon chaos of steep shadowed shopping streets ascends sharply into a sudden glimpse of the vast Peak that overwhelms the city.

I walk very slowly to keep the sweat below crisis levels. Turn and rise into the covered footbridge that crosses Connaught Road. A light breeze sticks hair to my lipstick and I emerge just as the sun hits the varnished brown of the granite on Exchange Square One. Each of the forty storeys is marked by tinfoil strips of wraparound glass that reflect the portholed windows of the opposite building, angled precisely into the adjoining space like a giant meccano board. I swear that each time I visit, the gap between the office blocks gets smaller as the whole island sneaks ever closer to its future parent: China.

Steiner's fledgling office is alive and ticking, a little community of expatriate profit. A couple of FX guys are haggling with the phones, the basket boys are in position like toy soldiers with their virgin shirts and matching haircuts. I slip into an empty chair and they break away briefly from the magnetism of their screens to flash their orthodentistry at me for a welcoming nanosecond. Sitting opposite these guys is like watching a wildlife programme about mammals you didn't know existed. My borrowed desk space on the little trading floor has a miniature phone board but no Reuters so I wander over to the mini-kitchen and make coffee, looking out at the harbour view towards the Ocean Centre and the New Territories.

I wonder about Pie Man and Rex and if he is off his food and if Al will remember to video *Twin Peaks* for me.

'I'm sorry, did I wake you?'

'No, no,' Pie Man stifles a yawn.

'Are you still in bed?' There is a scuffle as he rustles the receiver from one space to another.

'No. I must have dropped off last night.' I picture him slumped in front of the TV underneath a sea of sweet wrappers.

'I was just thinking about Rex.'

'He's good, he's right here beside me.'

'I was wondering if he was eating all right.'

'He's been gobbling it all up. Actually I gave him a treat.'

'Oh yeah?'

'Just a little treat.'

'What?'

'A Kit Kat.'

'You gave him a Kit Kat? Are you fucking crazy? Chocolate is poisonous to dogs.' There is a sound of interference or maybe static. Then silence and a sucking sound as if he is working his lips.

'I, eh, didn't know.'

'Jesus. Is he all right?'

'He's asleep. D'you, eh, want me to wake him up?'

'No.' Though really I do want to speak to Rex but not with Pie Man listening in.

'I'm sorry, Geri. I had no idea—'

'I know you didn't. I should have said.'

'I'm really sorry.'

'Don't worry. And, hey, don't think I don't appreciate it, what you are doing.'

'That's OK.'

'So what else is he up to?'

'He ate my cereal that I left on a chair.'

'You have to put food on tables. I mean, Rex knows tables, but sometimes chairs—'

'OK.'

'So did you let him off the lead?'

'Yes. He – did his *thing* – you know, on the footpath. A woman who saw gave me a filthy look. But I just couldn't do the bag.'

It's all turning into dog hell. 'Well, I'll be back tomorrow morning.'

'Actually, Geri, having Rex here has made me think about getting a puppy,' he says.

'Well, I wouldn't rush into it.'

'You think it's a bad idea?'

'No, I just – it's a lot of responsibility. And dog walkers are expensive. And then if you were going away for the weekend or something—'

'I don't go away much. Ever really.'

'And dogs get lonely.'

'So why do you have Rex then?'

'Because I already have him. Because—'

'Because you had St—' and he stops himself.

'What?'

'Nothing.'

'Go on say it. *Say it.*'

'I was going to say that you had Rex because you had Stephen.'

'He wasn't our fucking love child, you know.'

'I'm sorry.'

'Sorry for *what* exactly?'

'That you. That he – I don't know, I mean I just don't know how any man could ever do that. To you.'

I stare out at the harbour, hear his breathing testing the silence.

'Yeah, well, I've got to go so—'

'But how is your trip going?'

'I won't know for a while yet.'

'Are you having a good time?'

'I don't really want to be here.'

'Where do you want to be?'

'You mean, if I had a choice.'

'Yes.'

'Oh, I dunno. Right where you are. With *Rex* I mean.' Obviously I don't mean with Pie Man.

'I'm sure he's looking forward to seeing you.'

'Well, give him a kiss from me.'

'You want me to kiss the dog,' he says uncertainly.

'No, no, it's just something I say.'

'I've never kissed a dog before.'

'Jesus, Pie Man, you don't have to. Just pat him from me.'

'Maybe I could kiss his fur. If it's really important.'

'Just leave the fucking dog, OK?'

Silence.

'I'm sorry – I—'

'When are you coming back?' he cuts me short.

'My flight gets in around 5.30 a.m. tomorrow. I have to go to the office so I was going to get Lisa to come round to collect him if—'

'I'm taking the day off tomorrow. So she doesn't need to if that helps.'

'Oh, right. How come?'

'I though it would be nicer for Rex.'

'You don't have to do that.'

'It's OK, it's fun and I'm due a day off anyway. So you could pick him up from here.'

'Thanks, well, thanks a million, Pie Man.'

'Colin.'

'What?'

'My name is Colin.'

'I know.' Although the truth is I'd completely forgotten.

A sunlit plane rises soundlessly over the water from Kaitek and I start counting the take-offs through the grey-blue window haze: looks like one every three minutes, that's 320 between 6 a.m. and 10 p.m., adding on for night flights and tweaking down to smooth out, let's say a round 400 every twenty-four hours.

Out across the harbour a white spinnaker bends past the flank of a rust-stained tanker. Behind this wall of slow motion, a Lego chimney spits a steady stream of horizontal smoke and the gappy rise of toy-town apartment blocks comes to an abrupt end on the mainland hillside, waiting for the next excited rush of investment from quick-footed local entrepreneurs betting on the avalanche of money that will surely descend upon the New Territories in 1997. Six nerve-wracking years of tension and bargain-hunting to go, while western pundits warble on about the risk of the Chinese government going all Commie and jack-booting it down the streets of Hong Kong to kickstart the market economy.

The very first time I came to Hong Kong five years ago and stood down there at the water's edge, I was struck by the thought that only the British could do something so crazily grandiose as transform a huge rock in the South China Sea into a magnificent power base. I stood transfixed by the Peak in a gaping neck-arch and years of myopic schoolbook history unravelled – a continuous loop of embittered bleating about Cromwell and disembowelling and famine, the coffin ships, the martyrs, the faces of The Six Men, the agony and the ecstasy of dying for your country – all collapsed into the astonishing revelation that The Enemy had, in fact, Bigger Fish to Fry. That all the time we were crawling in and out of hedge schools and mustering futile insurrections, the British Empire was gripped by the tentacles of a dizzying ambition that explained the stunning irrelevance of Ireland. Even after Home Rule and a bellyful of potatoes and Rural Electrification, the story of Ireland was still all about the same thing: a Self as defined by the Other, an island clinging onto the victim psychology of an identity crisis, trailing a stone-age language through the jostling visa queue of emigrants, licking our own sores as we clutched our one-way tickets in a stampede for the next plane out of there.

Dad, what do you remember about World War II? I asked, tracing a pencil around my schoolbook photo: June 1944: Allies land on Normandy beaches.

He looked down at his plate, shuffled a cooling mash of carrots to the side. *I remember there were no bananas.*

So when Mrs Collins slapped the chalk dust off her skirt and told us to write an essay entitled 'Analyse the reasons and background to Ireland's neutrality during WW2', I added a paragraph at the end:

During the Second World War, Ireland remained sheltered from the earth-shattering events that were unfolding across Europe. The government's insistence on neutrality was based on the belief that 'England's difficulty was Ireland's opportunity', and large numbers of Irish people ended up inadvertently supporting the Nazi cause simply because they were opposing Ireland's most bitter enemy: Great Britain. The effect of this was to minimise the significance of the Second World War in Irish folk memory so that the country was left untouched by a tragedy that cost the rest of the world 50 million lives.

I resisted the temptation to mention the bananas.

Mrs Collins kept me back after class to tell me that I had completely misunderstood the neutrality issue. She said it was beyond the pale to even suggest that Irish people supported the Nazis and when I reminded her that we were the only country apart from Japan to send a sympathy message to the German government when Hitler died she told me that was irrelevant. She also told me not to use emotive words like 'earth-shattering' in history essays.

'Geri.' Tom Castigliano kisses me on both cheeks and I recognise his scent; I could do a blindfold test on all these guys who air kiss me. The Ivy Leaguers are always the cleanest, they know how to scrub everything away.

I follow him into his glass cube where the TV shows James Baker who has pitched up in Cairo to deliver a grim warning that time is running out. If Saddam Hussein is going to withdraw from Kuwait he will probably wait until he is on the brink before he moves. He looks up, making sure he's got the camera's attention. Our worry is that he will miscalculate when the brink is.

Tom frown-nods at the screen like he knows this already, as if he has actually written Baker's speech. This is a business school behaviour essential – the ability to be completely unsurprised by news demonstrates that you have conducted a comprehensive scenario analysis and discounted all possible outcomes. And just so there will be no misunderstanding, let me be absolutely clear. We pass the brink at midnight on January sixteen.

'Well, let's hope the translator gets the time right,' I say. 'You know, just in case Saddam is out clubbing.'

Tom switches off the sound, slings his leg over the desk and says, 'I hear Goldman's are sending—'

'Someone out here to cover Felix. Yeah, the whole fucking world is sending people out here.'

'So when are you going to join us?'

I shrug, run a finger along his desk, the wood warm and chocolatey.

'Hey, Geri, take it from me,' he spreads his arms wide. 'Asia is where it's all happening. This is the dawn of a new era. There's a deal pipeline like you wouldn't believe waiting in the wings. We've got a great chance to open up the Asian debt markets – all these Honkie companies are killing themselves to get some cheap dollars to bankroll expansion plans in China.'

'New World Order,' I say, looking at the rows of the Revolutionary Guard marching across the screen beneath a huge statue of Saddam.

'What does Felix say?'

'Oh, he wants me out here. He's keen.'

'Customer's always right.' He pats the desk. 'And the Grope?'

'We haven't talked about it. Yet. All this came up first.' I turn for the door and Tom walks me out to the corridor.

'So you're all set?'

'Yeah, all set for the simple answer to the simple question.'

'What's your gut?'

'Best not to have a gut. Felix will smell it and rip it out.'

An exhausted sigh escapes me in the elevator, startling a motionless suit. I wipe my hands carefully on powdered tissues and prepare a dry-palmed entrance into client space. The doors slide open onto the thirty-first floor and the entrance to Felix's office faces me like a vault. Felix told me these double doors were inherited from a previous occupant who dealt in gems – dull brushed steel engraved with intricate swirls and scrolls and no visible locks: a sealed tomb or the entrance to a treasure trove.

'Miss-Morroy-how-nice-to-see-you-please-take-a-seat,' Anna-Li murmurs a quiet welcome from behind her lacquered desk and indicates the armchair lying like a pool of quicksand from which you may never emerge. *Designed by a local furniture maker,* Felix told me on my first visit five years ago as he watched my flailing attempt to extricate myself from its embrace. *Reminds me of a Venus flytrap.*

I stand facing the window, the marble flank side of the adjoining building and a slightly different angle on the harbour view. There are no rubber plants, no glossy brochures advertising Felix's funds or his investment approach, no artwork, no ashtrays, no concession to the visitor. Anna-Li makes a note in the silk-bound appointments book on her desk and glances up beneath her long black lashes. But the fixed smile does not disguise the killer bitch that lies beneath her poreless skin, she is the Rottweiler gatekeeper who would rip my throat out on Felix's command: the past five years would count for nothing if he decided to pull the plug; Anna-Li would be impervious to my begging calls and let me dangle with a dead line buzzing in my ear.

She closes the book and rests both hands on the cover, her face unreadable, and I recast her in a Bruce Lee movie, wearing one of those tight silk dresses slit high on the thigh: she bends down to offer me a martini tray then straightens up and snap-kicks me right in the face.

'Geraldine.' Felix has perfected the Asian art of soundless arrival. 'How very pleasant to see you so soon again.' He bows, and I follow his lead down the corridor but my heart sinks when he steers me past the boardroom and stops before a door padded in grey leather. The first time Felix invited me into his inner sanctum it was like being propelled into someone's bedroom at the end of a bad date. A long windowless gallery cast in gloom with pinprick spotlights carefully trained to illuminate Felix's macabre collectibles. It has the dry airlessness of a mausoleum, a refrigerated chamber from which you might never emerge. On the right-hand side and shrouded in darkness is the closed door that opens into Felix's private office with its burst of light and a vista stretching far out into China. Tucked away in the left-hand corner is his prize catch: a glass-domed podium with an old letter displayed inside, the nicotine-yellow paper cracked along the top edge, neat dense lines of tiny-lettered black ink handwriting cover the page. *That,* he explained, *is reason in decay. Descartes' desperate attempt to accommodate an article of faith into his principles.* He tapped a bony finger on the glass. *He had a rather amusing exchange of letters with a Jesuit on the subject of transubstantiation – a correspondence that resulted in the unfortunate Père Mesland being banished to a Canadian mission where he died in ignominy.*

'I would like to show you my latest acquisition,' Felix gestures behind him, 'but that can wait till after our discussion.' He pulls out a chair at the oval table in the centre of the room and I sit down opposite as indicated, place my hands flat on the lacquered surface, trying to keep my eyes averted from the walled collection that I know so well.

One hundred and twenty four identically framed black and white photographs, each with a tiny inscription. Ladysmith – Mafeking – Elandslaagte – Colenso – Kimberley. *Are you familiar with the Boer War, Geraldine?* Felix asked the first time he took me into this room and my prepared murmur of polite appreciation dissolved when a closer inspection of row upon row of riderless horses revealed tethered heads bowed in exhausted defeat, the sharp jut of bones through their malnourished hide: a storyboard of animal holocaust. The centrepiece is a heap of marooned skeletons protruding from the bleak Transvaal plain. *A wonderful tale of incompetence,* Felix nodded in slow approval as we stood at this shrine to animal agony. *In 1899 General Roberts doubled the number of British horses to half a million. Unfortunately he omitted to provide sufficient fodder and two-thirds of them died of starvation.*

He settles opposite me with his back to the collection and places both hands on the table top, mirroring the way I'm sitting.

'I thought perhaps you had a one-way ticket, Geraldine. That you had come to give me the good news I have been expecting?'

'Not exactly. There wasn't really time to discuss the relocation – as soon as I got back they asked me to come out and see you again.'

'Do you know what the Romans did to the bearers of bad tidings? They had them flogged.'

A man in a black suit glides in bearing a tray. A slender white teapot and a single cup that he sets down on the table beside me. He stands back, awaiting instruction. Felix flicks his hand and the man turns away, the padded door sighs behind him and I picture myself scrabbling at it for all eternity.

'So, Felix, can I ask how you knew Kapoor was in the room when I called?'

'It is my job to anticipate what I do not know.' He leans forward and pours me the green tea that he knows I despise. 'So now Mr Kapoor has you running errands? Or did your boss propose you for this special mission?'

'It was the Grope's idea.'

'And how is your master? Still running in those… marathons?' the question suspended under a raised brow.

'Three hours, 59 minutes in New York. A personal best.' And we pause for a moment's silent reflection on Felix's personal best to date: two billion dollars under management, the largest private honey pot this side of the International Dateline.

'My little carrier pigeon. Our liaison has boosted your profile no end. I am gratified that my investment in you is bearing fruit.'

'So you already know why I am here?'

'Tell me, my dear, did you meet with Max Lester?'

'Yes.'

'Then you will know he is a most unpleasant individual. Very uncouth.'

'He's very keen to talk to you.'

'Everyone wants to talk to me all the time. But now that you have met Mr Lester you will understand why a meeting is impossible.' And I have to smile at the image of Max-a-Billion's Stetson in this room.

'I didn't know you owned 13% of Vulkan Valve.'

'You must learn to look around corners, Geraldine, to be more curious about who you do business with. I imagine Mr Kapoor was unimpressed.'

'So how come you own so much of the stock?'

'Your handlers didn't tell you?'

'Only that you'd owned it for a long time.'

He sighs. 'A dreadful disregard for history. Your generals send you into battle unprepared.'

I wait, inhale the silence. It is an art that takes all my concentration. The spotlights seem to shimmer above him.

'Let me tell you a story,' he says, folding his hands on the tabletop. 'My grandfather, Otto Man, was an engineer and a German citizen who came to England to find work in 1913. When war broke out he found himself interned on the Isle of Man since it was MOD policy not to have the enemy running about loose. Otto was released two years later on the condition that he found "work of national importance". So he took himself off to London and found a job at a machine tools business.

'But Otto longed to be his own boss. In 1917 he started his own machine tools company and called it Vulkan Valve. You might know that "vulkan" is the German word for volcano and on one of the very rare occasions that my grandfather spoke and I actually listened, he told me that he had been fascinated by Pompeii as a child. Vulkan was a tremendous success. They quickly diversified into radio; in fact they designed and manufactured the first portable radio in Britain. Vulkan began to manufacture all sorts of electrical components and by the 1930s had moved into defence, making shells, bomb cases, fuel pumps for aircraft and a huge variety of radio transmitters. The Second World War was a gift. Production exploded and at its peak the Vulkan workforce was over 10,000. They had a vast underground factory hidden in a section of the Tube tunnels between Newbury Park and Leyton-stone – the twin tunnels were five miles long and workers used bicycles to get around it.

'After the war, Otto intensified the focus on Avionics and Commu-nications and Vulkan became increasingly important to the UK's defence programme. But it was then that Otto's problems began. In the 1970s they had been selling surface-to-air missile to South Africa and

Vulkan was threatened with a ban by the US government under the terms of the Nuclear Proliferation Treaty. Otto was fiercely opposed to doing business with unstable regimes but Vulkan was making 20% of its revenues in South Africa. My grandfather argued with the board over the future direction of the business company and the issue was put to a vote. Otto opposed the board's recommendation and he lost. So he resigned his position in 1973 after an incident that he referred to as the night of the long knives.' Felix picks up his Mont Blanc and unclips the lid, examining the inkless nib.

'An empty protest really, since Vulkan went from strength to strength. And Otto spent his last few years brooding alone. His wife, my grandmother, was a distinctly humourless and slothful woman who died early. My father was their only child and he had died while I was still at school, so there was no one to bother Otto in his final years. But he was a potterer and prowled about in a Georgian manor house with a view over the South Downs, full of broken fishing rods and crumbling books, photos of dead relatives, broken watches, clutter everywhere.' Felix pauses, inclines his head to one side.

'Otto was dying when he summoned me to come to see him. Of course I barely knew him and he summoned up all the tedium of childhood – train sets and signals and batteries. He was an excellent engineer but tremendously dull, a man excited by mechanical moving parts. Partial to playing rather loud marching music.'

Felix leans forward a little. 'Have you ever seen a dying man, Geraldine? Otto was quite shrivelled, almost cadaverous. There was a curious texture to his skin, like melting plastic. I stood there by his bedside, his only surviving relative. And he told me I was to inherit everything, including his 13% shareholding in Vulkan Valve. And then he charged me with doing whatever I could to take revenge on the board on his behalf. "In your lifetime there will be a moment where you can strike. You simply have to notice it and seize the opportunity and take away the thing they want."'

'What did you say?'

'Nothing,' Felix shrugged. 'But Otto was the kind of man who took silence for assent.'

'So it was a sort of deathbed promise.'

'I thought it was the most appalling melodrama. These men who endow their lives with so much significance.'

'So after he died?'

'I met the Vulkan board for the first and only time at the funeral where the CEO delivered a rather effusive eulogy. As far as the members were concerned, I was a young philosophy postgraduate, they were condescending. A year later I left Cambridge and came out here. And eventually I used the shareholding in Vulkan Valve as collateral to start this business.' Felix spreads his arms wide, palms upwards like a consecrating priest. 'So you could say I owe everything to Otto.'

'That's quite a story.'

He nods, returns his hands to the tabletop. 'But background, my dear, is not always essential to the development of the plot.'

'So your 13% stake—'

'In fact, your information is a little out of date. I have been having some fun with the stock. You might even say I anticipated all this interest in Vulkan.'

'You've bought more?

'You ask so much, Geraldine,' he shakes his head, 'yet give so little in return. I sometimes wonder what would have happened to you if I hadn't taken an interest? You might have languished away undiscovered.' Felix smiles again as if the thought of my decline amuses him no end.

'So how much do you own now?'

'All told my interest is 20%.'

'And the board owns 10%. So if you joined forces you could make life very difficult for Max Lester. Have you spoken to Vulkan?'

'I do not need to speak to the board of Vulkan to know that they are fiercely resistant to the idea of a takeover. Most especially by an overseas company like Texas Pistons who are only interested in the defence side of the business. Such a bid would be considered to be extremely hostile.'

'Of course if you were to abide by your grandfather's deathbed wish, you'd side with Texas Pistons. You would use this takeover to "take away the thing they want".'

Felix sighs. 'My investment strategy is always guided by the simplest principles: Value. Price. Surely you know me well enough to understand that I cannot be held hostage by the request of a dying man.'

'Even though you owe all this to Otto?'

'There you go again, Geraldine, allowing the background to cloud the plot, scampering off after a red herring.'

'You don't feel any obligation to him?'

'"We do not triumph until we cast aside our humanity and make decisions on a logical basis."' Felix adjusts himself in his chair. 'I would be failing Kant if I abided by a dead man's request.'

'So what do you think about Max Lester's bid?'

'There *is* no bid. There is nothing on the table. So far there is just idle chatter,' he leans back and folds his arms. 'Or perhaps *you* have come out here to tell me what Mr Lester is prepared to pay for Vulkan Valve? Though I doubt very much that Mr Kapoor would entrust his carrier pigeon with such sensitive information.'

I look down, study my green tea. Regroup. 'What do you think of Texas Pistons?'

'A very impressive operation with excellent R&D. An acquisition of a company like Vulkan would be eminently sensible for them. Scenario analyses run by my people indicate that Vulkan is considerably under-valued. We are very optimistic about long-term prospects for MSTAR – this little skirmish in Iraq will fill their order book. And I myself see a very healthy long-term outlook for the industry of war. American foreign policy will keep factories in business for a long time to come.

'However,' he raps the table, 'I do not believe that Max Lester is at all interested in the electronics business. It is the defence product that he has his eye on. And therein lies a potential problem. If Texas Pistons get control of Vulkan they'll strip the company and focus on the most profitable elements. A lot of people in England will lose jobs. Naturally this is of no concern to me but it will mean lobbying pressure. More serious of course, is the reaction of the MOD. The defence business is a national asset and politically very sensitive. A bid from a non-UK entity like Texas Pistons would end up being referred to the Monopolies and Mergers Commission. Which would be very tedious, drag on for months.'

'So what will you do?'

But the laziness of the question annoys him. 'No doubt my answer will do wonders for your career,' he snaps. 'But you forget that I am still waiting for *your* answer to *my* question.'

Felix stands up abruptly. 'And now you must come and admire my latest acquisition.' I follow him slowly, let a reluctant gaze signal the outer reaches of an apprehensive interest in the large rectangular painting that seems out of place amongst all the photographs.

'October 25th, 1854. *The Charge of the Light Brigade*, "C'est magnifique, mais ce n'est pas la guerre,"' and I return his faint smile with a blank look. Felix taps the frame. Horses gallop across the canvas in a frenzy of war: blue-jacketed riders with lances drawn in the cannon dust, a yellow haze of muzzle flash in a battlefield valley where crawling corpses flounder in their own blood. 'The Russian general Liprandi thought the British must be drunk, to ride out to be slaughtered. Of course it did wonders for their reputation in the rest of the Crimean war.'

He leans admiringly into a foregrounded soldier who is raising his sword at a clutch of riderless horses. 'Did you know, Geraldine, that a horse will only panic when he can no longer feel the weight of his rider?' To the left the dead figure of a soldier is slipping from the saddle of a white-eyed horse whose flanks are smeared red, his arched hooves rearing above the trampled body of a fallen trooper who sprawls, helpless, staring up at the terrorised sky.

'Three hundred and thirty-five horses killed. And apparently almost as many again when Warner Brothers made their film.'

Something seems to flicker in the painting and I blink rapidly; my eyes are pricking and I turn away, retreat to the safety of the table.

'I had a call from a familiar of yours this morning.' Felix stands, arms folded by his wall of death. 'I believe "ex" is the appropriate term.'

'Stephen called you?' I twitch as if the chair was electrified. 'Why?'

'Oh, you know how everyone wants to talk to me. And these are interesting times. He asked to see me and, as you know, I rarely agree to meetings. But Mr Graves was – perhaps still is? – such an important figure in your life and the welfare of my business associates is very important to me. It was only curiosity that made me agree.'

'Stephen came here?'

'You just missed him. A very charming man. Very well-bred, as they say. Tell me, Geraldine, was that the attraction? The good genes? The shires?' He slides into the chair opposite me. 'Not really from the same side of the tracks, though, are you, my dear? I can see how that would be problematic. Mr Graves is clearly not a connoisseur of rare breeds, he was unable to appreciate what he had.'

And then everything shrinks small and distant as if I'm looking through the wrong end of binoculars, there's a sudden alcoholic surge in my sleepless veins, a battering ram in my skull. I exhale over the cold tea, my right hand floating up from its prone table-top position, leaving fingertip sweat circles on the varnish. I try to smile across the lacquered plain, but my eyes drift upwards to the starving horses nailed to the wall. I think I hear myself stall in the middle of a sentence that might have started out as a reply to some question of Felix's, opening and closing my soundless dry mouth but I can't be sure if I have actually spoken. I look down at my tea and a vision of the Grope, eyes fixed on a shimmering horizon where his triumphant chariot thunders out of a dust cloud to drop the warm carcass of a deal that he has cinched at Kapoor's feet. I see Stephen's commanding profile set against the arresting backdrop of a Stealth bomber and there is something else unarticulated, a connection that I sense but cannot see. And then it is gone, or like a phantom, it never was.

My upturned teacup rocks in its saucer, a spreading slop of liquid quivers on the table and it seems I'm standing though I don't remember rising from the chair. There's a pounding in my ear, the thud of distant cannons and the beginnings of a dizzy sobering radiating from my gut. I flop back down. My head lolls in the air-conditioned stillness. An involuntary trembling sneaks its way around my jaw and I look up to see Felix watching me closely.

'I have been a little concerned about you of late, Geraldine. You've lost some condition, in fact you look rather peaky.' He leans in, narrows his eyes. 'I think a change of air is exactly what is required.' He lays a chilly hand on mine. I look down at the slow spread of goose-bump prickle along my forearm, picture the future he has in mind for me: a lifetime in the chained embrace of his soundproofed Peak-top condo, naked and convulsing over a steaming bowl of Chinese food, some animal organ draped over my suspended chopstick, Felix's face obscured by a camera lens, his pale body spasming in a jerky wank.

'What will you do with Vulkan, Felix?' A simple answer to a simple question.

Felix unfurls both hands as if weighing the range of possibilities. '"All men would have to be perfectly wise before one could infer from what they ought to do, what they will in fact do." Perhaps you recall the reference?'

'Descartes' letter to Elizabeth,' I whisper.

'You are out of your depth in unfamiliar waters, Geraldine. And you are blindly thrashing about. The plucky Irish getting stuck into battles they never win. My intelligence tells me that various parties have been nibbling at the stock. Perhaps there is another shark circling? So I am waiting here in my little den for the interested parties to show their hand.' I picture Felix in his sunlit office framed by the hazy backdrop of the New Territories, savouring his strategic moment, weighing the balance of power; his drifting gaze coming to rest on a wall-mounted spear.

Aasagi: Removed from the body of a fallen Zulu warrior at Rorkes Drift, Pretoria, 1879.

'So what will you do with Vulkan, Felix?'

'Have I not been the most gracious of benefactors? Asking for so little in return? I am beginning to feel that my business is not sufficiently appreciated, Geraldine. Perhaps I should begin to look for service elsewhere.' Felix inspects his pen, head angled to one side and offers me his version of a smile, all those little teeth fighting for space. 'Like God, I can give and I can take away. I can pull the plug on your career.'

'Why would you want to?'

'Sometimes we act simply because we can. To see what happens. When I was a boy it was how I learnt about the world. Cause and effect, my dear. A very pure curiosity.'

'So what will you do?'

Felix leans forward and makes to rise from his chair. 'My analysts tell me that the right exit price for Vulkan would be up 30%. And who knows, perhaps the stock may even go all the way there without Mr Lester's help.'

7

lobster trap

tuesday 15 january 1991
15:15
hong kong

I PICK MY WAY SLOWLY across the sunshot stone of Exchange Square Two, checking each passing suit just in case Stephen is still lurking about waiting for a chance encounter, as if he could come strolling along at any moment. High above me in Exchange Tower One, Tom will be clock-watching and restless, but he'll read it as a good omen, assume I am still holed up with Felix. On the other side of the world the Grope will be pacing his glass box, waiting for the simple answer to the simple question. He'll call up Kapoor, tell him to *relax, she's got this guy in her pocket*. The bankers will be staring at the silent speakerphone, thumbs jabbing at their HP10s, reworking the spread between best case and worst, running numbers over and over to pass the time. Max-a-Billion will be prowling his suite in the Ritz, waiting for the call. I should go back to the office, but I am not ready.

I plough on through the sticky airlessness down to the Star Ferry terminal and take a seat beside an old man hunched over a paper cup, slurping noodles from wooden chopsticks that rise and fall in a continuous rapid knitting. I sneak three miniatures out of my bag and crack open the lids, drain them one by one. The old man turns and glares, mutters angrily, jabbing an accusing finger. Then he gets up and shuffles off.

There are worse places to be than Hong Kong of course. And worse reasons for being here than the threat of contingency that Felix has so neatly aired. *Quid pro quo.*

The ferry dips and rolls in a tanker's wake and I slide sideways on the wooden bench. A little girl in front turns around and stares at the tears that are spilling now down over my cheeks. She prods her mother's arm, and she also turns; the girl points at my face and the woman bundles her around and they too move away. I do not know what my tears are for since there is no accessible sensation other than the desire to lie down, to sleep, to reach the end of something.

A watery vision of Central wobbles on the receding horizon. Out there somewhere is Stephen, he could be looking down at the water or else already in a cab to Kaitek heading for the afternoon flight. Did he think of me when he stood in front of Felix's steel door? No, not for a second. Zanna is right: it is so over and I am gagging on a dead intimacy, clinging to driftwood like the castaway I am. Felix's taunt nags at my ear. *A very charming man. Very well-bred as they say... Not really from the same side of the tracks, though, are you, my dear? I can see how that would be problematic.* It has taken 182 days of stunned mourning to accept that Stephen and I had never been looking at the same thing, that the lost city of my world is a place he never even imagined.

Oh, but the aura of the unattached is like a smell that seeps into your days. There's no homeward rush after the last ticket is booked and the floor slowly empties and you're lulled into a fitful sleep to the drone of the US desk, the occasional hoot on the open line to New York, the muted roar of applause where some match plays out on low volume TV. At night I lie awake with price histories hovering in the darkness in front of me, replaying trades and patterns on a three-dimensional grid that stretches back years. An obsessive surveillance, or a place to hide, a fear that something has been overlooked or perhaps there is always some new data that could be mined or – worse – some old data that can be re-cast even when it's too late, the deal is long since done. I still cannot stop myself cluttering up my brain with useless digits, formulae, algorithms. To discard would be to forget, or maybe it is a way of forgetting the important stuff. Like what exactly Stephen and myself talked about the first time we met and all those lost conversations – I estimate 2,304 hours minimum – yet the fragments I remember would barely fill a page. There is an ephemeral quality about the whole relationship now as if it evaporates on examination.

But our Venice finale still screams at me in vivid colour. Every time I replay the closing act I tell myself it's desensitisation I'm seeking, that I'm hoping to reach a point where I can fast-forward, that I will become jaded by the story of my own abandonment. Instead I review it in salacious detail as if I might find some unexplored detail, some new prick of pain. Maybe there is a hidden code in the final act that will transform the story and reveal its true meaning. Didn't I learn that lesson at close range from my own family all those years ago: how the ending becomes the whole story. How it becomes the new beginning that shapes the rest of your life. Isn't this what I have learnt from my own mother? How the last act becomes the defining moment, all that happened and all that you remember: the family in the grip of a crisis, the healing that never happened.

But it's not those memories that rise now from the water's swell, it's the closing scene with Stephen: 182 days ago, at 5.15 a.m. on 17 July 1990, I was standing smoking on the balcony of Stephen's apartment, waiting for him to show up for our 7:10 flight to Venice. He'd spent the past twenty-four hours in competition for a 350 million-dollar deal (for a major European conglomerate whose identity, as usual, he refused to reveal). I was standing smoking in the cool quiet, looking east along Cheyne Walk and thinking: fucking hell. Imagining Stephen huddled with his team in a conference room, spinning their wheels in the agony of The Wait. When all the counter-proposals have been made, all the margins squeezed to shrieking point, when a whole universe of scenario analyses has been explored, when there is nothing to do but Wait For

The Call from some bastard CEO who will shatter the silence with his ring, and say the deal is yours. Or tell you that six months of work has been for nothing, snap you like a twig and leave you howling through gritted teeth.

I could picture the tired trolley of cling-filmed sandwiches beached in the corner of the room, the conference table littered with steel thermoses and bottles of water. No smoking. Even under Maximum Deal Stress, Stephen does not make any concession to human frailty. Spread around the outer circle of the room is a gaggle of multinational Junior Analysts, recently parachuted down to earth from their cosy nests at Wharton, Harvard, Columbia, INSEAD at $105,000 apiece; the fledgling investment bankers who are normally left alone in the office late at night with strict instructions not to play with any matches. Their fresh-faced ambition is being slowly crushed by the tedium of bag-carrying and eighteen-hour days. Tonight they brush up against the Holy Grail of Banking and wonder if they will ever do more than worship at the altar of Stephen Graves, whose foot-last rests in a shoe mortuary at John Lobb of St James, whose meteoric rise to glory has already passed into City mythology. Stephen Graves, who didn't just come top of the class of '83, but who simultaneously, in an impressive demonstration of impeccable time-management skills, cut four strokes off his golf handicap, became intimately acquainted with the off-piste terrain around Chamonix and read the first volume of *A La Recherche du Temps Perdu* (in the original French, of course).

I could picture Stephen with his feet up on the conference table, shooting the breeze with his henchmen Julian (INSEAD) and JJ (Stanford) and entertaining the peripheral audience with anecdotes about the personal idiosyncrasies of the Competition and an endless cascade of stories that include:

Great Deals I Have Done,

Great Deals I Have Stolen from the Jaws of the Competition,

One Great Deal I Lost Through the Scummy Tactics of the Competition, and

Close Shaves During My Off-Piste Adventures on Mont Blanc.

The young associates in the cheap seats inch their pallid faces closer, trying to memorise the names that flow from his tongue, straining to follow the short-hand circumlocutions of a rich history, trying to disguise the fact that they keep missing the punch lines, taking desperate but careful cues from Stephen's inner circle, who lounge in preening intimacy with the boss, but would never dare to put their feet up on the table.

It was 17 July 1990 and this was the closest they'd ever come to a Master of the Universe.

As daylight crawled into the airless room, the ringing phone finally broke the news: the deal would trade away to Goldman's. Stephen took the blow like the man he is.

So when he finally double-parked on the street below at 5.37 a.m., I was thinking how appropriate that we should be leaving for a long weekend, how the baggage of the Lost Deal would be good company for the Ailing Relationship. Although neither of us had actually admitted it might be a last-ditch attempt to resuscitate our union, I knew this even as I booked the flights. When Stephen stepped into the hall, I tried not to focus on his distracted registration of my presence and the departing plane. Instead I counted backwards and calculated that it was thirty-three days since we last had sex and immediately buried this thought in case he could scan it on my forehead.

After the near miss of the flight and the wrong seat numbers and the search for the hotel vaporetto, Stephen said that it was a shame I hadn't booked the Danieli, but I decided to ignore this as we cruised along the Guidecca. And when the Cipriani came into view through the spray, I could almost convince myself that Venice might provide us with inspiration. Standing on the quayside as the porter unloaded our suit-carriers, I actually managed to amuse Stephen by doing the pointing boy scene from *Death in Venice*. He laughed and I realised that this was the first time either of us had really made the other laugh in a long time. Over a lunchtime Bellini, I watched elegant women pick their way past expensive shops behind the shaded columns of the Piazza San Marco but Stephen was wondering aloud if we should be here at all, what with the summer heat and the crowds and the fact that he's been there, done that. I was reading aloud from the guidebook and planning: tomorrow the Doges and then Arsenale and Stephen was getting edgy about the intensity of an itinerary of things he has already seen and the snippets of history that we would both forget.

Leaning over the Rialto Bridge, he declared that we were definitely not going on a gondola, but even though it looked pretty tacky I still cherished a fleeting hope that he might change his mind, though I knew he wouldn't, because the idea of paying some man to sing at him is more than he could ever bear. Over coffee, Stephen said he wished I wouldn't keep saying how great it was that there are no cars and I told him that one of the pluses about being on holidays was being able to relax your mouth and let anything fall out. But he didn't consider this an excuse for being boring or unselective, there were certain standards. So I took the opportunity to remind him of his ex's mouth which was permanently spewing out mind-numbingly dull observations about the world in which she lived and Stephen said, 'Yeah, well, that was the main reason I dropped her,' and I said, 'Well, it took you a year,' and he said, 'Enough,' and I said, 'Good. Because I can't think of anything else.'

A frozen silence shuffled behind us as we stumbled through a maze of cobbled streets. A little worm in my head turned and whispered: the end is nigh. But I have never been graceful, could not just lie down and accept that there wasn't a way to rescue this. A cluster of pigeons burst apart when we rounded a sudden corner onto a tiny sunshot piazza and I stopped to stare at a crumbling yellow wall, the hopeless fragility of all these things so lovingly built.

Stephen stepped forward, level with my view. '"I have been familiar too long with ruins to dislike desolation." Byron on Venice,' he added and turned away and I thought of all the things I could say, the good and the bad, the relevant and the irrelevant, trying not to focus on the personal resonance of his quote. But the distance between us appalled me; he was accelerating away out of my reach, too far gone to turn around and so Venice became the backdrop for the sour dissolve.

In the evening we went through the motions of getting dressed up for dinner, so at least we could look good even if there was no chance that we were going to enjoy ourselves. Maybe rituals are therapeutic. Maybe it would actually have been worse if I just lolled on the bed in a pair of jeans and said I can't be fucked to get dolled up. Stephen looked great but I struggled for a way to say this that didn't sound ironic.

The porter's smile followed us across the lobby. He said have a nice evening which felt like a smack in the teeth. 'Right, let's go for a drink,' said Stephen. Like there was something else we might do instead.

Four or five drinks later on San Marco, every other table occupied by well-dressed couples who seemed to be mind-staggeringly in love, we were sitting silently side by side facing the piazza. We were both being over-friendly to the waiter, me smoking a cigarette about every six minutes, according to Stephen's watch, which I could monitor by narrowing my eyes and pretending to study the scene beyond his head. The waiter changed the ashtray, which was very small and of the cheapest glass. I was thinking why do they have such cheap ashtrays in a city where glass is an art form and in a cafe where the drinks average six quid a shot? And what about economies of scale and how many ashtrays get knocked off tables by careless drunkards. I was trying to remember a book I'd read about an Englishman of some artistic or literary merit, who came to Venice for a holiday or maybe it was to live with a boyfriend or his father, who might have gone to the opera while he was here or maybe it was the theatre, but all I could really remember was that I'd read about somebody in a book walking across the Bridge of Sighs, and then out of nowhere I was blinded by a threatening well of sudden tears, teetering on the brink of a weeping that might never stop. Holding my breath, I forced myself though a rush of numbers: last year's peak on the Nikkei Index 35,000, Dow Jones 2750, FTSE 2400, Rex's next date for vaccination 22/3/92, but I figured I was only picking questions I knew the answer to, so I did a few quick currency conversions to sharpen up.

'Are you hungry?' said Stephen and I thought about saying no, but appetite is a weapon wielded by sulking women.

'Sort of.'

'Pasta or something?'

'This *is* Italy,' I said, but it came out more acidly than I meant.

We started walking, managing not to brush against each other despite the rush of crowds. In the restaurant, I curled the top left corner of the menu and decided on fish, which both of us knew I don't like, but maybe a little unpredictability was just what the situation required. So I ordered the skate and looked to the right at the yellow lights moving across the dark water. Stephen chose the wine and I drank most of it. I considered the two days left and the vague possibility of making an effort. Perhaps the potential for change lay somewhere out there on the glittering horizon and we could make a dash for it, if only there was a lifeboat of energy and conviction.

I said, 'Sorry about the deal.'

'Not now,' he said, fingering the label on the wine bottle.

And although I was staring regret in the face, there was a roadblock between the thought and the feeling. Stephen was floating away and I could not find the words to haul him back in.

Stephen ordered another bottle of wine. The waiter commiserated with my uneaten skate and I explained that I had a very small appetite. Then Stephen said on cue, 'Why did you order it anyway?'

And I said, 'I just did,' examining the tablecloth. There was a faint red wine stain, just barely visible and I wondered if it was Irish linen because it felt very good quality but I didn't know enough to tell and then Stephen said, 'Well, I guess this is it.'

I remember I looked up and directly across the table to his profile staring out at the navy sea. I followed the straight line of his nose, toying with the idea of pretending to misunderstand, asking what did he mean, wondering if he was more courageous than me, if I would regret the missed opportunity of being the first to throw in the towel. Then he turned his face towards me, looking serious and vaguely irritated, like when he's stuck in traffic or when I've said something that he disapproves of. He didn't look angry, he wasn't frowning.

He said, 'Well,' and I was uncomfortable with his eyes, so I studied the tablecloth again for a while before I said, 'How d'you mean?'

'I think you know.'

'Yes, I know what you mean.'

'Then we might as well... knock it on the head.' His voice was low and even.

'If that's the way you want to put it.'

'Geri, I'm only saying what we both know.'

In the silence that fell upon us I explored the absence of sensation while imagining him coming round to pack up the clothes he had at my flat. Would he gather up the disorder of my stray possessions at his place and bring them over, or would I have to collect them myself and end up saying goodbye twice? I thought about the confusion of CD ownership, knowing that we would both say, 'You take them, it doesn't matter, I'm sure they're yours anyway.' We wouldn't look each other in the eye anymore. And a whole baguette would never get eaten up now. And I wouldn't have to make sure there was always champagne in the fridge.

And what would we do about sleeping arrangements tonight? Would Stephen offer to sleep in the armchair, like men do in the movies and would I say, 'Don't be silly, we don't hate each other, do we,' and would we actually end up having sex just so we could remember the last time we did it?

And when would the hurt be? Would it be tonight or tomorrow or in a few months' time?

'I'm going to try and get a flight back tomorrow,' said Stephen. 'It would be easier.'

'OK.'

'A couple of days on your own might be nice,' he suggests in a tone that encompassed just about everything.

'Sure. OK by me.'

'After all, you're the one with the guidebook and I've been here before.'

I realised this was his closing witticism when he raised his hand to call for the bill. He was wearing the cufflinks I had had made for his twenty-ninth birthday and I thought what a boring fucking present to give someone after three and a half years even if they were expensive. I reached for my handbag and he said, 'I'll get this,' and then we walked quietly back through the narrow streets, past the outdoor orchestra still playing light jazz at 1 a.m.

In the hotel room, I poured myself a large vodka and stood by the open window doing an emotional minesweep over the black water. I counted eleven distant moving boat lights. When I turned back into the room, I thought Stephen had sawn the bed in half until I realised that the double was a twin.

A silver light slipped through the window. In sleep Stephen always took up the whole bed, lying diagonally like there wasn't room for another person. On his back, one arm behind his head. Relaxed. Apparently that's not how I do it, not still and peaceful but writhing annoyingly around the bed. This makes me difficult to sleep with according to Stephen who is, of course, qualified to judge this issue after more than four years of experience.

Two bodies in a bed, the sum of collected facts and shared experiences, years of familiarity binding you together, the desire to tell and to hear all, the need to be known and explored, to shed your lonely individuality. In the beginning it wore us out: I couldn't get enough of the gift of his skin, the sensation of touching, like pink-lidded puppies nuzzling into each other's warmth. For the first few months, it only got better, clothes scattered on the floor, the bed always unmade, me thinking this is like the adverts where the couple doesn't care that it's lashing rain and they've got no umbrella. Maybe you take too much in the beginning and use it all up, or maybe beginnings are all there is, the rest a slow slide on gravel, lower and lower until you no longer see the top: why it started, how it began.

One hundred and eighty-one days ago, at 7:48 a.m., in room 303 in the Hotel Cipriani, Venice, I woke up face down in the pillow, and I knew without looking that Stephen was already gone.

After a half hour shuttling back and forth between Central and Kowloon, watching the orderly draining and refilling of passengers, I am flatly damp. I disembark, make my way past the busy shops with their the doll-like mannequins, hips and waists so slender, feet like babies'.

My step is slow in the thick air as I reach Mandarin and the doorman bows, his gaze lingering just a second too long as I lurch a little to the right and into the lobby chill. And there, walking quickly towards me and checking his watch, is Stephen. I stop dead as if I could be camouflaged by remaining still. The bell chimes faintly, the lift doors slide open behind him and he looks up to catch me with my mouth hanging open. A waiter's airborne tray glides between us and then Stephen draws level. His eyes as brown as ever, head tilted in the interrogative, the faint chin cleft is unfilled: he has been preserved intact, immaculate and exactly as I remember him.

'I might have known.' His smile is hesitant but it is warm, the slight dimple appears as he closes the gap between us and I catch the air rush of a familiar scent.

'So you're after my clients now?'

He grins. 'I should have guessed Felix would tell you I'd called.'

'You *do* know he only agreed to meet you out of curiosity?' And he frowns, his Stephen puzzle-furrow. 'Felix just wanted to check out the guy who dumped me.'

'Nothing could surprise me after all you told me about him.' Stephen smiles – kindly, unruffled, unshakeable as ever. He is looking right at me, so I look away. Please let me not be churlish now. Let me rise to the occasion and show how much I have grown.

'So how's Rex?'

'He's fine.' *Like you care.* 'Great, happy as a lab.'

'Lisa looking after him?'

'No, she's away.' *Like it's any of your business.* 'He's with a guy from work,' and for a fleeting moment I am tempted to invent a new boyfriend who is not only gorgeous and rich but babysitting Rex as we speak. 'Actually, it's Pie Man, the quant guy.'

'The fat guy?' *Why am I admitting to hanging round with fatboy?* 'A last minute thing for this trip. Rex sort of knows him.' *I don't have to explain. You left us, remember?*

'So you just got in today?'

'I'm not even supposed to be here. I was here last week, got back Saturday and then got sent out again.' And suddenly I want Stephen to know that I am travelling up the food chain, not just selling water to ducks these days. 'On a Special Mission.'

'Really.'

'For one of your heroes, in fact.'

'Oh yeah?'

'Kapoor, actually.' *Go on, look surprised.* And Stephen does in fact seem to miss a beat, I know him well enough to notice the slightest double take before he inclines his head in graceful acknowledgement.

'Well, well.'

'She must be going up in the world, is what you're thinking.'

'You were always destined for stardom, Geri.'

But that wasn't enough to stop you from dumping me, was it?

'So are you here for a few days?'

'I'm done. Flying back tonight.'

Me too, but I don't say this.

'You busy now?' He gestures with his hands, looks around and it seems like a genuine enquiry rather than a protocol line.

'I'm due in the office. To report on my Special Mission.'

'Oh, right.'

'Why?'

'I thought perhaps we could – that I could take you out for a drink. If you had time to kill and if you would – like to?' And I am struck by the awkwardness in a rare rephrasing from the man who so fluently despatched me in Venice. There is a steady drift down the lobby into the Captain's Bar and the promise of an afternoon buzz, the red hide is snug and softly animal and invitingly kitsch. But it pulses with the reminiscence of other warmer times and since this chance encounter is an opportunity to rewrite my own ending, I do not trust myself to navigate safely out of reach of the past.

'Yes, I'd like to. But not here.'

Out in Repulse Bay the clifftop air at the American Club feels lighter but isn't. Executive wives in tennis skirts thrash around on the pink courts, gathering in G&T clusters in the terraced heat to discuss the relative merits of birthing in Hong Kong or Tokyo, trying to pretend that dim sum is really nice once you get used to it and that all the slender young Asian girls don't bother them. A couple of years in expatriate nirvana before rock fever sets in. The island is a playground, a watering hole.

'You remember we came here that time with Tom Castigliano?' Stephen gestures with his wine glass. A rare collision of travel schedules three years ago had us overlap for twenty-four hours in Hong Kong and I watched from the viewing gallery while Stephen and Tom played squash, thinking which of the two is the most fuckable, legs slamming across the wooden floor, shouts bounding off the glass, Stephen doing a Borg kneel when it was over and both waving up to me before they disappeared to the showers. And while I lay back in the shaded heat, I could feel the soft sweep of Stephen's hand under the fold of my skirt, trace the smooth slide of his fingers along the inside of my thigh, taste the heat of his tongue as my lips parted and I pressed into the surge of him swelling deep inside me until the light blackened behind my closed lids. My eyes opened onto their double silhouette against the sudden sunset and Stephen said, *Time to wake up.*

I run my finger around the steaming ice bucket.

'You want to go inside?'

'I'm fine.' The terrace is sticky. Drips trickle down the neck of our second bottle into a small, damp pool on the stone.

'Felix is insisting I move out here.'

'Well, I guess that was always on the cards.' Stephen nods over the rim of his glass. 'But?'

'Who said there was a but?'

'So you *are* keen on the move?'

'There are worse places.'

'You don't sound too enthusiastic.'

'Obviously there's Rex to think about.' And even as I say this I know how pathetic it sounds. This vision of me home alone clinging to a fucking Labrador. A surrogate child, like Zanna says. But Stephen just smiles, a slight twist of the mouth – this is what happens when someone knows you so well they can write your script; in fact they *do* write it. And then they stop listening. Arrested development, a relationship on autopilot. You no longer grow.

I am nailed, explored and accounted for. 'You remember Diane down at the Abingdon Vet clinic, who looked after Rex that time? Well, I spoke to her about finding a home for Rex.' This is a total lie, I didn't, I haven't, but it occurs to me right now that this is a moment that's heading my way.

'You found someone?'

'Diane said no problem, they'd be a queuing up for a dog like him.'

'So you'll be moving out here soon then?'

'I haven't said yes yet, though Felix thought I'd come to see him with the good news today. When in fact I was sent out here to get a simple answer to a simple question.'

'So did you get it?'

'Mission accomplished. Geri got the simple answer to the simple question.'

'Congratulations.'

'Which I really should deliver.' I grind my cigarette out in the ashtray. 'But you know what? Fuck them.' I am seized by a sudden fury at being catapulted around the globe at everyone's whim. 'They can wait. I'm tired of playing messenger. And for all they know I could be having a late lunch with Felix.' Stephen smiles indulgently at my little show of force and I reach for my wine glass and knock it back as if this adds conviction. Is there nothing in my repertoire that he hasn't seen before?

The waiter brings another margarita. And water. And more wine. And for a moment I want to lunge forwards and rip the smooth skin from Stephen's face just for being so adult about our unexpected meeting, so utterly relaxed, holding out a way forward where we can be ex and civilised.

'I need sunglasses, the white tablecloth hurts my eyes.' Stephen reaches into his pocket, brings out a pair of Ray-Bans.

'So typical of you to come prepared.'

'You know me, always at the ready.'

'How about a cognac?'

'You don't like cognac.'

'Zanna told me I need to start liking new things. So I'm practising.'

He raises his glass and something in his easy charm makes me want to jab him. 'So how's the family, Stephen?' He gives me a sardonic arch of the eyebrows. 'I'm guessing your mother was gutted when you told her we were history.'

'Oh, you know Lucy, she will never like any woman I bring home. But let's not go there, Geri.' He rises from the chair with a smile, a little rap on the knuckles, a gentle warning about picking sores in public.

'Sorry, just kidding.' But I'm not and I fumble for a cigarette in my handbag and watch him walk away across the terrace towards the loos, stopping to murmur something in the waiter's ear. I used to wonder if Stephen and I would still be together if we could have stopped arguing about things like the fact that I think his mother hates me.

She doesn't hate you, he said, slamming the car door on the end of what turned out to be my last visit to Esher just over a year ago.

I am NEVER EVER EVER going to that fucking house again, I announced, unaware that my prophesy would soon come true because I would never again be invited.

This car stinks of dog, he snapped.

Your mother is such a bitch, I replied, leaning my head back into a night-drive fantasy about Lucy being strangled by the pearls that Stephen bought her for Christmas, reliving the strained aperitifs in the hand-mottling cold of the dining room. Lucy ingesting little bird bites of food into the black O of her perfectly made-up mouth, demonstrating her mastery of the art of elegant eating and me using my fork like a shovel because my mum never told us not to; the effort of being on my best behaviour driving me to drink far more than everyone else, Lucy slicing into her husband's monosyllabic contentment to say, *Geoffrey darling, why don't you pour Geraldine another glass of wine.* Stephen making a throaty snorting sound while his red-haired sisters swivelled their bobbed heads to take in my empty glass. Lucy's mouth creased into a straight line, eyes narrowing as I struggled for an amusing put-down when she asked about my little flat. Like I lived in some bedsit in Catford.

All this time Rex wasn't allowed into the dining room because of the cream carpet and I could hear him whining out in the hallway. Then there was a sudden furious scratching and everybody froze because Lucy just had all the doors refurbed, so I said *It's OK*, but got up too quickly, felling my glass. *Oh, shit, I'm so sorry*, and Stephen said *Shit* and jumped to his feet, wine snaking towards his trousers and Lucy said *Geoffrey* and Sister One was already rushing for the door and Rex came flying in and

I was tugging at his collar saying, *I'll get you a whole new set, Lucy, don't worry. They're antiques,* she murmured and Stephen snapped, *It doesn't matter,* as I was overwhelmed by an urge to whip off the tablecloth and carve my initials into the slab of rosewood with a silver fork.

She doesn't hate you, she just finds you difficult, said Stephen, sinking into the couch back at my flat, but I could never resist the pointless pursuit. *Do you find me difficult?* He flung his head into the cushion. *Let's not get into this.* But I hacked on. *So you do?* And then he lost it and it just got louder, forcing Rex to hop down from the couch and stand whimpering in between the two of us until Stephen said *I might as well leave now.*

'So tell me, Geri,' Stephen slips back into the chair, 'why don't you want to live in Hong Kong?'

I hear Zanna's home truth from a couple of nights ago. *I know why you don't want to go.*

'I guess I'm running out of reasons to object. And Felix is getting impatient. In fact the simple-answer-to-the-simple-question that I have not yet delivered comes with a price tag attached.'

'Contingency?'

'Oh, Felix didn't exactly spell it out. He just reminded me he owns my ass.'

'You mean if you deliver your answer you will be committed to moving out here?'

He picks up his glass and holds my gaze just over the rim, those knowing eyes. Behind him the hazy sun seems to lurch suddenly to the east but it is me, slipping, the collision of margaritas and wine and whatever the fuck else that is sloshing around in my sleepless drunken brain. And I need the loo but the terrace seems like a perilous crossing, the effort of rising from the chair too much to contemplate. I'm sticky with sweat, my hairline warmly damp and a comforting trickle down the back of my neck.

'Fact is Felix can pull the plug on my career any time he wants. All he has to do is stop giving me business.'

'He likes you.'

'You mean he likes *toying* with me. Just like you did.' Stephen inclines his head and I light another cigarette. 'Sorry, scratch that – NO – don't say a word. Just think of it as my cheap jab with a sharp object for leaving me in a hotel room.'

'You're right,' he says solemnly. 'That was unforgivable.' His hand hovers above mine and he hesitates, giving me time to pull away. But I appear to have no neural signals, all transmission has failed and I don't move, just watch his hand slip over mine like a holster. Looking like a perfect fit. And we are both staring at this still life when the waiter returns with the cognac. Stephen lifts his head to my shaded eyes, removes his hand and turns away to look out over the terrace and a gathering haze. He is gently biting on his lower lip now, an old habit of thoughtfulness.

'You should be careful with Kapoor, Geri.'

'I've had close shaves with bankers before.'

'Touché.'

'Anyway, Felix says, as usual, that the answer lies with Kant.'

Stephen grins. 'Remember the time you said that to the Grope?' We laugh. It is almost like the old days. He stops laughing and squeezes my hand. The sun seems suddenly much lower.

'I'm glad we met,' he says.

'This doesn't mean anything.'

'There's always history.'

'So let's drink to that.'

Stephen sits on the high stone wall while we wait for the cab. 'Not a bad place to be I guess, if things do get worse.'

I nod, drop my cigarette on the drive.

'Two days to expiry,' he makes a small explosion with his mouth and hops down to the ground in a confident no-hands way, landing in exactly the spot he had targeted, a true investment banker. I lift my head, but he's already looking down at me, standing so close that I am level with the second unfastened button of his shirt.

In the cab I sit at one side of the back seat, a full person-gap from Stephen who is staring straight ahead with his elbow in the open window, and it feels like all the air is being sucked out of the car by this stretch of leather in between us. When the cab pulls up at the Mandarin and he takes my elbow, the steps are somehow deeper, wider, longer; there's the blur of a doorman between the closing doors. The bell sounds, the lift shudders, I'm standing with my back to the wall as we ascend and Stephen guides me out onto the soft hush of the corridor, pulls me forward, stops to slide a hand over my breast and I am looking up only at his eyes, then we slam against the door and somehow get inside and I let his shirt follow the curve of his shoulders and flutter to the floor. Stephen grips my arms from behind, turns me over to lay face down on the cool sheet, his tongue drawing a hot slow line down the middle of my back, both hands curve over my cheeks and I thrust my ass upwards and backwards, spread my knees as his fingers glide in to check what I already know, that I am wet and ready, and for a while I cannot tell what is sliding and pushing so deeply inside me, except that the moment is coming and we are hurtling headlong towards it as the Peak glitters and sparkles in the window.

In the wakeful aftermath I lie in the crook of his arm, my leg slung over his. Lights burn away the dusk, quick and fleeting in its sudden transition. Stephen raises his arm and sweeps the hair gently back from my forehead and I close my eyes to the release that deadens my limbs, the onset of an exhaustion that might actually lead to sleep. Now, here, safe, returned to something resembling peace.

'So you're worried that Felix will force your hand,' he says and I wish he hadn't spoken. That we could just lie here mute and close and still.

'I dunno. That's the kind of weird fucked-up person he is.'

'You think he has you over a barrel with the simple answer to the simple question?'

'Felix has something that Steiner's wants very badly. And of course the only person he will talk to is me. So *that's* why they sent me out here. The Grope's bright idea to fast track his route to the board.' I sigh. 'All I have to do is deliver the goods. And then the Grope can tell Kapoor to tell his client he can have what he goddam well wants if he pays up 30%.'

Stephen does not respond, he lies beside me breathing evenly, my head resting still on the steady rise and fall of his chest.

'Or else I could stay in London and go down in history as the saleswoman who threw away her monster client all because she didn't want to go to Hong Kong.'

'You could always find some other clients.'

'I could always leave the City and start a puppy farm.'

He laughs, 'Come here,' and pulls me in tight and on top of him. My hair falls forward and he pushes it back. I look down on his face, there as it should be, but what were the odds?

'Geri,' he says, a little frown rippling across his brow.

'Shh,' I warn, 'don't speak. I don't want you to speak.'

'I'm sorry.' And I want to ask what for? Is it for the old past or this present moment that is already fading, or is it even for some future that has not yet come into view?

But 'Shh,' I dip my head. I kiss him into silence.

22:30

'WHERE THE FUCK ARE YOU?' The Grope must have been sitting right in Julie's lap since the call transfer is instantaneous.

I'd been staring at the clockface for a full minute before I understood

I'd slept for nearly three hours, which would be a cause for celebration if it wasn't for that fact I could tell without moving that I was alone, that Stephen was gone, had left for his flight and that I had been once again abandoned in a hotel room with a stale and empty bed like the remake of a bad movie. Only this time with a critical message gone undelivered and me running late for a plane. The red button on the phone flashing warningly, three folded notes shoved under my door.

'I got held up.' Standing there by the mirror with the reflected disarray of the bed sheets behind me.

'You saw our man.'

'Yeah, I saw him.' *Saw him.* There is a disorientating echo on the line that makes me feel dizzy, like a little schoolgirl parroting her answers at the back of the class.

'Well, what've you got? On a no-names basis,' he adds in warning. Like my fucking hotel room is bugged or something. Like the Mandarin hotel might be recording my line.

'My man says our information is out of date. He now owns 20%.' *20%.* And I think a low tooth whistle rolls back at me.

'He believes the target is undervalued.' *Undervalued.*

'And?'

'My man says he has not spoken to the board. He knows they are hostile but he will go his own way.'

'So?'

'He only cares about price.'

'And?'

'He says the right price is up 30%.' *30%.*

'Up 30%?'

'Up 30%.' And it feels like we could swap the echoed number back and forth in chorus.

'Up 30%,' he repeats again, since it is after all the simplest messages that often go unremembered.

'I have to get to the airport.'

'Fuck the airport! What's your best guess, Geri?' The Grope couldn't care less if I'm road kill as long as I deliver the goods. 'What's your gut? That's where he trades?'

'My man is always guided by pure self interest.' Much like yourself.

Honkie cabbies rarely speak English except for hotel and street names, which are all in English anyway, so when we judder to a halt in the god-awful tunnel with the entire weight of Hong Kong harbour pressing down on the brickwork, I ask my driver if he thinks we'll make it to the airport on time and he grins at me, nodding, 'Yes, yes.' I suppose I look like a half-wit to him as well. A warm trickle of spunk seeps out into my knickers and I shift so it won't leak into my skirt. I wonder if I will still stink of Stephen's sex when I step off the plane at Heathrow in fourteen hours' time. The cab inches forward and I think of *The Year of Living Dangerously* when Mel Gibson was trying to get to the airport for the last flight out of Jakarta, Sigourney Weaver waiting in the open door. Although I know from experience that this traffic jam is standard for this route this time of night, there is always the chance that the airport has been shut down for security reasons and we will have to turn back and there will be troops on the streets in Central because China has just airlifted in the military because they can't be bothered to wait till 1997. And in all the chaos of foreigners trying to check back into the Mandarin I will find Stephen who is also abandoned and we will leg it round to Steiner's office where Tom and myself and a bunch of other expats fill rucksacks with tinned food and chocolate. We'll take a train out to the New Territories where we'll buy donkeys from the locals and start heading towards – where? Tokyo, the Soviet Union, wherever we figure the best chance is. We'll have to learn not to wash so that dogs can't track us down, but just in case, everyone will agree to destroy their passports, figuring that Brits and Americans are definite targets, but I'll keep mine in my underwear saying that Ireland has never threatened anyone, though this will really piss Stephen off as he'll think I might be compromising their safety.

Then Tom gets shot by the Red Army, and the rest of us get arrested and thrown in rat-infested prison camps, where we break stones under a white sun glare for three years three months and three days, before being liberated, by which time Stephen has gone insane and the rest of us have forgotten our English.

Fuck him.
Fuck them all.

8

the coefficient of restitution

wednesday 16 january 1991
09:45
london

'HOW LONG'S A PIECE OF STRING?' snorts the cabbie. Because, wouldn't you just know it, on top of everything else we've hit the school run as well as the rain. The A4 corridor is jammed with eastbound traffic so from Heathrow to the City could take the whole fucking morning. 'Could be it eases up after the Hammersmith flyover,' he shakes his head at the world conspiring against us and sinks down behind the wheel, abandons all talk.

An unscheduled stop in Bahrain to fix an unspecified technical problem had us sitting on the tarmac for three hours staring into a desert night, a stone's throw from the theatre of war and exactly where no one wanted to be. A million troops just down the road while Saddam and his boys larged it up in Kuwait, checking their watches.

We all know he's not about to make a graceful exit; volte face is clearly not the guy's style. You don't grow that kind of 'tache and commission giant statues of yourself only to back down in front of the whole world. Death is nothing, history is littered with the corpses of guys who just kept bringing it on.

The man in 8A bent the stewardess's ear in anxious complaint and it was easy staring out the porthole to imagine a fireball rolling towards us down the runway. I could have become a war statistic gunned down in active service. Geri Molloy: she gave her life for a simple answer to a simple question.

The rain whips and lashes at the cab window like some vengeful god willing me to consciousness. I think about Stephen, how his plane was undoubtedly NOT delayed and landed on time hours ago, how he'd already be showered and scrubbed and back in the saddle at Unwin & Leider. And will he even be thinking of me and what does it all even mean? Was Hong Kong the goodbye we never had or was it tinged with a regret and the glint of recovery? And why did he leave without waking me, or did I not actually tell him I was flying out too? The truth is I cannot recall exactly what passed between us, my memories are smothered by a flight load of booze and the pill I found at the bottom of my bag. I know what lies beneath, this is not the bugle call for some new dawn.

The cab vibrates, the engine drilling right into my skull. I smooth my creased skirt, my hands shaky. I am crumpled and sticky carrying Stephen's bodily fluids across the globe.

The radio putters war news as we inch towards the flyover.

And in early morning trading shares in Vulkan Valve—

TURN IT UP, I yell at the cabbie.

Yes, let's have a look at the morning markets and breaking news on Vulkan Valve. And over in the City we have Peter Jensen. Peter, can you tell us what's happening?

Well, Sara, so far there has been no official announcement but even as we speak Vulkan shares continue to rise. Dealers report very heavy volume with the stock up now to 221p which is just over 10% already. Speculation is rife as to what's behind this sudden move, Vulkan had already been performing very well in the run up to potential hostilities in the Middle East and there's been a lot of media coverage about a new portable radar that is expected to boost their sales. But there's some serious buy interest this morning so it looks like Vulkan Valve is very much in play. Dealers are hoping to hear some kind of statement from the company very soon. Back to you, Sara.

'Good news?' says the cabbie over his shoulder. I am hanging over the back of his seat, my head stuck in the Perspex window.

'Yep.' I flop back in the seat. Looks like the party has already started. So once Max-a-Billion got the nod that Felix Mann would be amenable to getting out at up 30%, he decided on a dawn raid. Or maybe this was the plan all along, that Texas Pistons would pounce and take Vulkan by storm, it would certainly fit with Max-a-Billion's Stetson style. Of course, I would be the last to know. I could be dead in a Hong Kong ditch and the Grope wouldn't care less now that he's seized his moment of glory with my simple answer to a simple question. Either way my work here is done and I am now surplus to requirements, am not even supposed to be involved. So it seems pointless rushing into the office.

'Slight change of plan.' I lean forward right on the crest of the flyover. 'Take me to West Hampstead instead,' and the cabbie doesn't say a word, just swerves to the left in time to catch the A40 exit.

Rex hits me with a breath-stopping whack in the stomach and although I saw it coming I am flung backwards against the wall. He skitters off down the corridor, does a 360 on the lino and then gallops back to hurl himself at me with a strangled howl. Pie Man stands grinning in a voluminous scarlet tracksuit that makes him look like a giant gnome. The trouser legs pooled in multiple folds around his ankles. Giant white trainers like snowshoes.

'Sorry to show up unannounced but I was on my way to the office and then I found out I didn't need to go anymore. So I thought I'd come by and pick up Rex.'

'Oh, we've – um – just come back from a walk.' He gestures at his outfit as if it needs explanation. The door of another flat creaks open and a nose and glasses peek out at the commotion. Pie Man gives a tentative wave and ushers me into the flat and a lingering smell of fried food.

Improbably daintily fringed wall lamps cast a weak pink glow over the hall and once he's shut the door, he flusters and flaps, touching things and saying, 'Well, Rex slept here,' and 'There's his bowl,' as if I'd come by to check up on him.

'Any chance of a coffee?' I ask and he disappears into a galley kitchen. Rex snout-nudges my hand and I follow him into the living room. A green Draylon couch bears the imprint of Pie Man's butt, a favourite spot hollowed into a big crater dip. Rex flops down on a shaggy rug by the radiator beneath the window and yawns contentedly as if he's lived here all his life.

There is a thick stack of newspapers on a coffee table and a scrap of paper on the couch with an intricately annotated graph of variables in Pie Man's tiny perfect hand. So at odds with his size, lumbering now through the door with a mug.

'Can I just check something on your TV?'

He rummages about between the couch cushions and hands me a remote that is brown and sticky around the buttons. Then Pie Man flops happily down on the couch and Rex hops up beside him, settling quickly as if we all live here now and life is sweet.

'Are you sure you don't mind him up there?'

'Oh, he's been doing it since he got here.'

'All that dog hair—'

'Oh, I'm not fussy,' Pie Man brushes imaginary Rex-hair from his sweatshirt, but this somehow just accentuates his size and he seems now more gargantuan than ever.

On the CEEFAX page I read what I already know about Vulkan in neon courier so I flick to the news. Tanks rumble and bump across the screen. Stealth bombers, the same old library footage looking very stale now. Stormin' Norman in his fatigues outside a large tent. A dust cloud, a camouflaged heap of something, those nets like sand crabs. John Major at the despatch box. Bush. Baker. A library shot of Saddam smiling thickly beneath a massive chandelier. And then back to the anchor-woman at her desk.

And now, let's hear from Charles Martin who is over in the City.

Well, Anna, it all got off to an exciting start this morning when shares of Vulkan Valve were chased up 12% within minutes of the opening. Speculation was rife that the company was in play; of course Vulkan is a big player in the UK's defence sector and a regular in the news these last few weeks as we move closer to hostilities in the Middle East. Well, news just in a few minutes ago finally revealed what's going on and I can tell you that Vulkan's shares *have* now been suspended, there *IS* a bid. Vulkan Valve *IS* the subject of a takeover.

'For Chrissake, get ON with it,' I mutter.

And we have just heard that the mystery bidder is—

'TEXAS PISTONS!'

British Electronics—

'WHAT?'

—who are offering 260 a share for Vulkan Valve. What's more, British Electronics emphasise in their statement that they have the full agreement of Vulkan's board. There's a press conference scheduled for later this morning but it's clear that the board will be recommending this bid to shareholders. And since the board of Vulkan Valve own 10% that should make it very likely that British Electronics will get this deal done.

'WHAT THE FUCK IS GOING ON?'

'What's the matter?' Pie Man struggles to his feet. Rex stands on the couch, barks.

'What about Max-a-fucking-Billion?'

And we'll keep you up to date on all that's happening with Vulkan.

'British fucking *Electronics*?'

'What d'you mean?'

'SHUT UP.' But the screen has already left the City and swung back to Anna and the war.

'It just doesn't make sense,' I turn to look at Pie Man who stands picking nervously at his sweatshirt.

'I don't know what you're talking about, Geri.'

'That's 'cos you're not supposed to.'

'I'm just going to open a window if you're going to—' He nods at the cigarette I have already lit. 'I get a bit out of breath sometimes.' He jerks open the window and I lean out looking down four floors below me into the back of the building where the rubbish bins are stored.

'Fucking goddam.'

'Is there anything I can do to – eh – help?' Pie Man's voice is small behind me. I lean further out into the cold light rainspit, imagine Max-a-Billion going beserk on the 21st floor, trampling his Stetson, his foot smashing into the screen. The Grope apopleptic about his moment of glory being snatched from him. His big chance to look good in front of Kapoor, his last-ditch attempt to make up for lost career ground. And I will be the perfect target for his frustration, given that I deserted my post and went awol on an island bender. Or maybe they *knew* this was happening all along. Maybe I was dispatched on a fool's errand, some sort of decoy for Felix? But that doesn't make sense, this has all the eerie feel of the unexpected.

There is a slow cold crawl up my legs, the sneaking suspicion that I might have missed something, that a secret lies buried in my lost hours adrift from the office; the red blink of the message phone, the answer I gave, the missing piece of the puzzle. But what? *You are out of your depth in unfamiliar waters, my dear.* Felix's voice comes back to me. *Everyone wants to talk to me all the time.* I stub out the cigarette on the window sill, let it drop to the ground.

'Where's your phone? QUICK.' I am snapping at Pie Man's heels as he shuffles out to the hall. When I snatch the receiver from him, he hesitates and then retreats slowly from my glare, watching me punch at the keys.

Zanna answers on the second ring. 'Hey, how was the trip, are you downstairs?'

'I need you to find out something right now. I need to know the name of the bankers acting for British Electronics?'

'Why are you asking me that?'

'Because I'm not in the office.'

'Where are you?'

'It doesn't *matter*, just look it up for me, will you?'

'I'm just on my way to—'

'Please, Zanna, I need you to do this.'

'OK, OK, hang on a sec. Yeah, I heard the news break about the bid this morning.' She taps away on the keyboard. 'What's it to you, anyway?'

'Just tell me.'

'And why aren't you in the office, anyway? I thought you were due in straight off the plane.'

'Come ON.'

'Hang on, Geri, Jesus. OK, OK, this should show it, the bid notice – yadda yadda, et cetera. Here we go – the bankers acting for British Electronics in their bid for Vulkan Valve are – blah blah blah – yes, Unwin and Leider.'

'No.'

'Yes. Unwin and Leider. That's what it says.'

'Stephen.'

'Stephen's *bank*.'

'Fuck—'

'What? Geri, what's the problem? What's going on—'

'I don't bel—'

If I was even half awake and concentrating I might have heard the clues that Felix dropped like sirens and that should have sounded the alarm in my ear.

Perhaps there is another shark circling. If I hadn't been shitfaced, broken hearted, broken down, malfunctioning, I might have actually paid attention to what was really going on.

My intelligence tells me that various parties have been nibbling at the stock. But I was mooning about my ex, distracted by Felix's bedside story about his dying granddad, imagining the malnourished horses leaping out from their frames, and so failed to raise my antenna and do what I should have been doing: my job.

Background, my dear, is not always essential to the development of the plot. Vulkan knew that Max-a-Billion was threatening to bid so they hired Unwin & Leider to mount their defence. And clever old Stephen came up with the idea of a white knight and found the perfect candidate in British Electronics – a good old domestic company that the MOD would just love.

The defence business is a national asset and politically very sensitive. Stephen wanted to talk to Felix because he was clearing the stage for the knight to come galloping to Vulkan's aid. Maybe he told Felix all about British Electronics. And maybe Felix *did* talk price. Maybe he told Stephen exactly what he told me.

My investment strategy is always guided by the simplest principles. Value. Price. Or maybe Felix refused to comment and Stephen was about to fly home empty-handed until Geri dropped the goods in his lap.

All I have to do is tell Kapoor to tell his client he can have what he goddam well wants if he pays up 30%.

There are any number of permutations. I could have been everyone's pigeon seeing as I have made a career out of doing exactly what I'm told by all the men in my life. Even when Stephen dumped me in Venice I rolled over in submission instead of throwing things at him or beating him to the finish line. And when Stephen pitched up in Hong Kong looking for an audience with the grand master, Felix could have decided to set me a little test just for the hell of it. It's exactly the kind of mind game that would amuse him: see if Geri reveals all in a desperate bid to win back Stephen's affection. Felix the puppeteer tugging at the strings.

Zanna's voice is tinny in my ear. I kill the sound, let the receiver fall and hunker down on the floor. The truth pools and surges and bursts through my fuzzy thinking with all the force of a blow to the head. Stephen would have guessed my special mission as soon as I name-checked Kapoor. He is smart enough to be suspicious of coincidence and alert to the opacity of simple questions and answers. *Geri got the simple answer to the simple question* – so Stephen needed to find out exactly *what* Felix had told me. And he didn't even have to ask me directly, he just had to fuck me and I spilled the beans with no prompting.

All I have to do is tell Kapoor to tell his client he can have what he goddam well wants if he pays up 30%. I was sleeping with the enemy and taken for a sucker.

I'm sorry. Stephen's last words come rolling back at me. But sorry for what? For Venice or the fuckover repeat that had just happened in my hotel bed?

I can see it all in replay, hear my own voice like the soundtrack of a disaster movie, the trail of hints snaking through the Mandarin lobby, the boozy late lunch, the glittering sea, the elevator doors, the familiar touch of his skin, the whole sorry tale of the seduction. And I know without doubt that this is the truth, no two ways about it: Stephen fucked me to find out exactly what I knew. It was not a remembrance of things past, not a nostalgia trip, it was an opportunistic premeditated fuck and I have only myself and my big fat mouth to blame.

'You're crying.' I spin round to what I had forgotten. Pie Man's blurry shape beside me.

'You got something to drink?'

'Some water? A cup of tea?'

'I mean a proper fucking DRINK.'

'Oh, right – erm – wait.' He backs away and it's true I'm crying real tears, snivelling on my shirt sleeve. Rex jumps up off the couch and comes over to snuggle on my feet.

'I don't know how much you want.' Pie Man holds up a bottle of Smirnoff and a glass.

'A lot.'

He pours and I say more and he pours some more and I take the iceless glass and a huge burning slug. I hold out the glass again. He watches closely while I take another giant slug as if he expects some immediate effect. I snatch the bottle from him and sink down to the floor.

'Very early for that,' he says with a nervous laugh but I can't blink the tears away fast enough. He disappears and then returns, holding a loo roll. 'I don't have any tissues.' He hunkers down and pats my shoulder, tentatively, nervously, like I might lash out. Rex yawns, opens his mouth wide as a crocodile, rolls over and sprawls on his back.

'Look at him.' Pie Man scratches Rex's tummy. I take another swig and lean back against the radiator.

'If you're in some kind of trouble, maybe I could help?'

'I just got fucked big time.'

'You can tell me about it if you want. But you don't have to.'

Rex stretches front and back paws so he looks like a golden carcass. His ears flop either side and his tongue lolls happily. Pie Man carries on scratching and I tell him my story.

11:24

'ARE YOU GOING INTO THE OFFICE?' Pie Man has been fiddling with the shoelace on his trainer while he listens to my sorry tale of betrayal, shifting restlessly as if his great red bulk cannot be comfortably distributed on the floor.

'You kidding? So I can get ritually executed by the Grope as he takes revenge for making him look an idiot?'

'So what will you do?'

'Carrying on drinking seems like a good option at the moment.'

'Maybe they won't realise. Maybe they don't know you told Stephen anything, maybe—'

I shake the bottle neck at him. 'There is no such thing as a coincidence. Kapoor is smart, nothing gets past him.'

He will piece it together and the stinking trail will lead to me. Kapoor would have filled in the gaps, heard the cantering hooves of the white knight. And he will be rueing the day that he ever even gave air time to the Grope's idea that Geri Molloy should be roped into the proceedings. The stench of rotten egg on his face, in the down draft of Max-a-Billion's white-knuckled fury and the deal that got away. Outmanoeuvred by Stephen Graves, the young buck he tried to hire, Kapoor finds himself staring into the rancid jaws of a rare defeat.

'Maybe Stephen already knew about the price. Maybe Felix actually told him.'

'Maybe, schmaybe. Doesn't matter anymore.'

'What do you think they'll do?'

'Fire my fucking Irish ass.'

Because I was asleep at the wheel and I failed on all fronts. Because I didn't sound the alarm straight away, because I didn't tell the Grope the *crucial* bit of info that Stephen Graves had been to see Felix Mann just before me. Because I cost them nearly twelve hours of dead time before I even made the call, because I was too busy bragging and drinking in Repulse Bay. And I wonder where the beginning is in all of this, when I first dropped the ball, how far I have slipped and how long this has been coming. Something unarticulated about loss here, something that I cannot process. But maybe this is not such an untimely death: maybe I would've only lasted another five years, an earnings loss of $7,908,024.37 – assuming a conservative 30% annual growth.

'What will you do?' says Pie Man.

'Maybe I'll just stay right here on the floor forever.'

'Well you probably shouldn't go anywhere when you've had so much—' Pie Man nods at the bottle.

'Maybe I'll just hide out here, be your flatmate, drink shots and watch movies.'

He giggles excitedly, his boobs quivering like animals under the sweatshirt.

So what's the difference? The Grope can fire me in absentia. He can even use the fact that I went awol off the plane as further evidence of my instability. Yes, they could hang me out to dry for this since I've probably violated any number of compliance rules.

I could try telling the Grope that I would NEVER let Steiner's down like that, that I would never do anything to jeopardise a deal, NEVER put my career on the line by letting some information fall out of my mouth no matter what the reason, time, place or person I'm speaking to. I could say that Felix himself must have told Stephen, I could swear on my mother's life and fling myself to the floor right there in his office. I could beg for mercy, blame it on some lapse of concentration or a crippling six-month insomnia, homesickness for my dog; I could offer to check myself into rehab or something, but whatever I say will be hollow and unconvincing.

So I could just tell the Grope what he's already guessed. That my ex-boyfriend fucked me so I would tell him what I knew and then he fucked me again.

And I didn't I see it coming.

'You want to know the funny thing in all this?' I say to Pie Man. 'That's *twice* Stephen has dumped me in a hotel room.'

'Wanker,' he spits and glances, incredibly, to see my reaction. 'Excuse me, but under the circumstances.' And he is on his knees on the floor and for a moment I think he is going to start crawling but he is hauling himself upright.

'Go ahead, call the fucker anything you want.'

'Bastard.' Pie Man stands now towering red over me, mashing an empty crisp bag in his hand.

'Nearly done.' I take a swig from the bottle and shake it, place it beside me.

'You should steady on there.'

'Ha, that's a good one.' The bottle sits on the floor like an omen and his eyes shift from it to me.

'You could get alcohol poisoning.'

'Do you have any fucking IDEA how much I can drink?'

'You don't have to swear so much.'

'You are so fucking bastard right, Pie Man.'

He stands working his lips like he's chewing on actual words or struggling to keep them in.

'"Subscribers here by the thousands float,"' I begin. '"And jostle one another down / Each paddling in his leaky boat / And here they fish for gold and drown." In a big bottle of Smirnoff.'

'What's that?'

'Jonathan Swift on the South Sea Bubble.' I take a long slug and salute him. 'Stephen always had a quote for every occasion. It's a prep-school thing.'

And I slam my hand full force against the radiator, my knuckles scream and so do I. Rex barks, slinks away to the couch.

'Geri, what?' says Pie Man but I am gripping my hand under my arm.

'Ice,' he says and thumps away, comes back with a frozen bag which he lays over my throbbing knuckles. The bag is freezer slimy and smells of potato.

'Tesco's Crinkle Cut Chips. I fucking hate crinkle cut.' Rex slinks over and sniffs the bag.

'Is it sore?' Pie Man breathes like a caveman beside me.

'Course it's sore.'

'Do you think it's broken?'

'Don't know. Don't care.'

He peeks beneath the freezer bag and we look at the healthy swelling rising between the knuckle dips. 'Can you straighten your hand?'

I wiggle my fingers. 'So what does that mean?'

'I don't know.' I laugh and he laughs too, nervously at first but then he sees I am still laughing and he laughs some more.

'Let's do something.'

'Bit busy,' I wiggle the bottle at him.

'Just wait, just wait—' He is scrabbling round on the couch, pulling at papers. 'You'll like this.' He plonks his big butt down on the edge of the coffee table. 'It's a problem I've been working on that—'

'Music!'

'What?'

'Let's have some MUSIC.'

Pie Man goes over and roots in a cardboard box and then leaves the room and returns carrying a dusty little ghetto blaster that he puts down on the floor in front of me and plugs into the wall. He pops in a tape, gathers up the stack of papers from the shelf. 'I was just doing a little bit of work on this when you—'

'TAKE A LOOK AT MY GIRLFRIEND, SHE'S THE ONLY ONE I'VE GOT.'

Pie Man lunges for the volume button, there's a snap and the music stops. Rex leaps up and makes for the exit but I am rolling on the floor. 'Fucking SUPERTRAMP!'

Pie Man's fat face stares down at me flat on my back, my arms stretched so far either side.

'SUPERTRAMP.' I flap my arms on the carpet. I am laughing so hard I might puke and I roll over to my side and hoist myself up against the radiator again. 'Seriously, though, I mean who the fuck listens to that?'

Pie Man's fingers are scratching furiously at the underside of the cassette. He grabs and rips and tears a loop of the brown tape, drops it to the floor and stamps on the plastic casing with the heel of his big snowshoe, then picks up the mangled pieces and dumps them in the corner bin.

'Fucking hell, Pie Man, that was a bit strong.'

'My name is Colin, *remember*?' he bends over me, jowls unpleasantly red.

'Sorry.'

He sits back down on the coffee table and picks up his papers. 'Now listen.' I have to bite hard on the inside of my cheek to stop from laughing or throwing up. 'In 45 BC Julius Caesar wanted to change the inconstant lunar year into constant.'

'Control freak.' I hiccough so violently the bottle slides from my grip. 'Wahey.' I catch it just at tipping point. 'Check it out!'

He gives me a stern look. 'OK, so Caesar wants to change time. The astronomical year was 365 days and 6 hours and he wanted to fix the equinox at the same day.'

'What you have to do is—'

'Which is what he did. But they had to ease into it. And that year of transition was called the year of confusion.'

'I'll drink to that.'

'Maybe you shouldn't.'

'What the fuck else is there to do?' I am staggering to my feet but the carpet swarms up to meet me and I lurch back and Pie Man is droning on, 'So what I'm thinking is if we—'

'Could give a shit.'

He stops talking, lets a cool silence settle while he tilts his big head back and stares up as if some crucial piece of the Caesar puzzle might be written on the ceiling. The radiator is cold against the back of my head.

'It's such a waste, Geri. You have such a gift and you just don't want to use it.'

'I'm busy.'

'You could do so much. I don't understand, I mean, I just don't get it. You're totally wasted on sales.'

'Absolutely wasted.'

'The cutting edge in finance is quant. And I *know* what you are capable of, what you could do. I can see how far you could take it. But instead you just—'

'Future is quant. Drink to that.'

'We could even work on lots of things together.' Pie Man's voice is rising and closing in. He leans forwards, balanced on the edge of the coffee table like a massive red troll.

'The two of us.'

'We could move to somewhere else as a – like a package, you know. You could use this – eh – crisis to change direction.'

'Two of us in a package.'

'The future is all about people like us, Geri. In a few years' time the big money will be chasing quants and everyone else will be old hat. Even people like the Grope – they haven't got a clue just how big prop trading is going to be.'

'Fucking HUGE.'

'Just think how much fun it would be, how much we could do together—'

'Sitting around playing with models all day long.'

'That's the future,' he beams delightedly. Wipes his palms on his tracksuit. Does not register my piss-taking tone, for he is tuned out and into some horror vision where I throw in my mathematical lot with him and we break new ground in value extraction, use our mega brains and my sales expertise to roll out the models that will transform the business and end up pasted all over the front page of the *Wall Street Journal* as Beauty and the Beast, the ex-Steiner's combo who changed the landscape for ever. And I will be so boggle-eyed I will become blind to Pie Man's grossness that I'll agree to marry him so we can pool our superior genetic material to start a little baby farm of maths geniuses. Pie Man has a vision of possession, where the two of us work on maths puzzles for all eternity.

'How can you not want that kind of future?' His hands flop by his side, deflating, the dream receding. 'Don't you even care?'

'Everyone wants a piece of me. Seems like nobody wants the whole.'

'Frege's principle of compositionality,' he sighs. 'The meaning of the whole is the sum of the constituent parts.' I lean my head back but the universe wobbles and it flops forward again. 'You need to sort yourself out, Geri,' he says, with a chilly tightening of the lips. 'You need to take a good, long, hard look at your life.'

And I do. Here on the floor, dog hair all over my suit, unwashed and unloved, wearing the same clothes, the same fucking underwear for forty-eight hours. And still drinking. My tights are sagging at my ankles, a toenail poking through, the pink varnish chipped and tired since when was the last time? When were all the last times that anything was OK?

'I need a shower.'

'What, here?'

'You've got a bathroom, haven't you?'

He looks doubtful.

'It's OK, I'm not fussy,' I grip the radiator and try to haul myself up but my knees fold under the strain. 'Gimme a hand here, fucksake,' and his big fleshy paw tugs me upright.

'TAKE A LOOK AT MY GIRLFRIEND,' I sing. Rex slinks away to hop on the couch. 'All right, Rexy wexy, all right.'

'Steady there, Geri.'

'Having made my fortune Col-IN. I shall – mark you – become a highly original person.' Up close his neck fat is white like something on a butcher's slab. 'That's a quote from Dos-toy-evskeee actually. *The Idiot*. Very *topical*.' He steadies me upright, one big hand tucked under my arm. 'Uh – oh, don't forget the bottle. Coming with me to the shower.'

'You sure you want it?' He leads me into a shadowy room with curtains closed and a rumple of duvet rising like an iceberg out of the crumpled bed.

'Wahey,' I swing on his arm. 'What's all this? You're not trying it on, are you?'

'I only have an ensuite,' he mutters and I grab the bottle from him.

'No sharp objects,' I laugh, prod him in the stomach. He stands waiting while I lurch against the bathroom door. 'So what, are you going to help me undress too?'

I am a room spin expert; the trick is not to try to balance, but to find support and claw your way on hands and knees to a safe space.

'If you're sure—' he backs away.

'I'll scream if I need you.' And I tumble into the bathroom.

9

dark matter

17:31

THERE ARE SPIKES DRILLING against my skull, my temple throbs on one side and all the way down my shoulder into my right arm, which I cannot move, since it is lost somewhere over the side. My eyes open onto darkness. A bed, unfamiliar, feels all wrong. I lift my head, let it fall. I may be sick, something in my overheated chest. A laboured kind of breathiness and then a sickly smell, sweet, warm; maybe I have already been sick. I use my left arm to explore, discover I am wearing some kind of towelling robe.

'You're awake.' The voice strong and very close. Pie Man's stale vanilla scent. 'You know you passed out in the shower.'

I tug on my right arm but it is still stuck down the side of the bed.

'Where's my arm?'

'By your side. You cut your hand on the bottle when you fell.'

'It's numb. Can't move it.'

'I've looked after it, bandaged it up. And put TCP on it.'

'I don't remember.'

'That's because you passed out, Geri.' Disapproval snipping the vowels.

'Sorry.'

'You were lucky I was here.'

'It was your bottle.'

'Nobody made you drink it.'

'Spare me the lecture. I can hardly see you.'

'I'm here.' He shifts, sitting by my side on the bed and I can sense his outline now, inhale the stale sweat. I gag on a stomach lurch.

'You've been out for hours.' His voice soft and further away as if he has tilted his head upwards.

'What time is it?'

'5:32.'

'What?'

'It's 5:32 p.m.'

'What the fuck? I never—'

'What's the last thing you remember?' The tone is harsh and the battering ram in my skull and the lurch in my stomach are sapping all my attention but I don't like the sound of his voice in the darkness or how the mattress dips like a rollercoaster when he moves.

'I can't see anything. Open the curtains.'

'It's dark outside.'

A watery quiver hits my legs. 'I'm going to be sick.' I lurch upwards but my right hand catches again. Pie Man grabs my left shoulder and pulls me over onto to my side, shoves something hard and cold beneath my cheek.

'Here, be sick in this.'

A doorway of light. An overhead lampshade comes slowly into view, the top of a corner wardrobe but I shut my eyes again. I do not move since I know he is here. I can hear his breathing and I do not want him to speak. Something bad is happening here, worse than the dry aftertaste of puke and the rancid stink of all I expelled.

The last thing I remember is the shower, a noise. My right hand throbs somewhere down by the side.

'You're awake.' Didn't he say that last time? And anyway, how can he tell? 'I know you're awake, Geri, no use pretending.'

'Where's Rex?'

'In the living room. I didn't think he should disturb you.'

'I want to go home now.'

'I don't think you're in a position to go anywhere. In your condition.' When I open my eyes, he is standing by the bedside, arms folded and resting on his massive stomach.

'Yeah, well I'm going.' I roll to my right but my arm disappears down over the edge. 'And what's the matter with my fucking arm?'

'Why are you ALWAYS swearing?' His hands are clamped beneath his armpits now as if he is trying to keep them from harm. And my skull vibrates like it will surely explode and blow my brains out all over the bed. 'Why can't you just STOP? For once, just STOP swearing and drinking and running around and wasting everything that's good.'

'Why can't I lift my arm?' He glances down the side of the bed and back at me, a grim little unpleasantness playing about his lips.

'Why?' I cannot keep the rising quaver from my voice.

'Because it's tied to the bed.' But I know this even as he tells me so I turn my head to the left where it is dark and wintry behind the curtains, the sound of belting rain.

I might have pissed myself.

Oh, but pull yourself together, Geri, this is *Pie Man*. This is the Pie Man you know, not some fucking psycho-killer like in the movies; this is just a fat-boy geek who slobbers around in the office all day eating jammy dodgers. This is a big guy who is really a very small guy underneath, so you need to get it together. Take a deep breath and play it cool.

'I just want you to stay still, to stop all this—' he waves a paddle hand.

'For my own protection, huh?' I turn my head back and offer him a feeble smile, try to show him I am not fazed by all this. 'Only it's making my arm go numb.'

He doesn't reply, but I hear Rex whine softly in the next room.

'He wants to come in.'

'No, he's staying there.'

'Maybe he needs to go out?'

'I took him out this afternoon. When you were out cold.' This last delivered viciously. 'Let's hoist you up a bit.'

His big red arms slide me effortlessly up in the bed and he plops a pillow behind me like a hospital nurse. He sits down on the bed, the mattress tips steeply and I slip sideways towards him. And there, over the side of the bed covered by the vast folds of a dark blue bathrobe, is my tethered arm. I pull at the sleeve. Rex's red dog lead looped round my wrist and disappearing under the bed. A big wad of bandage around my palm.

Focus on the specifics, Geri. Focus on solutions. Stay in safe waters. Do NOT digress.

'So is it a bad cut?'

'One slice and a few scratches.'

'I might need stitches.'

'It's not deep enough.'

'There could be some glass in there.'

'I don't think so.'

'Yeah, but I should get an X-ray. You know, in case there are slivers and they could travel up to my heart or something.'

'You don't need that.'

'You're not a doctor.' I smile, winningly. But Pie Man has a new resistance to my attempted warmth and these little gestures that would normally have him fawning and blushing have no effect. There has been some kind of transformation while I was unconscious, a steely immunity to my charm. And I do not like what I see.

'It would be a waste of time just sitting there for hours in casualty,' he mumbles.

I WOULDN'T MIND AT ALL, I want to scream. Anything that gets me out of this fetid danger zone, all sorts of unravellings going on.

'I had to rescue you, you know, Geri.' He shakes his head. 'But you don't even remember what happened, do you?' His lips compressed in tight distaste.

So I wing it, try to recreate the moment of astonishing heroism where he saved my life while I was blind drunk in his bathroom. 'I think I remember slipping.'

'I heard the thud and then a smash and I called out but you didn't answer, so I was really worried. I even hammered on the door but you still didn't answer. Then I was going to break it down but it turned out you hadn't even locked it. And there you were on the floor.' He spreads his arm. 'The vodka bottle was all smashed and there was blood on your hands. I don't know how you didn't cut yourself to pieces. I mean you could have done yourself some serious damage, Geri. It was awful to see.'

'I'm sorry.'

'Then I lifted you right up so you wouldn't roll on the glass.' He nods in memory. 'You know how heavy an unconscious body is?'

'Like a dead weight.'

'Yeah, like a dead weight.'

'You must be very strong.'

'You're not that heavy.'

'Well, about eight stone. Maybe even more.' I want him to be impressed by his gallantry in the face of my dissolution, so this sordid little story can have a nice ending and we can skate on past the nasty plot twist of captivity.

'I carried you in here. Sorted out your hand. TCP, bandages. Cleaned up the bathroom. And all the while you just lay there.'

I shake my abject head. 'I'm really sorry. Really.'

'And you had no clothes on.'

A chill snap of my spine. He is glaring at me, an unreadable needle between anger and disgust.

'You were completely naked.' I let my eyes drift down from his unreturnable stare to the stained duvet. I try to push away the horror flashes for this is the Pie Man I know, but I am already body scanning and in the searchlight of failed memory I am squeezing my thighs.

I cannot tell, I do not know.

'That's why I put my bath robe on you.'

'Thanks.' A croak, a little paltry thing.

'You don't even remember.'

To continue to pretend would be fatal, he is not stupid. 'You're right, I shouldn't drink so much.'

'No, you shouldn't.'

'Maybe I have a drink problem. And a pill problem.'

'You shouldn't sleep around either.' He lurches up from the bed, the mattress rolls me back to the left and centre. 'Doesn't it bother you at all?' Pie Man is up and pacing now. 'I mean don't you care how you behave? Don't you have any self-respect?'

I don't answer, worry my fingers at the sleeve, contemplate screaming.

'Don't you see how you can end up?'

I nod. He twitches his head violently.

'You slept with Rob.' How does he know? 'And don't go denying it because I saw you that night in November. I saw you both leave the bar and go to his place.'

'You were watching? You followed us?'

'Maybe I was worried about you. You were drunk.'

'I *know* Rob.'

'You *know me*. But look how you've ended up. Passed out, cut up and tied to someone's bed. Don't you see what a mess you are making of your life? It doesn't have to be like this.'

'Well, maybe you've taught me something very important then. Don't ever trust men you think you know. Thanks. Thank you, P – Colin.'

'And then you went to Hong Kong, halfway round the world, and slept with Stephen. After all he'd done to you. After he'd been a complete shit, you still had sex with him again.' He shakes his head roughly as if the repellent thought is stuck in his ear. 'What were you *thinking* of?'

'I don't know. I guess I was still in love with him.'

'Or maybe you're just a bit of a slut.' His mouth creases into an ugly leer. 'A bit of a slapper. As Rob would say.' Rex whines and scrabbles at the door.

'And then you come round here and end up lying in my bathroom and I'm supposed to—'

A little moan of fear escapes my lips. The taste of tears.

'I know what you're thinking, Geri. Why you look so scared and so pathetic – so HELPLESS. You even think that I would – you actually think I'm *that* kind of person – GOD!' He flings up his exasperated hands. 'You don't even know what happened. YOU DON'T EVEN REMEMBER. Even if I *did* have sex with you, you wouldn't remember.'

Rex barks and Pie Man whips round in annoyance. Rex barks again louder. Scratches furiously at the door.

'He can hear my voice. He'll keep on barking.'

Pie Man thumps away, Rex comes flying in and leaps onto the bed and licks my face and then settles down beside me with a contented whimper, tail beating happily on the duvet. I am safe, I have my dog now. He will give me strength. Pie Man stands in the doorway watching.

'Could I have a glass of water? Please?'

The phone starts ringing just as he returns. It could be Dr Who calling with a question. It could be Pie Man's mum or dad checking up on him. It could be the phone company or it could even be all the people who are supposed to love me who have somehow figured out what is going on. But no one knows where I am, I am awol between Heathrow and the office. If ONLY I had told Zanna on the phone, I might be spared whatever it is that is coming my way.

I keep sipping the water while Pie Man broods thickly, leaning against the wall opposite.

'Could you open the curtains?' He hesitates, but he does it, sweeps them back onto a rectangular frame and a blotched January night sky. A line of rooftops planted with TV aerials is stacked against the city glow. We are not overlooked. I could wave my free arm for all eternity and no one would see.

I could make Rex bark repeatedly. This is easy if you're playing with him, but I only have one free arm and anyway Rex has learnt to trust Pie Man, so if I tip him over the edge that could be it. In the movies women always do it wrong, take stupid chances, run up blind alleys. In real life it has to be different. But in real life you don't expect to be tied to a bed in West Hampstead with a fat guy in a red tracksuit who is leaning now in the doorframe, working his mouth.

Maybe he is not sure how this should continue. Maybe he doesn't have a plan beyond teaching me a lesson. Or maybe his resolve is weakening. He is not in charge. He does not even want to be in charge. He is just trying to show me he can be in control. He is chewing now on the inside of his cheeks and then I remember: he isn't eating, he hasn't eaten in all the time I've been here. Maybe he stuffed his face while I was out cold but I haven't seen him eat a thing and Pie Man is *never* not eating.

'I'm hungry.' I tell him, loudly. He straightens up and approaches, swallows once, swallows twice, big earnest motions that dip his head. 'In fact, I'm starving. I haven't eaten since I can't remember. Could be days in fact. *That's* why the booze went straight to my head.' He's licking his lips now, as if my comment were some sort of auto-suggestion. 'So have you got anything to eat? You must be hungry too.'

'I can't in front of you.'

'Course you can. We'll eat together. I can help you cook.'

'You're only saying that so I'll let you go.'

'No! Well, yes, I mean obviously I don't like being tied up, who would? But I'm just saying we could have dinner together, maybe even—'

'DON'T FUCKING TRY THAT!'

Rex leaps up, barks, looks uncertainly at me.

'Don't' – Pie Man kicks the bed frame – 'DO – that.'

Rex barks again, his legs rigid in confusion. This is the man he has lived with for two days who has fed him and walked him and let him sit up on the couch and eat Kit Kats. Rex shrinks back down beside me with a soft growl. My stomach flips over and I am shivering.

Remember, I think inside, remember in the movies where they always go wrong. Don't antagonise. Stop talking. Say nothing or say only very soothing things. Do NOT argue. Be passive.

'I know that you would never, ever, *ever* go out for dinner with me.'

'Not true.'

'YES true.'

Rex presses tight against my hip, he trembles at intervals with a faint grumble on the exhalation and keeps Pie Man under nervous surveillance with a stiff-necked gaze that tracks his every movement. His fight-flight instincts are foxed by all this human chaos, he might hurl himself at Pie Man's jugular if I let him but I would not trust Rex to carry through to the bloody end – I suspect he is all bark, no bite, the killer instinct bred out of him or destroyed by my softie nurturing.

'There are things that—' he is sliding an agitated hand up and down his arm. 'There are things you understand, things I can talk about to you that I can't to anyone else.'

'You mean like maths stuff?'

'But you don't even care.'

'That's just what I say.'

'Why?'

'Because it always made me feel like a freak show. Even at school they thought I was a freak, a cheat. I never wanted to be different. Just wanted to be like all the other girls.'

Pie Man approaches the bed and flops down on the other side of Rex. He lies in a backwards sprawl, a doughnut of neck fat cushioning his head as he tilts it up to the ceiling. The red sweatshirt rises and falls with each harsh breath.

Rex turns to me with a low beseeching whine and I nod and smile and mouth 'Good Boy', tickle the favourite spot beneath his chin. I dare not even whisper aloud and interrupt this meditative strategy that could restore Pie Man to an equilibrium, perhaps some abdominal breathing technique that he has learnt. Maybe he is imagining a peaceful blue ocean, sun streaming down on a magically slimmed body, warm lapping water at his toes. Or better still, standing in front of a gleaming tower of monitors, screens flickering with a web of charts and numbers flashing live and dangerous in the world where he is king of minds and hearts.

'I don't like losing my temper,' says Pie Man in a voice that is small and squeaky. I scratch Rex's head and he settles on his front paws with a sigh. We are inching towards safer ground.

'But you shouldn't wind me up.'

'I'm sorry.'

'When I get hungry, it affects my mood. Sometimes it actually feels like I'm going mad.' He lunges to his feet and exhales sharply, staggers a little.

'The truth is it's this—' he pats his wobbling gut, 'that puts women off.' He clutches mournfully at a flesh roll. '*You* said it.'

'No, *Rob* said it.' And I have no problem emphasising Rob's culpability in this so he can one day be the one captured and tied to a bed.

'You laughed when he said it. I remember.'

'I laugh at anything. I'm an idiot.'

'You think I'm fat.'

'No—'

'You're lying.'

'Not totally.'

'I knew it.'

'OK, OK, you're overweight. You're fat, even. But that's not a permanent condition. I mean, you can lose it. You can change.' He turns half to the wardrobe mirror as if projecting his imaginings, a slim fit six foot two inches but then he spins away, the dream doesn't take shape.

'Were you – a big kid?

He nods, a big lumpen nod.

'Were your family?'

'No, no. Just me. My dad was like a rake, could eat anything. He hated the way I was. Always trying to get me to play football and run about.' And he shivers, sets off a trembling of belly excess, maybe the memory of all those years as the fat boy secretly munching at the back of the class, pushed around the playground at lunchtime.

I can picture exactly how it would have been, the hollow victory of the five A levels and the university scholarship falling on deaf ears. Apart from the maths teacher who'd probably never had a star pupil before, his mum and dad smiling in bewilderment like you do when someone is talking to you in a foreign tongue. *There's nothing wrong with normal,* his dad would've muttered, remembering all those Sundays when he kicked a ball in the garden and his son lumbered after it like a legless walrus until they slammed through the door and the consolation of a fry-up in front of the telly. I imagine Pie Man trying to love what his dad did, like the funnies, the Marx Brothers, Laurel and Hardy, all that slapstick bungling and the sense that maybe they were laughing together until the screen went blank and the moment was gone, leaving nothing in its wake except *Match of the Day*, little men in colours worrying at a ball as if their life depended on it and his dad slapping the arm of the chair. *D'ya see that?* Afterwards an emptiness much like hunger as he sat cradling the biscuit tin on the couch, heard his dad creak across the landing and the bedroom door slam. His dad lean like a bean. Hollow legs: *I don't know where he puts it*, his mum said admiringly. Hollow legs, hollow men.

'You have no idea what it's like to be always hungry. It's like a fierce burning pain. And if I don't eat I get into a rage like I might break something.'

I sneak a glance round, there are traces of an old supply trail – a flattened pack of Jaffa cakes lies on the floor by the wardrobe. What might once have been a fruit bowl on the dressing table, full of loose change and paper clips. This is what I am thinking: how much is there in the fridge, in the cupboards? I remember Frosties on the counter, Rex's bowl on the floor. Is there enough food? What happens if we run out of food? Has he bought enough to last for this impromptu kidnap event, and will he be afraid to go out to the shops and leave me on my own in case I escape? Or scream the house down, which I surely will.

'Maybe it's your metabolic rate.'

But he is not listening, he is scrabbling fiercely at his brows as if they are gripped by some infestation. 'You think you're so smart. So cool. So—' he loses the word. 'You and that moron.'

'You mean Rob.' I will give him up as a moron any day. 'I'm not like him.'

'You shouldn't be like him, but you are.'

'No.'

'Swinging it about, thinking you own the place, thinking you're above us all. Well, you're not.'

'We're not.'

'All your money, all you've earned. All your big bonuses. I don't care. The clock is ticking, you know, and it's people like me who are going to be running the show soon. At least *you* should be able to understand that. Moron doesn't even know his time is up.'

'"The most disgusting and hateful thing about money is that it even endows people with talent, And it will do so till the end of the world."'

'The whole point is you *do* have talent.'

'I was quoting. Dostoevsky. *The Idiot* again, as it happens.'

'What do you actually care about, Geri? What do you actually value? Nothing important. You waste your natural gift, you drink yourself silly all the time, sleep with lots of different people and hang around with – with losers. You probably have sex with your clients as well.'

'No I don't.'

'I don't care if you do. *You* don't care what you do. You're pathetic. You don't even have a job anymore; all you have is a dog.'

I scratch Rex's head. This is not the right moment to cry but I cannot will the tear back and it rolls in slow uneven motion down to my lip.

■ ■ ■ ■ ■

I'm thinking how all stars die, just in lots of different ways. The biggest ones die soonest and in the most spectacular fashion. A red super giant that explodes into a supernova and for the briefest of moments shines brighter than all the other stars in the galaxy put together. But collapse is inevitable, it all ends in a black hole so dense that not even light can escape.

Burnout is final. That's how it goes.

'Open the robe,' he says.

I look up but his is not a stare I can hold, something in his extinguished eyes makes me think of the tabernacle on Good Friday when the light has gone out, when God is dead and we are left alone with our darkness.

'Open the robe.' Rex growls faintly, a little ridge of fur stiffening on his spine.

'I've already seen everything, you know,' Pie Man is breathing hard. 'And you're not even all that great.'

He reaches forward and opens the robe, slides it apart right to my shoulders. 'Your tits are small.' Lips curled downwards like he's looking at a piece of dogshit. 'Not what you'd call sexy.' There is something like nausea rising in my lungs and I swallow hard though maybe spewing all over my skinny tits would be the best thing that could happen right now. His eyes narrow and blackening, his fat finger prods my collarbone and begins a slow trail down the middle of my chest, he is watching me clench my teeth, his finger slipping slow and steady down over the swell. It stops, hovers just above my breast. I close my eyes.

Out of my limbs a sort of spasm, I am trying not to shake. Rex stirs, turns his golden head and I open my eyes to see him twist his neck and look at me. Sadly, it seems.

'If you hurt me, he will bite you.'

Pie Man doesn't register my voice, his eyes are closed and all air sucked out of me now, my throat in some kind of traction, he slumps forward making some kind of moan and I scream 'HELP' but his hand clamps down over my nose and mouth, my jaws so wide I cannot bite into the flesh and I am kicking underneath the tangle of sheet and Rex is barking, Pie Man is saying 'All right Rex, all right Rex,' and Rex, who is backing away, off the bed, then Pie Man's curdled face close up, holding my head in his hands.

'If I wanted to fuck you I could have done it while you were passed out.' He pushes me back and sideways, my temple snaps against the board and it is this that roars my brain and I swing my left arm wide, high, close, my wristwatch catching his cheek, but he does not release me, just holds it in easy victory. I am so completely disarmable.

'Don't you get it? Don't you understand anything, Geri? Any man can take whatever he wants from you.' A pronouncement or a forecast. A lesson taught or delivered.

I hear my own whimpering and Rex's nails clicking away on the wooden hallway. He wants no part in this humiliation. And so I am truly alone. This has the feel of my soul shrivelling up to die. Pie Man lets my arm slip, grabs a pillow and strips the case from it, twists it and stuffs it in my whining mouth, ties it fast and hard behind my head. I am gagged, bound, the sound of my own shortening breaths against the cloth. He pats his cheek, inspects the little smear of blood on his fingers. My saliva coming fast and free. I cannot swallow, I will be sick and I will choke, so I close my eyes. I must will myself out of this body, detach and disengage like a shuttle that sheds its casing, my own self unhooked from all this. For this is only one possible world. In another I am running free now, like Setanta whose feet never touched the forest floor. My hair is a streaming banner behind me, Rex bounds alongside like a fearless warrior hound, and in this world I can ford the deepest rivers, scale the highest mountain, I am untouchable, uncatchable, I am soaring above it all.

The mattress heaves upwards. Pie Man rises without looking at me.

He turns and leaves but does not close the door. There is a rustling sound from the galley kitchen and I strain to listen. He is muttering to Rex, he could be reassuring him with food, bamboozling him with biscuits to make him forget that I lie bound and gagged in the bedroom. But I get to work on the pillowcase gag, scrabble and tug and it slips down my chin just as he walks back into the room.

'Corporate Slave Animal,' I tell his approach and he stops by the bed, takes in the pillowcase lying crumpled around my neck. He nods. But at least his hands are empty. I am too scared now to keep silent, to leave him alone with his thoughts and I am a salesperson after all and I am not without resourcefulness. This would be the wrong time to cave. So let's just be clever about this, Geri, let's keep talking, keep him interested, and steer him away from thin ice to safer ground. Let's just stay alive till the next best thing.

'Corporate Slave Animal,' I repeat. 'You know Kenichi-san out in Tokyo? It's what he calls the office workers. It's a way of thinking about things. When you don't own yourself anymore.'

There is a fading flush about his cheeks, a patchy unshavenness and a whiff of stale flesh. And in the slump of his shoulders, his flab seems to be pulling him lower as if a great tiredness adds to the weight. He takes a step towards the window where the night sky is washed with light glow. His lips move, he seems to be whispering something and then he yawns, a great long hippo gape of the jaws, that from down here on the bed seems to play in slow motion.

'You're tired,' I say, 'you haven't slept.' He shakes his sagging head and looks wildly around the room and the chaos he has created. And I realise that he needs me to show him a way out of this. So I must tread carefully, proceed with caution. My heart batters against its cage. 'You look exhausted,' I say again and pat the bed. 'Sit down.'

He nods at me, at the mattress and then lowers his bulk onto the bed so that he is facing the window with his back to me. 'Lie down,'

I tell him and he reels backwards like a felled log, his head at right angles to my hip. And the light sinks, as if a dimmer switch has been thrown over the city. From this view his hair is thick and brown, dull and choppily cut, an uneven stab at layering around the crown. His lids close, perhaps he is just exhausted by event, by all that has happened to him at the hands of others, defeated by the bit players and the jocks who steal the spotlight and get the girls. His huge red legs anchor him to the floor and now he spreads his arms wide in cruciform.

Rex appears in the doorway, head cocked in uncharacteristic hesitation as if he is weighing up the alternatives. But instead of bounding over to the bed he stands silent and watchful. There is a new sobriety here, a new attentiveness to the situation, as if he has finally arrived at the gates of adulthood. He pads demurely over and hops onto the bed with an impressive delicacy, positioning himself democratically between Pie Man and me.

'You want to know about my circus trick?' Pie Man doesn't answer. 'You want to hear the story?' He doesn't even open his eyes, but there is a quality of stillness that I will take for assent.

'Long multiplication was the beginning of my unmasking.' Rex turns over to lie on his back with his paws in the air. I scratch his tummy and he sighs contentedly in a trusting sprawl.

'Mrs Donovan, fourth class. So I was nine.' A sea of plaits and bobbles. Desks with sloped lids, stained with old ink.

'Geraldine Molloy, show me how you worked it out.' She slapped the ruler on my desk.

'I did them in my head.'

'Don't be a silly, Geraldine. Those sums are far too complicated to do in your head. Now show me where you worked them out.' She slid the ruler underneath my orange copybook and lifted it, as if there might be something hidden underneath. 'Open it up and show me.'

I opened it slowly to reveal the graph paper, a pristine universe of unsullied squares, the backdrop for all the numbers I could project in my head.

'Right then, Geraldine.' Mrs Donovan stiffened inside her cardigan.
'So I suppose you can work out 276 times 98 in your head?'

'27,048.'

The girls shuffled in their chairs. Orla sniggering behind me. Mrs
Donovan tightened her grip on the ruler.

'Or 322 times 59?'

'18,998.'

Her hand twisting at a pink button. My fingertips damp, barely
pressing on the wood, a hot buzz of defiance blazing at my neck. I
tipped my chin upwards.

'Ask me another,' my little girl voice swelling thick in my throat.
Emer's thumb drifted into her open mouth, the way it did when she
was nervous. Mrs Donovan staring down at me the way you'd take
the measure of a snarling dog. Suspicion glittering in her dark irises,
the deep furrow of her brow. That she might be the butt end of some
unpleasant prank here, some trick played by silly girls to make teachers
look stupid in front of a class that was growing restless now, gripping
the desk edges with excited fingers.

'433 times 78.'

'33,774.'

'45 times 23.'

'1035.'

She stalled. A little quiver in her peach lip. I stood up, stepped to
the right so I could see the test questions on the backboard behind her
and I reeled off the answers in loud sing-song:

'And 872 times 63 is 54,936.'

'469 times 86 is 40,334.'

'777 times 99 is 76,923.'

The wall clock ticked. The girls held their breath all around me. Pink
blobs appeared on Mrs Donovan's cheeks like she'd been slapped.

'You're not even checking my answers,' I told her.

Through the corner of my eye I could see Orla suck in her cheeks
with the effort of suppressing giggles, she threw a covert glance at Emer

and then there was a loud explosion from Marian, helpless over by the window and then they were all at it, the whole class laughing their heads off and I was laughing too and looking round, laughing at them laughing at me, for they too believed I had found some clever trick.

Mrs Donovan banged her ruler down on my desk, slammed so hard it snapped and a piece clattered to the floor. She stood clutching the broken stub like a knife. No one was laughing now. The bell hammered above the door.

There was a little plaque that read 'Headmistress' on Mrs Murphy's door. A half-eaten Rich Tea beside her teacup.

'No one likes a cheat, Geraldine.'

'I wasn't cheating. I was doing the sums.'

'Enough now,' Mrs Murphy raised her hand. 'Concentrate on your lessons. Your brother was always a such good boy. Why don't you take a leaf out of Kieran's book?'

In the playground the girls were playing hopscotch. Orla stopped on one leg.

'God, did you see Donovan's face, I though she'd burst.'

'What did she say?'

'Did you get lines, did you?'

'Where did you have the answers?'

'Had you the sums up your sleeve or something?'

'Did you learn them off by heart?'

'Will you show us how you do it?'

'Will you do it again tomorrow?'

'I didn't have anything up my sleeve. I didn't learn them off by heart. I just did it, like I said.'

'Yeh, course you did.' Orla tugged her plait frowning.

'I worked them out in my head.'

'Course you did.'

Emer picked at her pinafore pocket. Marian bit her fingernail, stared.

'I DID.'

'Liar.'

'What did you say?'

'You heard.'

'Say that again.' I pucked Orla with my elbow.

'No one can do those sums in their head. Mrs Donovan said so.'

'I can.'

'You're such a show-off,' she said, hands on hips. 'It's a trick.'

'It's not a trick.'

'Like magic or something,' she flicked her plait behind her shoulder. 'Like when they take rabbits out of hats.'

'Or pennies behind your ears.'

'My dad can do that.'

'It's a trick.'

'Yeah, it's all tricks.'

'It's not.'

'Is so.'

'NOT.'

'SO.'

'Not.'

'Liar. Cheat.'

'BITCH.' I pushed her hard. Orla wobbled backwards, then flew at me but I grabbed her plait, thick and rough like rope, yanked as hard as I could. She screamed, 'GETOFFMECHEAT', and I kicked her shin. She was on her knees and I jumped on her, ground her ugly face into the tarmac, the girls were yelling, 'Miss, Miss, come quick,' and I was screaming 'I AM NOT A CHEAT' and Orla lay there roaring until the teachers' hands like clamps on my arms dragged me away.

■ ■ ■ ■ ■

'Now, Geraldine,' prompted the headmistress. I stood beside her desk facing down the audience that was arranged in a little semicircle before me. My mother sat fidgeting with the clasp of her handbag. There was an empty middle chair where Orla should have been, but instead she squirmed on her own mother's lap, trying to make herself small and cuddlable, a big pink scratch on her cheek, a plaster on her knee with iodine smeared underneath, a bruised shin. Eyes sparkling with the righteous thrill of the wounded.

'Geraldine?' Mrs Murphy's voice was sharp.

I stretched my neck as high as it would go. Facing down my mother's tight lips. Refusing to offer the expected apology.

'She said I was a liar.' I looked down the line of my nose at Orla who sniffled, dabbed her nose with her hanky. Her mother ran a comforting hand over her head, arched her brows.

'Geraldine,' my mother urged in a whisper.

'Come along now,' Mrs Murphy's pitch rose in warning. But I was rising higher and higher, floating above them all. I was unreachable with my new-found disdain, up there in the thin air.

'Well then,' the headmistress sighed, shook her head and stood up.

'Do you want to stay and watch?' I snarled at Orla.

'You will be QUIET,' Mrs Murphy rapped her knuckle on the desk. Orla was shepherded away bawling. My mother stared aghast at this daughter-turned-sinner and then backed out the door.

'I have never had call to use this on any girl before,' the headmistress picked up her cane from the coat rack. 'But you leave me no choice.' She looked grimly at the shiny bamboo. 'Now hold out your hand.'

I did not flinch at the first stroke. She paused, checked my face for some sign of remorse but I held firm, waiting. Her lips tightened sourly and she whacked again, this time harder and I kept my head high and watched her closely and I knew that she hated what I had made her do – three – four – five – but I was stronger. Though I didn't know where all the cussedness came from, I had discovered a deep and velvet well of power.

■ ■ ■ ■ ■

Rex is whimper snoring, I pat him into stillness and Pie Man's red mountain stirs. 'Why didn't you talk to your mum and dad? Surely someone would have—'

'Sshh,' I tell him. 'Don't interrupt.'

My father talked to me in the dining room that Saturday and told me to be a good girl and not to be getting in trouble at school. I told him they said I was a liar and a cheat. 'Ah, well now,' he said. 'Keep your head down, Geraldine, and just get on with your work. Take a leaf out of your brother's book,' he said, just like everyone else. My father didn't take girlfights seriously and anyway he was checking his watch, the three o'clock at Newmarket would be on telly soon.

I wanted to tell him I was afraid, that this thing with numbers felt like a birthmark, a deformity that singled me out. I wanted to tell him how the numbers followed me, how they hovered even on the edge of sleep. How they swirled across the wallpaper, wobbling and swooping into position. How I lay awake at night taking comfort in what I would later discover are called prime numbers, hunting them down like hidden treasure that you pick and weigh in your hand, testing their shape and properties, lining them up on my bookshelf atop the uneven sweep of volumes. 7 above *Black Beauty*, 29 above the *Children's Bible*, 73 above *Little Women*. Sometimes I paraded them in a ring on the floor of my bedroom and each time I found a new one I arranged a steeplechase of primes – the highest didn't always win. I wanted to tell my dad that sometimes I felt the numbers were choking me and that there might be something terribly wrong with me since I could not leave them alone, like a feverish compulsion to scratch at your skin till it bleeds.

But I didn't have words to describe it so I just promised to be a good girl and he patted me on the head and went into the kitchen. I eavesdropped on the staircase.

'Sure isn't it great if she likes sums,' he said to my mother.

'She was cheating, George, the teacher said so.'

Later my mother was doling out rashers and egg. 'What are you looking at?' I said. Kieran raised a startled head. I offered her my most insolent glare.

'That's enough out of you, madam. You'll get up to your room right now with no tea.'

I scraped back my chair.

'I'm very disappointed in you. Your brother never got into trouble like this,' she called out as I slammed the door.

I stomped my protest upstairs and lay on my bed with the curtain billowing in the open window, the sound of summer evening football, the punishing chant of other children playing on the road until the day dissolved into a pale grass-scented evening, the downstairs mutter of adult TV and the clatter of washing up. I poked my head under the curtain and watch the girls play a last game of German jumps in the fading light. Áine Kenny stood with the coloured rubber bands twanging at her ankles. Last Sunday she sang a solo 'Ave Maria' at Mass, her voice a startling sweet that had all the parents reeling in the pews. On Tuesday Emer walked on her points across the entrance hall, one chequered square at a time. All these girls could do the special things that girls do.

I heard the closing click of Kieran's bedroom door and then the music seeping through the wall. 'It's not fair,' I said from the threshold while he lay reading on his bed, lost in his book, his favourite Russian stories tucked inside a tattered green hardback. But Kieran didn't hear, he was with Chekhov on the shores of the Black Sea or gazing at the chandeliers in St Petersburg. I flopped down on the floor, kicked the skirting boad. 'I don't want to be different.'

'So don't be,' he shrugged, turning the pages. 'Just pretend.' I rolled over on my back and looked at him upside-down. His extra eight years put him in an unimaginable place. 'Just keep your own secrets.' He smiled and considerered my upside-down face. He was pulling further and further away from me and soon he would be gone. 'Now be quiet and I'll read you this story.' And I knew it would be a sad one because Kieran was always reading sad stories. He read aloud to me in the watershed hours between school and teatime, even long after I was able to read myself. I can still see him sitting on the floor with the thick green book and Tchaikovsky on his cassette recorder. He picked stories that made us both cry, as if constant immersion in raw emotion and pathos was some sort of poultice that would keep us tender and vulnerable, so that everywhere you looked the world was flooded with casual injury. Scabbed horsehide and slinking dogs who bare their cringing teeth at a raised hand, Scott's ponies sinking up to their necks in the snow until the crack of a bullet laid their misery to rest in the Antarctic wasteland.

I used to lie on the bed digging my toes into the soft press of his pillow imagining the starving she-wolf lying in a bitter March snow, suckling the cubs who prodded her emaciated belly with their paws. And I cried, retreating to the numbers in my head, multiplying my way into the future in a hypnotic sequence of numbers that only got bigger, while Kieran sat motionless in the fading afternoon, the book open on his lap, a single tear rolling down his cheek.

Pie Man breathes the noisy labour of the obese. There is a sprinkling of powdery white across the red mountain of his sweatshirt, rising and falling like some great dormant rumbling, molten lumps on the verge of sudden ignition.

'So I took Kieran's advice,' I tell him. 'I took my secret underground, thinking maybe darkness would stunt its growth.'

'You mean you pretended?'

'Though sometimes I really couldn't hold it in.'

Maths class aged twelve and the intolerable discomfort of an error transcribed by the teacher from the textbook onto the board. That's wrong, Miss. Seeing the mistake before knowing why or how – the shape, something wrong with the shape. The class gawped and sniggered while the teacher stood beached in a shaft of sunlight, before packing my impertinence off to the headmistress and I wrestled with the urge to beat her brains out with the wooden edge of the chalk duster. My erratic test results fitted the profiler of a cheat and teachers issued occasional warnings. I was sullen and unresponsive. But the nuns didn't worry themselves about underperforming girls since there was an endless supply of average men who would provide for them. I was alone since no one could follow me into that other-worldly space. On the other side of a blackboard or at the end of an equation hovered a universe vast and unknowable, like the frozen steppes where a sled would whoosh me away to a place of no return. And that's how it would be, there would be nothing for me to be except different.

'Your brother gave you the wrong advice,' says Pie Man softly. The red mountain rises and falls. 'You should ask him what he thinks now.'

'I can't.'

'You could try,' he says coaxingly, gently, as you would encourage a small child.

'Kieran's gone.'

Darkness has fallen. And I am being dragged now back into a past I'm supposed to have shed. The whole point of leaving is that you don't take the shit with you, but there it is seeping under the door like floodwater.

'Tell me what happened,' says Pie Man. 'Finish the story.' And it seems that is all the prompting I need. But I don't have much to remember: I was so young and everything is wearing out. There was the sandpit in the back garden where Kieran used to cover my legs completely and then tickle me. Oh, everyone loved him, the boy with chestnut hair and ocean eyes. All the mothers on the road used to say he had eyelashes like Tony Curtis in *Spartacus* and I'd see his name tucked inside the scrawled hearts on the back door of the girls' toilets at school. Sometimes on my way home, he'd cycle past me with a bunch of friends, making a whooping noises and doing wheelies, ties streaming from their necks. Kieran lagged behind, a back-pedal distance between him and the others, looking round at me with a secret smile, though he never stopped, never broke ranks.

Jesus, Mary and Joseph, my mum shrieked the day he strolled through the front door brandishing his Leaving Cert results, an excess of As, my mother screeching he'd be getting into Med then. Kieran stalled in a threshold shrug, his accommodating grin and the lack of an alternative suggestion, unable to resist the grinding force of academic success, my mum racing out onto the road to tell the neighbours about the fledgling doctor, the first generation of university material.

A week into his first term, I came in from school to find her standing by the sink, tears rolling down her cheeks, saying it broke her heart to see the Weetabix packet lasting three days now he wasn't having all this meals at home.

I remember the first time he came home late, I was lying in bed imagining him crumpled in a gutter with his brains spilling out all over the road, clutching the crushed bike as the tail lights of a drunk driver faded away into the night. Then I heard the slam of the back door and my mother tiptoeing down the stairs, Did you have a nice time? she said, while Kieran puked his guts out in the toilet. She let him miss Mass the next morning and lie in till noon, cooked a big fry to help him get his strength back. *He's only pissed you know, Mum, he's not sick,* I said as she handed me the tray. *Wash your mouth out, miss. Your brother is studying day and night and he needs to let off a bit of steam. You could take a leaf out of his book, I'm telling you.*

Strange books everywhere, littering all the rooms with their anatomical detail, red and blue cross-sections of skinless body parts, skeletal quizzes at the breakfast table, the curved shelf in his bedroom collapsing under the weight of future responsibilities. But Kieran didn't talk anymore. There were unfamiliar voices on the phone. And he'd stopped reading to me. Floated past on the stairs like I was invisible.

There would be a ring at the doorbell and he would disappear for a whole night and come back thinner. He was leaving us for another world. Once I sneaked into his room, crouched down by his shelf of spine-crinkled Russians and slowly, methodically tore the first eighteen pages of *The Idiot* in half, the satisfying thrill of injury, the dust-sweet smell of tattered yellow pages, their transparent flimsiness, such a tenuous link with immortality. Hurting is a very easy thing to do.

And then I was eleven, nearly twelve, walking home from school. I stopped in our front garden, there was a dead sparrow on the grass, I·can still remember the grey underside of its wing, the way it was so small, the way the feathers looked, the raindrop lightness shattered by a broken wing, but the image doesn't hold. What I hear instead is my mother screaming and me running inside and upstairs where Dad was splitting open the bedroom with an axe. *Hurry George Hurry Oh God George,* my Mum's jabber, *God help us*, hack hack, the wood splintering a jagged opening, Dad's hand shoving through, the click of the key, *Mum, I'm scared,* my hands pawing at her back, *Oh George*, and the door burst open onto a fallen chair, a shoeless dangle, the trouserless legs below the naked body of the mangled face that filled the space where the light should be. The shape, the body, a swinging carcass.

Kieran Molloy
Beloved son of George and Patricia
Brother of Geraldine
Taken to God March 2nd 1979

Later, a lifetime later, after the front door had finally closed on the procession of priest and doctor and neighbours, we were left alone with our horror. *Why'd he do it?* I tugged at Dad's sleeve and when he didn't answer I kept repeating the question, louder, louder. *You must know, you must know why*, but he didn't even move, I thumped his back and Dad led me from the kitchen, hugged me limply and then shook my shoulders, *Geraldine, shush now, shush, don't be upsetting your mother.*

In my mind we are all still in that room, suspended in that moment:

a family in the grip of a question never answered. And that is how it would always be. Nothing we could do, that moment defining past, present and future and rendering it all meaningless. The pain binding us together and keeping us apart. Time passes but the scene doesn't change. A teapot frozen in mid-air between the cardboard cut-out of my mum and dad, stone-faced and absent, seated at the kitchen table. The things I knew she touched secretly when alone, sitting on the cold narrow bed, running her hand over the dry electricity of memory, her insides scooped out and filled with pain. So she had to lose herself in a wilful dementia or shrivel up and die.

Kieran was in a coffin swamped with coloured wreaths in the cool sanctuary of the church. My whole class filed through in craning curiosity, the subdued thrill of event that I remembered so well from my only other funeral experience the previous year: Helen Murphy, leader of the Heather Patrol and with the longest hair in our class, who died of leukaemia, aged ten. In the pew I held my mother's handbag while her clawed hand bit into Dad's arm. I followed their shuffle out into a heartless rain in the new scratchy black coat that Aunt Joan made me wear, while men in dark suits shunted the coffin into the jaws of the waiting hearse. My mother's wail broke the crowded stillness, a flock of birds burst from a tree and I pushed through the mourners and ran and ran and ran, through the car park, down the hill, slamming my feet on wet cement until I could run no more and lay down in Mullens' driveway.

It was the day the tinkers set up camp on Chestnut Road and never left.

Pie Man lies with his mouth open and gasping in erratic snores. Rex's gold is silvery in the lowlight, his front paws still raised and bent and twitching a little in dream. A million heartbeats and it's all over.

I pull at the duvet but I can't contain my shivering. I will drift into exhaustion, but there is only a drift backwards, the unceasing pull of a past. An unravelling all around me, an unbearable sadness that has nowhere to go.

'Go on,' says the red mountain. 'Finish the story.'

'After Kieran was gone I learnt to stop concentrating.' It was really a surrendering to dream. In the grey drizzled mornings of English class I could feel myself slipping into a beckoning open grave, in wistful pursuit of the elusive nightingale, scribbling tiny notes in the margin of Keats's reverie, flicking soft, worn pages to the condemned Pearse, his love for God, mother and country fused into an alluring vision of glorious death and eternal life. Late at night watching the orange street light seep under the too-short curtains, they all collapsed into one exhausted tangle: *I do not grudge them: Lord, I do not grudge / My two strong sons that I have seen go out / To break their strength and die, they and a few / Now more than ever seems it rich to die / To cease upon the midnight with no pain / In bloody protest for a glorious thing / They shall be spoken of among their people / The generations shall remember them / And call them blessed; / Blessed are the meek for they shall inherit the earth...*

My mother's first few weeks in hospital, that time when it still seemed reasonable to believe it could be temporary but was really the beginning of her irreversible decline. And all these years later she is still there. On Christmas Day just gone my father drove me down to the hospital for our first joint visit in five years, buzzed through a thick glass security door. A giant foam lozenge that serves as a couch in the centre of the ward. Dad leaned forwards in the couch, arms folded on his knees, head lowered, sleeping or praying or avoiding, looking more like an inmate than a visitor. Two nurses stood chatting over by the station, their shoes like great dollops of cream and I wondered: do they see it? All the broken relatives, the battered families thrust into despair? And what do they think about the inmates we visit, the home-wreckers who choke on the mess of their own lives, unwilling or unable to stop its cancerous infection, like creeping parasites of destruction.

Their existence whittled down to the gaps between medication, days measured out by little white cups. Once I sat in the middle of the ward and watched while a woman set fire to the hem of her pink dressing gown and the nurses sprayed her head to toe with foam. And I thought: why not just let her burn?

A nurse patted my father's wreck of a shoulder and he wandered off for a cup of tea.

'Mum, we've come to take you home for Christmas lunch.' The foot of my mother's bed was just visible from the doorway, the blinded window casting a weak strip of horizontal sunlight across the grey carpet.

'I… didn't have any breakfast.'

'You didn't want any, remember? You told the nurses you weren't hungry. And anyway it's Christmas dinner in a few hours.'

She hummed, a flat snatch of sound or extended sigh. The noises that she makes now startle me. She was always such an exact communicator, not given to redundant emissions.

'Tell Kieran to come in here. Tell him I want him.'

'Mum, you know Kieran isn't here anymore.'

I heard the snuffle from the bed, and I knew that this was just the prelude to the familiar head-banging that would descend to an inhuman moaning, a steady unchecked flow of tears and snot dripping down her chin and I walked over and put the box of tissues on her bedside table just as Dad arrived, rubbing his hands in false cheer. 'It's a fierce cold day outside, you're well tucked up in here, girls,' and he sat on the side of the bed and patted her hand, stuffed a wad of tissue onto her heaving chest. 'There now, don't go upsetting yourself, Pat,' he droned in a practised soothe.

'She asked for Kieran,' I snapped. But he didn't look at me, just kept on stroking her hand. 'Jesus, Dad.' I turned and walked past the glancing smile of the arriving nurse.

'D'you know what would do you the world of good, Patricia, would be to get out of that bed and have a cup of tea with your family.'

I backed out of the room, signalled for buzzer release.

■ ■ ■ ■ ■

By my last year at school, Mum had been permanently installed in hospital and I took to practising smoking in Kieran's bedroom, home alone after school, dropping cigarette ash on my uniform, going over the distant final moment I had spent with him. At 4:45 p.m. on 1 March 1979, I had met him wheeling his bike up the road. I asked how he could bear studying for six years just to end up looking down people's throats all day? He said it didn't really matter what he did, looking at me with a smile that didn't seem connected to his lips. Hours later I heard his low-volume Tchaikovsky, but I didn't see him after that, just the crusts of dead toast on his plate when I came down to breakfast after he had left for an early lecture.

The next thing I saw was his broken face.

In all the family floundering over the entitlement of grief, I didn't figure in the pecking order. My mum had granted herself a private abandonment. My dad finally gave up on the struggle to find something useful to say. *God love him, wouldn't he have made a lovely doctor?* I began spending afternoons lying on Kieran's bed playing his tapes, reading the Russians that he loved, suspecting the dead authors of a morbid intimacy with him, searching for some secret buried deep in Dostoevsky, Chekhov, Esenin and Tolstoy, some hint of what they might have been whispering in his ear. I read them all, quickly, thoroughly and it seemed that it was everywhere, death stalking the thin pages.

I listened to his music, waiting for a sign. Staring up at the light fixture, re-enacting Kieran's last moments, I wondered how long it took to lose consciousness. Wouldn't a second-year med student have calculated all this? And why didn't he write a note? I couldn't believe he had nothing to say as he fingered the rope. I wanted to ask someone but there was no one to speak to about the shame and the guilt, what it meant. Eventually the batteries gave out on the little black tape recorder so I smashed it to pieces with a hammer in the backyard. Then I built a bonfire of his books in the corner of the garden and piled high all their Russian misery, their unhappy families, their ever-present suicide, whispering to him from their graves like sirens in treacherous waters, stealing him away. I watched them burn and I swore I would never be moved by a story again. I had recurring half-dreams, bloodstained water running over my hands down the sink. I kicked at Kieran's bed and screamed: what about the ones you leave behind? How do the undead ever move on? He had taken everything along with his life.

Dad stared out the teatime window until we both gave up on the wordless strain and picked at our plates in front of the TV, the evenings passing in a blur of sitcoms and canned laughter. I slopped through my homework, cutting every grade down to the bone. I slouched into a wilful and persistent under-achievement at school, learnt to hide my oddity behind a teenage mask of jaded non-engagement. My father sighed at my report cards and then just stopped bothering to read them. In his eyes a disconnect. A not-there. And as the years passed I tried my hardest not to be a comfort to him. Getting pissed, getting stoned, staying out all night. Sometimes I met him Sunday mornings in the hallway on his way to Mass and it was almost as if he wasn't sure who I was. 'You lucky bitch,' sighed Emer, twirling a bottle of blue nail varnish. 'You can do whatever you want.'

I low-balled into Arts at UCD. I skipped lectures and spent three years looking for answers in the stale air of the library. I read everything, a spine-numbing search through the chronicles of mankind's obsession with the mysteries of universe and mind, as if understanding could somehow kill the pain. But I never found an answer to my question. The one that stuck was Stekel's address at the 1910 symposium of the Vienna Psycho-Analytical Society: 'No one kills himself who has never wanted to kill another.' Suicide as murder transposed. I'd sit staring out the window at the stagnant lake, thinking, who was Kieran trying to kill? But the fact is my memory was fading, I was forgetting but I was still clinging onto anger. It seemed a safer place to be.

And then one afternoon in my final year I wandered into a campus milk-round, and was captivated by Steiner's sleek linguistic promise, the shoe-shine dazzle of applied corporate intelligence, the groomed and barely harnessed ambition. There was a pristine glow about the evangelical speakers that cast a dull pall over the whole auditorium, the campus, my life, my hair. And in the crisp white collars and impeccable suits I saw the first glimmer of a quick route out of stagnation to a place where I might want to be, where my special talent would be my passport. Something within began to shift, the first stirrings of a survival instinct. I had found a stepping-stone that would bridge the aching gap between the past and future.

A month later I stumbled off a plane onto a trading floor, where a hygienic-looking American managing director failed to ambush me in an interview chat about calculus and I thought, looking at the photo of his ranch in Wyoming: a performing dog can make good money in a place like this. And I did.

After three years hunched between my book towers in the library, it was a breeze to catapult from the back of the class to the number-one slot. On the day of the results the lecturers who had spent months issuing me warnings flitted round my First in effusive bewilderment, while the rest of my class slunk past, shooting resentful glances from under their mortar boards at the bandit who had stolen the show. The head of Ethics asked me if I'd like to come and have tea. The departmental head sidled up and asked if I'd considered a doctorate. But I could sense the circular emptiness of academic struggles, two thousand years trying to answer the same fucking question. I showed him my interview letter from Steiner's and his face creased into a sneering derision.

But I had a hunch that the energy of a repressed fury could fuel a great career, and I was right. I had found a kind of sheltered housing, a nice desk to rest my weary head, a little slot that fit so snugly, a place to call my own. An audience that would applaud my circus trick, a showering of corporate affections to fill the empty space: promotions, money, a cloak of power. Home is where the work is. Consumed by fourteen-hour days, a busyness that replaced distraction with exhaustion. And then one day, I realised I wasn't looking for answers anymore. Mostly it was like the past was someone else's movie. I had found a new virtual life, a historyless reinvention that I could almost believe in. To be so desired, to be so exactly loved that it could be quantified, that I could see it in the numbers – a big, fat, back-slapping cheque at the end of each year, isn't that all the proof a person needs? Like someone who wants to fuck you every minute of every day just to prove the extent of their love.

The window is aglow with the city's pulse. And in the top corner a sliver of moon. We may have slept a little, knocked out by the drone of stories and dream and the foul taste of the past. Pie Man stirs, swallows, passes a palm over his face and holds it there in the shaft of hallway light. His watch says 22:02. Rex yawns, raises his head and licks my free hand.

The mattress shifts. Pie Man shuffles round to my side, bends down and unties the dog lead. He lifts my arm and rubs it tenderly between his hands as if willing it back to life. And then he turns away, steps out into the hall and I hear him click the latch on the front door and retreat into the living room. I sit up. Rex stands, stretches and I swing my legs round and onto the floor but remain sitting, listening. The draught steals along the floor to my toes, there is a faint sound of footsteps down the corridor, a door closing with a distant bang. I grab at my scattered clothes, dress quickly. Rex watches, a low impatient whine. I grab my bag and creep barefoot into the hallway.

Pie Man sits on the couch in the living room, his fat head buried in his fat hands. He doesn't move. I pick up my shoes and edge backwards to the door. Rex stands guarding the space between us but Pie Man remains bent like a figure on stage who will stay till the curtains close. Rex trots ahead and I turn and I run down the corridor, the stairs, Rex taking the skittering lead, through the front door and out onto the night street.

10

clawback

wednesday 16 january 1991
22:26

Out of the crooked timber of humanity,
no straight thing can be made.
Emmanuel Kant

THE DOOR OPENS ONTO A creased and anxious caution.

'Geri—' Stephen pauses with a phone dangling in his left hand. Rex sits beside me, shockingly demure, not hurling himself at Stephen, not even looking at him, just leaning against my leg.

'Come in,' Stephen swings the door just a little too wide, looking into the space behind me as if expecting I'm not alone.

My lips part into what might seem like a crazed grin since I can't seem to find my voice. I step onto the mat and then sideways into the hall and out of his force field. Stephen mutters something into the receiver and hangs up.

He crouches down, 'Come on, Rex.' And Rex growls, low, faint, but a warning all the same. Stephen straightens up and moves back slowly and Rex slinks past him to my side.

Stephen scans me up and down – with my coatless shoulders, my bare legs, I am visible trouble in his hallway. He opens his mouth then clamps shut on whatever words he was about to speak. He is trying to read my agenda: is this howling revenge for the fuck or the fuckover? But even I do not know why I have come except that standing by the cab window with the rain whipping at my cheeks, my voice was dying, fading out like the sound of not being me anymore and Stephen's address was all I could produce.

'You – eh – you've cut your hand.' He looks at my bandaged knuckles. 'And your wrist is all swollen. Or something.' And the years of solicitous upbringing almost propel him towards me but he stops short. My teeth start chattering loudly as if a switch has been thrown. To touch him would be a high-voltage fry.

Stephen recovers his poise, shifts into crisis-aversion gear and announces that ice would be just the thing for that wrist. He disappears into the kitchen, urging me to shed my coat and sit down. He doesn't offer the living room.

All along the hallway are neat stacks of cardboard packing boxes that appear to be full. I stand rooted in the corridor, watching his grey T-shirt as he moves between the freezer and the cupboard, rattling on in an upbeat distant monologue about how he was just making some calls and watching *Newsnight* and the countdown to the war. He is keeping up a steady stream, as if his chatter could keep disaster at bay, like a charm to ward off evil. Like the way you'd try to calm an unannounced crazy who shows up late at night on your doorstep with a dog who used to love you but now clearly hates your guts. His bare feet squeak as he turns towards me with a Pyrex bowl of ice and a roll of kitchen towel. 'Here, this'll help.' I step obediently into the kitchen, drop my bag on the floor and sit down over a mug of black coffee. Rex slips under the table and settles in a ball at my feet.

I tear off three sheets of the white paper and fashion them into a jagged bag of ice, I pat and press it hard against my wrist. 'It burns.'

And Stephen says that will help, it will stimulate the blood flow and minimise bruising. Then he asks me in a quieter voice if I want to tell him what happened. 'No.' I raise my head to look at his face for the first time.

'Are you sure?' He considers me gravely. As you might examine an injured pet.

'Yes. I'm sure.'

■ ■ ■ ■ ■

I first stepped into this apartment on 3 July 1986, strolled straight into the kitchen, sat down on this very table right here, and lit a cigarette. Stephen leaned in the open doorway, jacket over his shoulder as I exhaled and said, 'So what are you going to do about it – kick me out?' He moved towards me, took the cigarette from my fingers and flicked it expertly behind him into the sink, lowering his head towards mine until it was so dark I couldn't see, but I could feel our lips part at precisely the same moment. For days afterwards I would slide my tongue around the inside of my mouth, trying to figure out how his kisses made me feel like coming.

'So you're moving?'

'Yes, actually,' says Stephen and looks behind to the hall as if he's checking the boxes are still there.

'Anywhere nice?'

'New York. To run the office there.'

'I'm not surprised. After this week's stunt you're ready for anything.'

'You're upset.' And he nods sadly, as if to say this is no more than he had expected.

'HAAH,' I hear myself laugh. Only Stephen could defuse this situation with an understatement that so completely captures the heart of the matter and the extent of the gulf between us. 'There is just one question I wanted to ask you.'

Anyone else would be wary of my rage but Stephen knows exactly where my boundaries lie and he does not feel at all threatened. I am not in the least bit dangerous. His assessment is, as always, correct, since it would seem that my anger has been entirely displaced by grief, a deep, low, raw and private gash.

'Shoot.' He leans against the door jamb, arms folded. Wriggles his naked toes. I look at him full face and, it seems for maybe the very first time, with clarity. Stephen is ready and prepared for all eventualities but answers are suddenly irrelevant. I see now that it was always the question that was important. All's fair in love and war and Stephen is precisely the man I know him to be.

'"My feet are at Moorgate, and my heart under my feet."' I offer up his favourite Eliot quote and he smiles. That will teach me to listen more carefully.

'And your question?'

I flick it away and he nods.

'But congratulations. New York is a big step. Even for you.'

'Thanks. I'm looking forward to a new challenge,' and with a professional smile he disappears down the hallway to the low-volume murmur of the TV.

The ice bag pulses and stings. I want to smoke. But I have done enough by showing up unannounced. I move towards the balcony doors, where I used to like standing barefoot, even in winter, turning my glass to keep the ice cubes circling until they melted, looking down on the street and the roofs of speeding cars heading north and south along Beaufort Street. In daytime you can just see a little brown section of the river from here. I used to stand in this spot and time the passing cars. The average number in a one-minute period between 1 and 2 p.m. at weekends is fifty-four. Between 1 and 2 a.m. it falls to seventeen and a third of those are cabs. The average rush-hour speed in Central London is 11 mph. The incidence of German cars is approximately 1 in 4, but of course that is very zone-specific, you can't extrapolate to a nationwide profile.

Night folds around me like an envelope, I can feel the cold rising ghostlike from the river, lapping like a wave around my feet. *Shut the door, it's freezing,* Stephen would say, so I'd close the door behind me, not ready to come in, not yet, needing to breathe. The hollow nightfall, the transition hours before sleep or not-sleep, before the sudden clarity that hits me at 2 a.m., where I used to think I could do some of my best work, if only there was something that needed doing. Night-trading I guess, but all the Asian openings were over there, not here.

Of course that is exactly what I should have done back then: switch countries. There are worse places than Hong Kong. I could have given Rex away temporarily to a good home, told Stephen to wait for me, to hold on, pretending that wasn't absurd, knowing the impossibility of maintaining a relationship at a distance. Or it would seem, even at close range. I hear the distant click of heels and lean over, looking down to my left where a lone girl picks her unsteady way along the pavement towards the Kings Road. Black or navy coat, white scarf, gloveless, shiny leather bag that keeps slipping down her shoulder, I half-shout 'HI', thinking it will somehow embolden or encourage, but she doesn't hear. If anything happens on Beaufort Street I will at least be a witness.

Rex twitches in sleep, makes that little whimper, perhaps he's dreaming we are still back in West Hampstead or maybe he's forgotten all about Pie Man now, maybe he's just dreaming of chasing rabbits in a field where the grass doesn't smell of car exhaust.

My arm aches, the ice pack is dripping cold lines of water. I lean over the railings and watch the girl disappear round the corner.

I can hear the TV and Stephen's silence down the corridor. I can smell the cold coffee in front of me and I look down at the table and a blue and silver plastic pen. Rolling it over between finger and thumb, I read:

Hotel Danieli   *Venezia*   *Tel : 00 41 522 6480.*

So he went back. With someone else, and to the hotel he'd wanted in the first place. And I remember the jolt as I smashed a heavy heel on the steps of the Cipriani on 20 July 1990, leaving an open-mouthed porter gaping down at the splintered entrails of gold plastic biro that I had ground into the stone. The only thing I could find that Stephen had touched and that I could break.

Rex barks so loud I jump. He hurtles into the hall, there is a scrabbling of keys and then a slam. I turn around in the chair to see her staring at Rex who does a U-turn and comes back to sit at my heel.

'You have keys,' I stare stupidly at the bunch in Zanna's hand. She opens her mouth, she is also staring at the keys and then she shoves them in her pocket as if the very sight of them is offensive. Stephen has come rushing down the corridor and is standing just out of my view, the third point in this triangle.

'It's not what you think,' she says. Stephen steps into view, they are standing shoulder to shoulder in the hall and I seem to be shrinking. Zanna's mouth takes on monstrous proportions. Stephen is gripped by a speechlessness that I have never previously witnessed. I am reeling backwards, scanning through our shared memories, searching desperately for the moment when I should have known, a point where it must have begun. But each scene self-destructs on contact as if these disconnected fragments never made a whole.

'I mean it, Geri,' she insists, 'nothing – happened till after.'

I make to walk out of the kitchen, through the gauntlet of two, when there is a loud explosion from the living room. 'IT'S STARTING,' shouts Stephen, running back down the hall, and we follow the call of the TV to a deep night sky illuminated by green flashes of anti-aircraft fire and an anchorman saying, We have John Holliday live from Baghdad telling us that the aerial bombardment of Baghdad has begun.

I hear the off-camera thud and John says, We can feel the ground of this hotel shaking as the attack continues. It's hard to tell, Bernard, but the closer targets appear to be government buildings. Can you see over there in the distance there are rose-red explosions about ten miles out of the city lighting up the sky.

The camera pans overhead for signs of the Allied bombers and Bernard's voice cuts in, I'm curious, John – you can barely hear any planes?

These are B52s flying at 55,000 feet, am I right?

Bernard taps his right ear. Sorry to interrupt, John, but we've just heard from Tel Aviv that Israeli civilians have been told to open their boxes, that's those boxes which contain gas masks and syringes of antidotes to nerve gas and a powder to decontaminate chemical weapons that—

Bernard is interrupted by the excited crackle of John's voice. It's like there are a hundred fireflies over to the west there, the blast that came through here a few minutes ago was like the blast you feel at Cape Canaveral when a rocket takes off, a huge wave of hot air came in right through our window here.

Stephen presses the remote and the scene jumps to a still of a concrete building with a live phone-in from some reporter in Saudi. The Al-Batin hotel is just a stone's throw from the Kuwaiti border, there's complete panic here, Trevor. A Saudi engineer just ran past me down the corridor shouting *war war war.*

Stephen flicks to BBC where Bush sits in the Oval Office, a flag draped by the window behind him and a smaller one on his desk. The world could wait no longer. We will not fail.

He jabs impatiently and Bernard returns. He is nodding vigorously at some army guy trapped in a video screen with two and a half rows of medals pinned across his chest. Make no mistake about it, this is serious hardware. We're talking F–16 Fighting Falcons, F–4G Wild Weasels, A–10 Thunderbolts, probably some F–15 Eagles and of course your F–117A Stealth bombers. That's on top of the B52s with twelve cruise missiles and eight short-range missiles apiece.

Zanna takes the remote from Stephen's hand and mutes the volume. Then she steps closer to me, reaches out a hand and reconsiders. Smoothes her fingers along her camel sleeve. It is the perfect coat for a crisis.

'I want you to know that I – that *we*—' she casts a prompting frown at Stephen, 'never deceived you.'

'No,' he nods, glancing at the screen. 'Absolutely not.'

'That nothing happened during—'

'Ever,' he adds.

There is a fireball in my throat, I am holding my breath lest it erupts but a small gurgling sound seems to come from my gullet. I am still shrinking, I am tiny now in this room between two giants. The floor rushes up to my face and I stick out a blind arm, Stephen's and Zanna's hands shoot out to steady me as you might a rocking boat, they hold me stable while the thud and boom of Baghdad's annihilation fills the air. And then I am propped between them, they hold me upright, like a toddler about to take its first steps. And I feel that this is somehow where I have always been, in a state of containment. But it is high time I took some of my own weight. I have been a willing captive for far too long. I have been holding my breath and there is logic now in the full and complete withdrawal of the occupying forces of the heart.

'We never lied,' Zanna stares meaningfully at Stephen who looks affronted, as if the idea of deception is so preposterous that it does not need addressing.

'There was no lying,' he confirms again, formally, like an expert witness.

I give her sleeve a little tug. 'Repeat after me, Zanna,' I say. She stares at me with a look of magnified alarm. Her face is moon pale, the TV light casts a flickering glow over the shadow-filled room. And I hear the flood roar as the dam bursts open between us and all our years are swept neatly away as we plunge into an uneasy silence, the strangeness expanding to fill the space between us. We have reached the breakpoint in our friendship and the stage is set for a bitter ending, a severance that will be final. Zanna's voice already petering out into the future distance.

'Repeat after me.' I manage a smile. She releases her grip on my arm, shoots a glance to Stephen and he lets his hand fall away.

And I do not stumble. The picture fades into stark contrast and everything is bleached out in a white light of grief. It is not what I thought at all. And I am the last to arrive.

Stephen picks up the ringing phone and snaps, 'Yeah, I know,' and then he kills the war show.

'I need to go to the office,' he announces.

'And I should too,' says Zanna.

Rex is already standing by the front door, his nose pressed into the seal. Stephen bends to pet him but Rex is having none of it. He snaps his head away with a regal stare and pads unbidden out the door, leads the way and down the stairs.

'You got your car?' Stephen takes the steps in a light run.

'No.'

'We – *you* – could drop Geri home first,' Zanna prompts. She stands passenger side in the open door gathering her long coat about her, her face sallow in the streetlight. Stephen hesitates, jangles his key and I know he's running the logisitics. Home is west, work is east. 'Or I could drop you at the office.'

'I'm taking a cab home,' and I turn away, feeling their eyes like leeches on my back. Rex gamely nuzzles my hand like he's cheering me on. There is something here about dignity and I am learning fast. Almost immediately I see the approaching yellow cab light bearing down like an angel to deliver me from this misery. The driver looks at Rex who sits on the pavement looking for all the world like the model dog and he says OK and we bundle into the back. Rex does not whine or try to climb on my lap but settles himself demurely at my feet. It seems he is ready to rise to the occasion, make the transition. He is ready for the hard stuff up ahead. The big dog stuff.

Through the window I see Stephen pull out and drive away with a hand signal salute, the sort of generic gesture that clearly signals there is nothing left unspoken, there are no outstanding issues or lingering doubts and all our history has been perfectly erased. Stephen is liberated from the trench warfare of our relationship and has moved on into the exhilarating embrace of new hostilities with a guaranteed pay-off. I watch the tail lights recede in the drizzle and I know that this is the last I will ever see of him.

00:46

AND THEN I REMEMBER THE KEYS.

I scrabble in the soft shell of my bag, rooting for the metal tag and then dump the contents of the bag on the seat to prove what I already know – my keys are not here. They are in the pocket of the coat that lies still in Pie Man's lair, unless he has burnt it by now to destroy all traces of my presence. One spare set is at Zanna's and the other is in the office, in my desk drawer and I am swearing at the bag, swearing at Stephen because it is in some way all his fault. I am too tired by far for this carry on, bobbing along the Kings Road after an eternity of captivity, this time of night, this time of *war* is not the right moment for anyone to have to wonder what the hell they're doing with their life.

'Actually we need to go to the City,' I tell the cabbie and he shrugs as if to say this change of plan is a mere detail compared to what is going on in the larger world. The radio keeps up its urgent commentary on the sketchy war news and I am cold, cold to the heart and bone and nothing but the reflection of my own circumstances visible in the pane glass. Rex rests his head on my shoe and yawns. I switch off the overhead light as we head along the Embankment and I see it is true that water shines silver under moonlight and that red cars have low visibility at night. In a few hours' time this dead zone will come alive, tubes rushing to fill the empty vacuum of empty platforms, the city in the grip of the alarm clock of war.

The security guard is watching TV with his feet up on the desk and his back to the counter. He slides the file towards me without taking his eyes off the screen. 'Hey,' he calls and when I head towards the lift Rex shows up on the security camera. 'I'm locked out,' I explain, 'and this is a real emergency.' He waves me on. War changes all the rules.

The deserted trading floor is a Pompeii of chairs at odd personalised angles. Cheap biros on open reports, crushed Coke cans, overflowing ashtrays and, above, the heat and hum of unmanned hardware, like an abandoned spacecraft looking for command. We don't switch off our life-support when we are leaving in the evening, just in case the machines might never start again in the morning.

My desk is a wailing wall of Post-its on the phone board. I yank open the trestle drawer and YES, there are my keys. Rex rummages in a bin, fishes out an empty yogurt carton and wanders off in search of food. I sit down, write my name on the open notebook over and over and over again until I have filled the whole page and then I shred it, float the pieces on the floor.

I get up and walk over to the bank of overhead TVs, turn up the volume on CNN where Larry Register is live from Jerusalem, toughing it out in a gas mask, waiting for scuds that might be laced with chemicals. The anchorman, who is safely tucked away in Atlanta, asks Larry if he really shouldn't be evacuating the building. But Larry isn't listening, he's busy opening windows and ringing up his colleagues in Tel Aviv to ask if they're seeing any scuds and dangling microphones outside to hear what's happening in the night sky.

There's a clicking behind me and I look over at a green sales line blinking on the phone board. I pick up the receiver onto a familiar long-distance crackle.

'Geraldine.'

'Felix.'

'You were lost and now you are found.'

'How did you know I would be here at this time of night?'

'We are at war, my dear, and you are running out of places to hide.'

'I wasn't *hiding*, Felix. I was being held against my will.'

He sighs, clicks his lips faintly. 'Your instinct for self-preservation has deserted you. You have been lurching about like a stray kitten, taking unnecessary risks.'

'I escaped. I got away.'

'You need protection. You won't survive in this jungle.'

Rex pads over and drops an empty sandwich carton at my feet. I lean down to scratch his head and reassure, but perhaps he has already forgotten the night's adventures.

'So Felix, did you know that Stephen would betray me?'

'Your own trusting heart betrayed you, Geraldine. Your pillow talk. You were the victim of your own indiscretion. Did you really believe that Stephen Graves was different to all the others?'

'You could have warned me when I came to see you.'

'I did rather sound the most obvious alarm when I told you that he had been to see me. But it seems he has the most appalling effect on your concentration. You were not paying attention. You have not been paying attention for some time, Geraldine. If you had been listening, you might have guessed that Stephen had found a white knight. The clue was there in our conversation.'

'Did you set me up?'

Felix makes a noise like laughing. 'My dear, you set yourself up all the time. There is always someone using you.'

A flood of war headlines surges across the screen. Larry turns to talk to a colleague, their heads so close it looks as if the snouts of their gas masks are kissing.

'I saw Stephen tonight. I called round to his flat.'

'How very dramatic. Tell me, was it an ugly confrontation?'

'He has a new woman. She is – was – my best friend.'

'Poor Geraldine, betrayed at every turn. You must toughen up if you are to survive this world of beasts. What a tawdry end to this theatre. And a very shabby performance by Kapoor, I must say.'

Tick-tick goes the greenback, steady under fire. Felix's breathing hisses in my ear. Larry's masked head is shaking mournfully now, like an S&M hopeful who has changed his mind too late.

'So tell me, Felix, what did you do in the end?'

'British Electronics is a much better bet than Texas Pistons. The MOD will not object to a domestic buyer.'

'And Otto's deathbed request?'

'Ah, Geraldine. The ethics of investment. Perhaps you should apply yourself to some real work in that area.'

I light up a cigarette, kick off my shoes and warm my feet in Rex's fur.

'Goethe once said that reading Kant was like stepping into a brightly lit room.' His voice is faint now, as if the receiver is some distance from his mouth. 'Did I ever tell you that I learnt German specifically to be able to read Kant without the screen of translation? He proved to be disappointingly ponderous and repetitive. A wearying excess of words. Very Prussian.'

I hear his fingers tap the Reuters buttons, like a secret code.

'I have a business proposal for you, my dear.'

'Too late. I'm guessing the Grope has already fired me in absentia.'

'On the contrary, the landscape has changed. I spoke to your boss a little while ago.'

'You spoke to him?'

'I wanted him to understand that Steiner's would lose *all* of my business if you were to leave the firm. And naturally the loss of my order flow would simply add to the long list of problems that have tarnished his reputation in the past few days. Especially if you were to resurface at the competitor of my choice.'

'What did he say?'

'Under the circumstances, he was very enthusiastic.'

'I'll bet.'

'There is one condition.'

'Oh yeah?'

'Your relocation would be immediate. I told him that you have twenty-four hours to arrive.'

My Reuters shudders and blinks. 'Why are you doing this, Felix?'

He pauses, a low vibrating hum like a distant tuning fork. 'Because I want to see what you will do. Because I find that I cannot calculate the odds. And this is a problem that engages me.'

'So you want to force my hand.'

'It is time for you to grow up and take charge, Geraldine. To put aside your childish ways, to decide, to make a *choice*. Become your own master.'

'Why me?'

'Perhaps you should think of me as a patron. You will never find a greater admirer of your talents. But you need to remain interesting for me to keep you alive. There are plenty of ciphers out there. I want you out at the coalface, here in Hong Kong. It is time for all of us to see what you are really capable of.'

Felix exhales in my ear. I stare at Larry's masked face. The camera jolts to an arm snaking a mic out of a window into the blackness. There is a muffled shout and then the long crescendo of an air raid siren.

'What do you really want, Felix?'

'What was Russell's desire? Do you remember?'

'"I have wished to understand the hearts of men. I have wished to know why the stars shine. And I have tried to apprehend the Pythagorean power by which number holds sway above the flux."'

'I would like a diversion from the monotony of consistent out-performance. And I am not finished with you. In fact we have barely begun.'

The anchorman urges Larry and the guys to be careful, a professional catch in his voice as he reminds us viewers that we are in the live presence of reckless heroism.

'But what about what *I* want to do?'

'I am not at all convinced that you are the best judge of that, Geraldine. And in any case, I am not interested in your grubby narrative. I am only interested in the development of the plot.'

'How the story ends.'

'If you will.'

'And if I say no?'

'You simply have to choose between sudden death and a glorious redemption.'

A screen arm reaches up to switch off a desk light and Jerusalem is plunged into darkness. The anchorman's voiceover explains that Larry believes they could be sitting ducks, that he has switched off the lights or maybe even smashed them.

'Remember Kant. "I ought never to act except in such a way that I could also will that my maxim should become universal law." Discontent can be our liberator, it can spur us on to our destinies.'

The anchorman tells Larry they'll be back soon and the screen freezes on a still of the lone mic dangling from the window. He tells us with audible disappointment that Larry might have left the hotel room. His latent survival instinct has kicked in and Larry has chosen life, cutting short this gripping dance with danger. I hear the collective sigh of a global frustration as the insomniac audience is denied the thrill of the office being blown up during a live transmission.

'My offer expires in twenty-four hours. What we have, you and I, Geraldine, could be a marriage of minds.'

Rex stands up and pads towards the double doors, turns his head to look back at me. 'Did you know that Nietzsche once described marriage as a grand conversation?'

'"Do that which will render thee worthy of happiness"?' I say and pick up my keys.

'You are losing something in the translation.'

'I'm leaving now, Felix.'

'My driver will be waiting to collect you at the airport.'

02:02

REX STANDS IN FRONT OF ME, ears cocked, listening to the ringing phone. I stroke his head but he's been restless ever since we got back home and wonder if he picked up this phone sensitivity from me. I once read about a girl who had a bird phobia and her spaniel copied it, fled whimpering from pigeons in the park. The ringing stops and the answerphone clicks and silently records my fate. I go into the bathroom and Rex follows me on high alert, scenting the winds of change.

I sit on the couch and wait for the Grope to call again. Rex hops onto my lap as I pick up the receiver.

'Geri, *finally*. Been trying to get you forever.'

'You could say I've been tied up.'

'We were – concerned. You were kinda off the radar there. No one knew—'

'You wanted to find me so you could fire me.'

'Hey, let's not jump to conclusions here. You went AWOL.'

'I was being held captive.'

There is a faint intake of breath as if he has just stopped himself saying something. 'Well, what can I tell you, Geri, it's been quite a week.' He sighs. 'Oh yes, quite a week.'

'I spoke to Felix a little while ago.'

'Great, that's great. So you're up to speed.'

'He told me you'd made a deal about me. That he'd made you an offer you couldn't refuse.'

'Look – the important thing is, like I said to Felix, Hong Kong was *always* on the cards, Geri.'

'So you're *not* firing me now?'

'Like I said to Felix, I know you'll do a great job out there. This is a terrific opportunity for you and I'm more than happy for you to be on the first flight out of here.'

'So Steiner's can keep all his business.'

The Grope sighs long and heavy. 'Geri, take it from me. This experience has been a lesson you will never forget.' His voice has already shifted into archive. He will be moved himself very soon and without a patron. 'This move is coming at exactly the right time in your career. You're a lucky girl in the eleventh hour.'

'My grandmother always said you make your own luck.'

'Sounds like a great lady.'

'She's dead.'

'Right.' He clears his throat. 'Well, I'll leave you to it. Let you get a couple of hours sleep. Julie will have your tickets ready as soon as you come in. And she'll sort out everything with the apartment, et cetera, anything you need. So you just get yourself on that plane straight away and start looking for a nice condo. Castigliano will give you a few tips, he's real happy to have you there, got all sorts of plans. See you in a few hours.'

I put the phone down on my new best friend.

11

futures and options

thursday 17 january 1991
10:46

'BEFORE ANYONE ASKS,' I wave my bandaged hand, 'I fell over and thank you, I'm fine.' Rob's anxious face relaxes into a grinning head shake. Al slaps me on the back and says he assumed I'd slipped off a bar stool in Hong Kong.

There is an air of focused energy about the brisk rows of white shirts and a steady war hum. Paper Union Jacks sprout from monitors and the backs of chairs all along the UK desk, they are even hung underneath the bank of overhead TVs. Over at SPUD there is a blank space where Pie Man should be. His desk is cleared of paperwork and freshly dusted. The screens removed. The geeks are clustered round their boss, trying not look as if they are missing a limb. And I know without asking that he is gone, high-tailed out of the complications, having calculated that his chance of getting away with everything would be much improved if he disappeared. He may have fled West Hampstead. May even have flung himself under a train. Or he could be sitting somewhere amidst a sea of Tesco bags, eating himself to death. But it's far more likely that he's already interviewing with Bankers Trust down the road who will welcome him with open arms. And Pie Man will take it all the way. One day I will read about him in the business pages. He has only temporarily left the stage. And deep down we both know my trouble is all of my own making. It is time to grow up and pick up the reins, time to take the next step, for history is what you make of it. And there is no such thing as a victim.

Rob laughs down the phone but he is still staring at me across the monitors, the scissors stalled in his right hand above a large cut-out flag on the front page of the *Sun*. I watch the red and green lights, remembering how we used to have touchscreen phones and how it took so long for the novelty to wear off and then we got Seaq on our PCs and that was fun for a while and then our disposable income took a leap and that was great too. But it seems like nothing lasts.

'You wish, mate, you wish.' His right hand extending the flex, his other now writing a ticket. And I'm thinking: you get born, you grow up and then maybe there is a moment when you realise that this is all there is, a hamster wheel of sensation and your whole life up to this point has only ever been about that lesson. Dreams of possibility start slipping like silk from your shoulders and there is nothing left to do except turn your slap-burnt face away and drink a little more, party a little harder, jam that nose right into the grindstone and watch the bank account swell. You carry on because the wheel keeps spinning and, hey, there is always the chance that you might find something worth having, that you wouldn't just end up sitting there watching your hands turn to dust.

The first day I came for interview at Steiner's, I spilled coffee down myself while I sat waiting in HR. By amazing good fortune I happened to be wearing a mandarin collar shirt that buttoned on the shoulder so I could reverse it. I was, as the secretary told me, ever so lucky. I guess I took this as confirmation of truth and never looked back.

I remember going to Principles and buying a black velvet suit with a cropped jacket for thirty quid, which was a fortune. The day I wore it, I thought I'd arrived. I thought I was the biggest power dresser on Moorgate. That suit was going to get me anywhere, would open all doors. But then every time I got somewhere, I felt it wasn't where I'd wanted to be. And now I look around me – the trading floor, the bodies – and I see that this is not a test drive, that I'm already way down the road. This is, I realise, the loss of innocence and I have to laugh out loud; whoever would have thought it? That there really is a time when you can't get it back, when you've jumped beyond the sand mark and into a new age.

'Hey, Castigliano, my man. How's it going?' Al stands up. 'Yeah, Geri's here, returned from the abyss, looks a little worse for wear but I'm sure she can explain all that.'

'Geri. Tried to call you at home but I guess it was a long night.'

Tom wants to tell me about a really cool apartment coming up soon 'cos Franklin is going back to New York and he'll take me to see it at the weekend and I picture a cab's slow climb up to Mid-levels where the rooftop swimming pools are too hot to use in summer. So much happening out here, Tom says. On my screen amid the urgent scroll of headlines is the news that city officials have cancelled the carnival in Venice citing concerns about the war and the threat of terrorism. I watch Reuters blink and embellish, and all possibilities seem equally likely.

Rob stands up, his curved palm slips a note to Greg the boot boy, who lopes wordlessly about the floor collecting shoes and sits on his orange box against the back wall of the trading floor, working the dazzle on the leather. Once I stuck my foot out when he was taking Al's and he hesitated, then nodded. Later, on my way to the loo, I saw all the Oxfords and Brogues arranged in a semicircle around Greg's box and his hand inside my pump, the spiked heel gripped tight between his thighs. He looked up, reddened and froze. All right Greg, I muttered and hurried away but when he returned the shoes, Greg ignored the note I held out and shuffled off and I knew that I had somehow crossed a line, stirred a silent ripple through the manwaters.

'Boys and girls, we have some news,' says Rob. 'Old Greg here is starting at Tullett's next week.' He slaps him on the back. 'They're giving him a shot at the big time.'

'No kidding,' says Al. 'Congrats.' Greg beams. And I wonder how the shoeshine boy will look in a shirt and tie, all larged up, a moneybroker.

'Movin' on up, movin' on up,' Rob sings into the receiver. 'Nothing can stop us – here Jonno, JONNO. I hear you're taking on Greg. So you need to get yourself round here to do my shoes instead. Arf arf.'

I turn to the window behind me, spread my hands on the cold sill. A small nameless city bird hurls itself from a rooftop and careers wildly in front of the window and then spins away towards a triangular shoal that dips in formation and dives gracefully out of view.

'All be over in a few weeks,' Al muses, patting Schwarzkopf's wall poster which is already looking a little tired.

'Only if you get the guy,' says Rob.

'Who?'

'Saddam, that's who. Got to finish the job, Al. You don't leave the bastard out there to play games. 'Cos next thing you know he'll rise from the ashes and you've got a whole army of towel heads rising up against you. I mean, you Shermans just don't get it.'

'Yeah, right. We don't get it. This is *our* party remember?'

'And we invented foreign policy, mate. Who d'you think founded Iraq anyway? We've been everywhere, civilised the whole world. Fucking *discovered* you lot, put you on the map. And I'm telling you right now: you haven't won a war if the fucking crazy is still IN CHARGE! Am I right, Geri? You're a Paddy, you tell him. Here we are years after we left that little pain in the butt island of Micks right next door and they're *still* giving us gyp. The I-R-fucking-A is still running around with Semtex blowing up kids. And why? I'll tell you why. Because we let them get away with it. When we should have killed every last one of them.'

What Rob does not see is that Joe has taken up position right behind his chair, the phone cable stretched out behind him. His narrow head is cocked to one side, a deep furrow between his brows. And the whole Jap desk has fallen silent, they're watching their master who has stepped outside his magic circle and who seems, for possibly the first time ever, to be paying attention to something that's happening outside his Jap bubble. Rob spouts on oblivious, wagging a pencil in one hand until he sees that Al is looking not *at* him, but *behind* him. He stops mid-stream and spins around.

'All right, Joe,' says Rob. But Joe does not look down, does not even appear to have heard him speak. He takes a step closer, a movement light and tense, as if he might spring up to head a ball at any moment.

'Al,' says Joe and we all turn to look at Al, whose existence Joe has never acknowledged until this moment. The phones flash and click and the Jap traders fan out like a silent chorus behind Joe and it seems like everything has hushed while we wait.

'You ever see *The Magnificent Seven*, mate?' asks Joe.

'Yul Brynner?' Al slides his hands into his pockets as if bracing himself for a remark that could topple him. 'Yeah, sure.' Joe nods gravely and Al grins, emboldened. '"In this line of work, we are not all alike. Some care nothing about money. Others, for reasons of their own, enjoy only the danger."'

'"And the competition?"' shoots Joe.

'"If he is the best with a knife and a gun, with whom does he compete?"'

'"Himself."'

We wait expectant but the impromptu theatre has ended. Joe steps a little closer, now he is right by Rob's chair. 'So you know what happened in the end?' his voice soft, his bright eyes trained on Al as if he is fixing prey.

'Sure,' says Al, affecting nonchalance with a shoulder shrug. 'They saved the village.'

'And how exactly did they do that?'

'How?' Al repeats, stalling. At Columbia they teach you to avoid stating the obvious, or at the very least to know when the obvious is exactly what is required. And so Al buys time while he scans through the range of permutations, wondering if this is just such a moment and if his reputation, which is – let's face it – not exactly hitting the high-water mark, could be rescued or destroyed in an exchange that has all the feel of a gun-slinging showdown. It's a binary outcome and the scent of a virtual humiliation is in the air. We are hanging by a thread here.

'Did they let the bad guys walk away?' Joe whipcracks the phone cord against his thigh. Rob flinches in his chair.

'No, they did not,' says Al. 'They killed them all.'

'That's right, they killed 'em all. Every last one.'

Heads bob in silent consensus.

'You always kill the bad guy,' says Joe. ''Cos if you don't...'

'The bad guy just comes back and kills you,' says Al on cue.

Rob exhales. The bewildered chorus that is the Jap desk exhale. Joe tips forward as if he is taking a bow for his performance and raises the receiver to his ear. 'You still there, mate?' he barks and spins away, back to his pitch, pulling on the black cord as if he is reeling himself into shore.

Al is already back on the blower beside me, squeezing his mini football, spinning some yarn about a bomb-proof tech stock to one of his Swiss clients. The PC screens flicker and the lights blink a power surge and I wonder what a life would be without all this. Once there was a five-minute cut on the floor and the place stopped and we just stood around looking helpless. Dead black phones hooked in metal desk clips like cardiac chargers. Without the screens and the chargers we are nothing. They feed us, give us the power to carry on.

I remember a jaded Saturday on an extended business trip to Tokyo when I took a spontaneous bullet train out of the city to kill a few hours that shopping couldn't. Stepped off at Nikko in the countryside air and walked northwards through tapered streets of shuttered houses. Crossed a footbridge over a clear rush of water where a passing crocodile of giggling girl guides stared at me and I stumbled on what looked like a cemetery. Row upon manicured row of miniature stone Buddha statues with red rags tied around their stone heads. That evening in a heaving whisky bar in Roppongi I asked Yoko-san what they were. *Self-immolators*, he replied in perfect East Coast. *The families come to tie the red ribbons, like you guys would bring flowers.*

So circle the wagons, it's time to go. Asia has long since gone to bed and Europe will soon be out to lunch while the East Coast files for the subway. A temporary hush will settle on the floor, while the screens still blink. A surreal silence, on the brink as we wait for the next move.

I grab my bag and switch off my Reuters. Al looks up puzzled in mid-flow so I smile, pat him on the shoulder, give him a little salute. He carries on talking, watches me walk around the desk to stand behind Rob who is making a whooping noise into the phone and tapping his screen. He waves Bud Light to run a ticket over to the stock desk and clicks mute.

'You had me worried there when you didn't show. What's up, G?' he brushes his hand lightly along the inside of my bandaged hand. 'You really OK?'

'Yeah, fine.' It isn't difficult to smile at him.

'Well, you look like shit,' he grins and his touch is gone.

He clicks the receiver. 'Fuck's sake, Jonno, keep your shirt on. I'm here.' And as I turn away Rob calls out where am I going because there is a block of that Amgen up for grabs but he's got to take it right now and what do I think, would Felix care before the stock opens?

'Dunno,' I swing round and spread my arms wide.

'But what do you think?'

'I think that if you can't take a risk, you might as well be dead,' I say and start the long private walk up through the bank of desks, past the hunched shoulders and the bobbing warrant traders.

The Grope leaps up, all teeth, when I appear in the doorway. Julie comes in to give me my travel wallet and he says something about a great result. He pats me on the shoulder – carefully as if I might shatter at his touch. Then as I turn to leave, he grabs my hand and he's shaking it and holding on as if he's clinging to a rock, and he seems smaller and oddly transparent as if he is fading into outline. He is vanishing, he is yesterday already and I know that I will never see him again.

I retrieve my hand and back out the door and I'm talking without saying anything, it's just my mouth that's moving, every other part of me is already gone.

But it seems that in the end all of this is easy now, oh so much easier than Rex grinning in the rear view at seven this morning, excited at having his full range of toys in the boot with him, maintaining an urgent whine all the way to Richmond Park. He ran off across the crisp dark grass and I followed him up through the spare wood and out onto the wide grassy slope that rolls down to the road. In the centre of the space in front of me a man flew a model plane, red with a grey stripe along the side. When it landed, he ran towards it holding his sports jacket tight round his body. He was short and fat and out of breath. I bent to pick it up for him, but he shouted: 'No no, leave it, I'll get it,' waving his hands like he was in distress. I stretched out my arm, thumb upturned and erased him. There was something crumbling inside me, this desire to cry.

I found the place without much of a problem with the vet's biroed directions on my knee. A long line of houses with deep gardens set back from the road and a stone's throw to the Park. Oh, but it was just the hardest thing. Rex leapt right out of the car as if he was arriving home or something and ran off to chase a collie bitch who came flying out from the back of the house. Leaving me with the woman who looked like she had sounded on the phone, sort of shapeless and with a creased, smiling face. While I unloaded Rex's toys and blanket and crate of dog food and his vaccination card and leads, she kept saying, 'Are you sure you won't have some tea, dear,' even though she knew I couldn't do that.

Rex came hurling towards us with the collie in hot pursuit and disappeared through a gap in the hedge. I lit a cigarette and, looking mostly up at the sky, said a few unnecessary things about his habits and stuff, things she didn't need to know but that I needed to tell her. A way of spinning it out. And then I stubbed the cigarette on the ground and said, 'Well, I'll be off then.'

She touched my arm and said, 'Don't you worry,' and she called Rex and he came to her panting, with flecks of saliva on the fur of his neck where the collie had been play-biting.

He stood lolling his hot pink tongue like a cartoon dog and I went to hug him, but this huge lump rose in my throat and my face got all hot so I mumbled 'Thanks' without looking at her and fled to the car. The woman stood on the pavement, Rex beside her with his ears cocked, tongue hanging loose and happy and I drove off and they got smaller in the mirror, the tears pouring down my face so that when I got to the corner I had to stop because I couldn't see and I had to scream just once to ease the pressure in my throat. Sitting there with the engine running and my head pressing into the steering wheel, these snapshots – Rex the fluffy puppy, Rex sitting in the bath, Rex cowering at the vet's, Rex slobbering over his tennis ball – they flashed past and I thought I'd lose my mind, but eventually I got the tears under control and headed on eastwards. Feeling, Christ, just feeling so much older. Like I was missing a limb or something. Like I was finally and completely alone.

12

scorched earth

12:21

THE STREETS ARE WARMING UP to lunchtime but the bar is empty when I walk in and find him behind his pristine counter polishing glasses.

'So, Faustino, what would you say if I told you I was kidnapped by a man for a whole day?'

He puts down the glass, folds the cloth over his shoulder and stares at me. 'He hwan money for you?'

'You mean ransom? No, he didn't want money.'

'What he wan if no money? He shakes his head, leans closer. 'He hwan you do sex?'

'Maybe. But he didn't force me.'

Faustino spreads his arms wide on the bar. 'What he hwan?'

'I think maybe he just wanted to teach me an important lesson.'

'Ah. Is very fucked up people.'

'Yes. Very fucked up.'

'How you get haway?

'I told him a story and then he just opened the door.'

He frowns, runs a doubtful finger along the fine line of his chin.

'You don't believe me, do you, Faustino?'

'Sure, sure. We all love good story.' He reaches down and places the Absolut bottle on the counter. 'You hwan double?'

'No, Faustino.' I offer him a hand. 'I just came to say goodbye.'

Zanna was on the phone when I walked into her office. She stood immediately and began to wrap up the call, with none of the usual imperious hand signals holding me at bay.

'Geri,' she said with strained formality when she'd put down the receiver.

'I came to say goodbye.'

'You're going already? Now?' I could hear the hesitation in her intent, she was testing our shallow waters, wondering if a breathing space could retrieve the situation. But we both know that there isn't a route map back to the beginning, that friendship is supposed to be about sharing the manageable best until the fun wears out and life really is too short to stick around patching up old baggage.

'My car's waiting downstairs.'

'I was going to tell you that I will be leaving too—'

'Going back to New York? Yes. It figures.' And I can picture her already tripping along Wall Street in her early morning sneakers, expertly outmanoeuvring the flooding suits.

She nods, twisting her lips to the side. 'In the spring. It's been decided.'

'That's nice,' I say. 'So you can both be together.'

She opens her mouth but reconsiders. The taste of humble pie hard to take.

'So what about Rex?'

'Dogs are like kids, you know, they need a stable home.' I touch the glass iceberg, press down hard on the jagged edges and when I turn my palm over there are little pink pressure spots.

'Anything you need a hand with just ask,' her voice almost a whisper.

'There is just one thing.'

'Go ahead.' She steels herself for the payback she deserves. Moves round the desk to face me and I realise for the first time that I am actually a good couple of inches taller than her, which is something I never noticed in all these years.

'Anything,' she says for she is ready. And this is the Zanna I know, who is always closing or seizing the moment, who never stands in a queue. There is a defiant tilt to her chin as she waits for my axe to fall, and the petty curiosity drains from me and is replaced by a surge of memory: the first time I saw her, the first time she strode onto the trading floor swinging that bob; I can see her fixing my mascara in the ladies at the Ritz, *look up, Geri, and for Chrissake don't blink*; I can feel her hand on my back as she looks over my shoulder in the mirror and I know that she is exactly who she purports to be. She is Rosanna P. Vermont and history may have separated us from a future but the past doesn't have to be revised. There is something about good faith in the air. She is not un-brave. She doesn't scurry off to hide in a cave. She will live and die by the sword and she will always face the music.

'What?' she says now, for Zanna is ready to count the cost.

'Repeat after me.'

.   She cocks her head.

'Repeat after me,' I say again and her puzzled face breaks into a smile.

'Repeat after me,' she whispers shakily and I see her eyes tear up. She twitches her nose against this unfamiliar sensation and I reach out to pat her shoulder but my hand flounders in the space between us and just brushes the side of her arm. Zanna bites her lip hard and I walk through the open door and out into the corridor with that last picture of her. The bitten lip, the useless tears, my flailing hand.

I will try to remember her this way just because I can. And I will try to remember us intact. It is a beginning.

■ ■ ■ ■ ■

I dump my suit carrier and slam the door. The driver says how it's not such a great time to be travelling and then we head off through the City streets. He keeps up a monologue about the war and how he wishes he had CNN and I'm thinking how these days never get fully light. We inch through the West End in a receding drizzle and every single thing I see looks like it's melting away.

I imagine Pie Man hunched over a café table in Liverpool Street chewing over some algorithms; he has scoped out what Bankers Trust are up to and he is electrified by possibility. He reaches for the second Eccles cake and his hand freezes, paralysed over the plate. He kicks back the chair, gathers his papers together and strides out. Hurries purposefully forwards and breaks into a run along Bishopsgate, he is chasing the shadow of a big fat boy and in a moment he will outrun him and take flight for the very first time.

I picture the Grope opening his display cabinet and fingering the mementos, releasing the ghosts, all sorts of past tense rushing up to greet him. They have talked it over and Lauren says maybe it's time. He hears the thunk of a chip shot on the green in Fort Lauderdale: Lauren reminds him of the grandchild they will be able to see. He flicks a speck of dust from the Stars 'n' Stripes. Better not to wait for the call, better to call time yourself. Better to throw in your own towel than have it ripped from your body. He turns away and picks up the phone to New York.

And down the road, in a high-speed lift on London Wall, Stephen adjusts his cufflinks. Accepts the approving nod from his reflection in the mirrored panelling. A bell chimes, the doors glide apart and a burst of executive sunlight blinds his eyes as he walks forward into the heavenly glow of the Chairman's office, his hand already outstretched.

All these endings streaming out behind me like a kite tail.

■ ■ ■ ■ ■

As we hit the M4 the driver makes a dash for the inside lane and silence invades the car like an extra passenger. My suit carrier flops against my feet and I notice it's light for a one-way trip. But the things I need for a life are things I do not yet own. And there is plenty of time.

'You never said where you were going, love,' says the driver, pulling up at Departures. I put my bag on the ground and lean into the open window to hand him the fare.

'A long way.'

'Nice day for it,' he says and smiles at a sudden January sunshine.

Terminal 4 glitters coolly inside. I stand still in the middle of the concourse and look up at the blinking lights on the board. DELHI – NEW YORK – HONG KONG – CHICAGO – SINGAPORE – HARARE – SAN FRANCISCO.

On the other side of the world I picture Felix at his desk with the harbour lights winking behind him, his face illuminated by the green glow of the screens, a faint smile playing about his lips as he calculates the odds. *It is time for you to grow up and take charge, Geraldine. To decide, to make a choice. Become your own master.*

I close my eyes and concentrate on my breathing and for the first time it actually works. I can feel an unencumbered rise and fall of the lung, waves breaking on a cooling sand, a caressing homesickness for a place I have never been. I am shedding the crinkled years like a stale skin.

At the ticket desk it is just as I expected – what with the war and everything there is plenty of long-haul availability, tickets for anywhere you want to go. I look up at the board again and the salesgirl waits patiently for me to say something and then smiles and taps everything into her screen. Swipes my credit card and slots the ticket into a wallet. Says, 'Have a nice flight.'

I walk back outside and light a cigarette, standing on the edge of the pavement breathing kerosene fumes in through my mouth, the muffled scream of planes and a chatter of arriving stewardesses trailing their overnights and clutching their hats against a sharp wind.

I open my bag, take out the two ticket wallets and hold them level in front of me. Read the itineraries printed on the flaps:

16:15 LHR – HONG KONG
16:30 LHR – SAN FRANCISCO

I think of the Big Fucking Ticket all those years ago that was the beginning of all this. And I have to look up and smile at the open skies, for this is the moment where I write the ending. So I let one life drop to the ground with a smack and walk quickly inside.

I am ready to take the wheel.

I am already there.

acknowledgements

THE STORY THAT FELIX TELLS GERI about Vulkan Valve was inspired by the history of Plessey, the British electronics and defence company which was the subject of a hostile takeover by GEC-Siemens in September 1989.

I am very grateful to the Yaddo Foundation, New York where I twice lost and found this book. Thanks to Mac and Michael for critical early support and to all at Serpent's Tail and Profile whom I omitted to mention on two previous occasions.

Very special thanks to Chris Seery for expert input on all things financial, encyclopaedic knowledge of the history of the markets in the '80s and '90s, forensic reading of the entire manuscript but, most of all, for years of friendship on and off the floor.

The poem is 'The Fall' by Anthony Cronin, New Island Press, 2010, which I first heard during his reading at Listowel Writers Week. All the good advice from Kant is from the *Critique of Pure Reason*, transl. Werner Pluhar, Hachette, 1987. The mathematical test Felix gives to Geri was found in *Genuis, Richard Feynman and Modern Physics*, James Gleick, Abacus, 1994. The 'scattered children of Eire' is taken from de Valera's St Patrick's Day address which I first heard in the British Library's sound archives. Full text available on YouTube. The quote about the Charge of the Light Brigade is from General Pierre Bosquet. The version of Descartes' letter to Princess Elisabeth of Bohemia in 1646 is from James Petrik's *Descartes' Theory of the Till*, Hollowbrook Publishing, 1992. Geri quotes from *The South Sea Bubble* by Jonathan Swift, *The Wasteland* by

T.S. Eliot and also blends lines from Keats, Pádraic Pearse and the Gospel according to Matthew. Bertrand Russell's quotation is from *Critical Assessments of Leading Philosophers*, Routledge, 1999.

An extract from what would eventually become this novel was published in *Contains Small Parts*, UEA anthology, Pen & Inc Press, 2003.